* * * * * * *

Bill pulled up behind Rutledge's pickup truck, shut off the engine and looked out the windshield for a moment before he got out. It was obvious Rutledge was not in a very good mood. He was staring at Bill with squinting eyes and had his arms folded tightly across his chest. Bill got out of his patrol car and walked over to Rutledge.

"Good afternoon, Mr. Rutledge," Bill said politely.

"It ain't afternoon. It's damn near evenin'," Rutledge said with a sharp tone to his voice and a disgusted look on his face.

"You reported that you found a body?"

"You know damn well I did. You wouldn't be here if I didn't. What took you so damn long gettin' here?"

"I was in Hill City when I got the call. It takes a little while to get up here."

"You should spend more time away from them coffee shops and spend more time out here."

"You found a body; so show me where it is," Bill said flatly with a hint of anger in his voice.

"It's over there behind the old tool shed," he said without moving from the side of his pickup.

Bill looked at the old man, then looked toward the tool shed.

* * * * * * *

Other titles by J.E. Terrall in
    LARGE PRINT

Western Short Stories
    The Old West
    The Frontier
    Untamed Land
    Tales From the Territory
    Frontier Justice

Western Novels
    Conflict in Elkhorn Valley
    The Story of Joshua Higgins
    The Valley Ranch War

Mystery/Suspense/Thriller
    I Can See Clearly
    The Return Home
    Murder in the Backcountry

Romance
    Sing for me
    Return to Me
    Forever Yours

MURDER IN THE BACKCOUNTRY

by

J.E. Terrall

ISBN: 978-0-9997823-0-9

This is a work of fiction. Names, characters, and incidents are either a product of the author's imagination or are used fictitiously, and any resemblance to actual persons, living or dead, is purely coincidental.

Printed in the United States of America
First Printing / 2016 – www.creatspace.com
Second Printing /2018 - www.creatspace.com

Cover: Front and back covers done by author,
          J.E Terrall

Book Layout/
Formatting: J.E. Terrall
              Custer, South Dakota

MURDER IN THE BACKCOUNTRY

To

Tom and Marilyn Novotny
Good wine, good food and good friends,
it doesn't get any better than that.

Historical note: The air force base located outside Rapid City, South Dakota, was known as Rapid City Air Force Base at the time of this story, 1948. It wasn't until 1953 it was renamed Ellsworth Air Force Base.

CHAPTER ONE

It had been only about fifteen minutes since Deputy Bill Sparks of the Pennington County Sheriff's Department entered his home in Hill City. He had already taken off his uniform, put his gun on the top shelf of his closet and was in the shower when his phone began to ring. He quickly stepped out of the shower, grabbed a towel and wrapped it around his waist, then went into the living room holding the towel around his waist with one hand while he picked up the phone.

"Hello," he said as he stood dripping water on the floor.

"Bill, this is dispatch."

"Hi, Mary. What's up?"

"The sheriff wants you to go up to the old Jasper Quarry. It seems old man Rutledge found a body up there."

"Did he give you any idea what happened?"

"No. All he said was there was a body at the quarry. You know he never gives us any more information than he absolutely has to," Mary said.

"Is Rutledge going to be there?" Bill asked as he looked out the window at his new 1948 Patrol car parked in the driveway with the sun reflecting off the hood.

"He said he would hang around until you get there. He sounded reluctant to stay so he might not be there by the time you arrive. The sheriff wants you to report in as soon as you find out what's going on."

"Will do. I'll be going as soon as I get dressed. I was in the shower."

"Okay. You're to call in if you need help."

"Will do," Bill said then hung up.

Bill went into his bedroom, dried off then got a clean uniform from the closet. He put it on, strapped on his gun belt, retrieved his gun from the closet then started out the door. He got in his patrol car and headed for the Jasper Quarry located west of Hill City.

It took almost an hour for Bill to get to the quarry. Most of his travel was on county roads which meant he traveled on crooked dirt and gravel roads. As he turned his patrol car into the gate at the Jasper Quarry, he saw Raymond Rutledge standing next to his old Dodge pickup. He had his back to the pickup and was leaning against the rear fender with his arms folded in front of him. He didn't look very happy.

Bill knew the old man would not be very happy that it took him so long to get there. He also knew Rutledge didn't care much for him, or for sheriff deputies in general. Bill had had a run in with Rutledge when he first became a deputy almost two years ago, and it had not gone well. Rutledge was arrested for trespassing and for not answering his questions. Bill took him to jail where he spent the night before seeing the judge. The night in jail did nothing to improve his attitude toward Bill, but he did finally answer Bill's questions in front of the judge before he was released and allowed to go home.

Bill pulled up behind Rutledge's pickup truck, shut off the engine and looked out the windshield for a moment before he got out. It was obvious that Rutledge was not in a very good mood. He was staring at Bill through squinted eyes that followed every move Bill made. Bill got out of his patrol car and walked over to Rutledge.

"Good afternoon, Mr. Rutledge," Bill said politely.

"It ain't afternoon. It's damn near evenin'," Rutledge said with a sharp tone to his voice and a disgusted look on his face.

"You reported that you found a body?"

"You know damn well I did. You wouldn't be here if I didn't. What took you so damn long gettin' here?"

"I was in Hill City when I got the call. It takes a little while to get up here."

"You should spend more time away from them coffee shops and spend more time out here."

"You found a body; so show me where it is," Bill said flatly with a hint of anger in his voice.

"It's over there behind the old tool shed, 'round back," he said without moving from the side of his pickup.

Bill looked at the old man, then turned and looked toward the tool shed. It was an old building that had seen better days. Part of the roof had fallen in, the door was crooked and dangling to one side by a single loose hinge, and the building was leaning sharply to one side as if it was waiting for something to cause it to fall over.

Bill knew a little about the old quarry. It had been closed for more than twenty years. If he remembered correctly, it was closed in the late twenties, or very early thirties. Over the years it had become a hangout for some of the local kids. They would drive up to the quarry to smoke and drink a few beers without anyone bothering them, except for the few times when Bill got a call and drove to the quarry to bust up their late night drinking parties.

"Wait here," Bill said.

"What the hell for?"

"Because I told you to," Bill said sharply. "Are you going to give me a hard time again? 'Cause if you are, I'll take you in as a material witness. A couple nights in jail might make you think twice about giving me a hard time."

Bill just stood there looking at the old man, waiting to see if he was going to give him any trouble. It must have been a couple of minutes before the old man finally spoke. During that few minutes, he was probably remembering the last time he refused to cooperate with Bill. He didn't like the inside of the county jail one bit.

"Okay, I'll wait, but I won't like it."

Bill didn't care if old man Rutledge liked it or not, and he didn't bother to comment. He simply turned and walked toward the tool shed. At first he didn't see anything. There was a lot of tall grass and weeds around the sides and back of the shed due to the wet spring which made it hard to see anything close to the shed. It wasn't until he walked around to where he was almost directly behind the tool shed that he saw the body.

The body was that of a man leaning up against the shed as if he had been sitting on the ground with his back against the shed resting when he was shot. It was hard to tell how old the man was because he had obviously been dead for sometime. If Bill had to guess, he had been dead for at least a couple of days. He had seen enough dead soldiers during his time in the Army in Europe during World War II to know the man had been dead for at least a day or two.

Bill remained several feet away from the body while he began looking around. He wasn't sure what he would find, if anything; but he might find something that would provide a clue to what happened there, or why the man had been murdered.

Not seeing anything that appeared to help make it clear what had happened, he returned to his patrol car and got out his camera. He took the camera and walked back to the tool shed. He began taking pictures of the tool shed, the body and the surrounding ground as soon as he was close enough for photographs to show the area around the victim clearly. The area had a lot of old rusted machine parts and miscellaneous junk just laying around in the tall weeds.

"Hey. When you goin' to let me go home," Rutledge yelled.

"When I get done. Now stay put and I'll be there in a few minutes."

Bill just shook his head in disgust then continued to study the scene and continued to take pictures. He noticed the dead man's shirt was covered with blood that had turned dark reddish brown. From the looks of it, the man had taken a load of buckshot to his chest at fairly close range. He bent down and moved in a little closer to the body.

On closer examination of the body, it looked like the man's hands had been broken as well. Bill knelt down and took a closer look at the man's hands. A look at the man's face showed signs that the man had been beaten before he was shot. He took a couple of close-up pictures of the man's hands, chest and face, all from different angles.

Bill stood up while still looking at the body. He took another look around as he thought about what might have happened to him. It was at that moment he noticed tire tracks in a small area void of any grass or other vegetation. He then turned and walked back to where Rutledge was still leaning against his pickup.

"Tell me, did you get a good look at the body?"

"Yeah. Why?"

"Do you know who he is?"

"Nah. Ain't never seen him before, besides he was pretty messed up."

"Are you sure you've never seen him before?"

"Yeah, I'm sure. You think I kilt him?" Rutledge asked sharply.

"No, but you seem to know a lot about what goes on around here."

"I ain't never seen him before," Rutledge insisted rather sharply.

"What were you doing around here, Mr. Rutledge?"

"I was just nose'n 'round the old quarry. It interests me."

"What were you looking for?"

"Nothin' special."

"Did you see anyone hanging around here?"

"Nope."

"Any strange cars or trucks around in the last couple of days?"

"Nope, none that I seen. Can I go home, now?" Rutledge asked.

"You mind if I take a look at your pickup?" Bill asked ignoring his request.

"What for?"

"Do you mind?" Bill asked sharply without answering his question.

"No. I guess not," Rutledge said knowing he really had little choice.

"Step away from your pickup," Bill ordered.

Rutledge reluctantly stepped away from his pickup when Bill approached it. Bill took his flashlight off his belt as he walked over to the pickup. He shined his flashlight on one of the tires of the pickup, then walked around the pickup shining his flashlight on each tire as he examined them. When he was finished, he was satisfied that the tire tracks he found were not made by Rutledge's pickup. The tires on Rutledge's pickup had almost no tread left on them, which didn't surprise Bill. However, the tracks in the dirt showed a deep treaded tire had made them, probably fairly new tires.

Bill then looked in the back of Rutledge's pickup. In the back he found several rusty tools that looked like they might have some use left in them. He also saw several rusty pieces of metal that appeared to be part of an old lawn mower. He turned and looked at Rutledge.

"Okay, you never did answer my question about what you were doing here. You want to try to answer it so I believe you?"

Rutledge paused for a moment while looking at Bill before he answered. "I was lookin' for thin's I could sell or use myself."

"Did you find anything?"

"No," he replied, but not too convincingly.

"I know you're a scavenger. What did you find? This stuff in the back of your pickup, maybe?"

"Okay. I found me a couple of rakes and some lawn mower parts I can use. I found the body when I started lookin' 'round the back of the shed."

"Where did you find those things?"

"They was in front of the shed, in that tall grass next to the door. I didn't see the body 'til I went 'round back."

"Did you touch or move anything at or near the body?"

"Nope."

Bill looked at Rutledge's face. Rutledge looked a little like a kid who had been caught with his hand in a cookie jar. Bill knew he had nothing he could hold Rutledge on, but he would talk to him again later.

"Okay, Mr. Rutledge.   You can go home. Don't come back here. You understand?"

"Yeah, I understand.   Can I keep what I found?" he asked with a more pleasant tone in his voice.

"Yeah.   You can keep it, but you stay away from here. You understand that?"

"Yeah," Rutledge said, then got in his pickup.

Bill turned and walked back to his patrol car. He sat down behind the steering wheel and watched Rutledge as he drove away.   When Rutledge was gone, he called in on the Army surplus radio the department had gotten for the patrol cars.

"Car eight, to dispatch," Bill said.

"Dispatch, go ahead."

"Mary, you might want to notify the sheriff that we have a homicide out here at the Jasper Quarry."

"Are you sure?"

"I'm sure. The victim was shot."

"I'll let him know.   Have you any other information."

"The victim is a male in his late twenties or early thirties would be my best guess. It looks like he might have been beaten pretty badly before he was shot with a shotgun at fairly close range. It looks like he has been dead for a couple of days."

"Oh, - - - ah - - - I'll tell the sheriff," Mary said with a slight quiver in her voice.

"Tell the sheriff I've taken a lot of pictures of the scene and that I found tire tracks near the body. I can't say for sure if the guy was killed here or somewhere else, but I'll make a cast of the tracks just in case. I'd better wait here until the body is picked up. I don't want anything to happen to it. We're lucky some of the wild critters around here haven't gotten to it, yet."

"I'm sure he will get someone out there to get the body as soon as he can."

"Thanks, Mary. That's all I have for now."

"Take care of yourself," Mary said.

"I will. Out," Bill said then set the headset on the seat.

Bill looked around. The sun was starting to set and it wouldn't be much longer before it would be dark. There was no doubt in Bill's mind it would be dark before anyone could get to the quarry. He needed to do something to protect the body. Bill started his patrol car and moved it to a position where he could put his spotlight on the body while still keeping his patrol car back far enough to prevent it from possibly destroying evidence.

While Bill waited for the Coroner to get there to examine and remove the body, he opened the trunk of his patrol car and took out a kit he had made for making plaster casts. It contained Plaster of Paris, a small jar of water, a stir stick, and an old meat loaf pan to mix it in. He mixed up a batch of Plaster of Paris then carefully poured it over the tire tracks. It wouldn't take very long for it to set, and he would have a cast of the tire tracks. While he waited, he turned the spotlight on the body. Once the cast was dry enough, he picked it up and carefully wrapped it in a couple of towels then put it in the trunk of his patrol car.

It wasn't long after he was finished making the cast when he heard a vehicle coming closer. A quick look at his watch showed him that he didn't think the coroner could get there so soon. He could see the headlights as the vehicle turned into the quarry. Bill stepped back into the shadows as he slipped his hand over his gun. If it was trouble, he wanted to be ready.

The car rolled to a stop, but it was too far away and too dark for Bill to get a good look at it, or at the license plate. It was clear that whoever was in the car had seen the light from his patrol car. The car suddenly backed out of the gate, turned back onto the road and sped away before Bill could get a good enough look at it to be able to identify it. He wondered if it was some kids coming there to drink and smoke, or if it was someone who had come for some other reason, perhaps to remove the body or destroy evidence.

Since he was at a murder scene, he didn't think he should go after whoever had turned in the gate. He needed to make sure the murder scene was not disturbed any more than it had been already, and that he protected whatever evidence might still remain. He doubted he could get to his patrol car, turn it around and give chase in time to catch the car, anyway. Bill also thought about making cast of the tire tracks of the car that sped away, but realized that there would not be any useable tire tracks in the gravel road.

Since Bill had done all he could until the coroner arrived, he sat down in his patrol car and looked out the windshield. He sat there staring at the body. He didn't want some critter disturbing any evidence, but he was also wondering who the man was and why he had been killed in such a violent and brutal manner. Was someone trying to get information out of him, or were they just mad as hell at him for something he did he wasn't supposed to do, or knew something he wasn't supposed to know?

It had been almost an hour since he had called in when he heard another vehicle on the road. He got out of his patrol car and turned to look toward the gate. He could see the headlights of a vehicle as it turned into the quarry. It was the coroner's truck.

The coroner's truck pulled up behind Bill's patrol car and stopped. The coroner got out of the truck and walked toward Bill.

"Hi, Bill. I hear you've got a body for me," Ralph said.

Ralph Wickum was the Pennington County Coroner. He was a short, stocky man in his late forties. He had thinning brown hair with a little gray in it, he wore heavy glasses which made him look scholarly. Bill knew him to be a man who missed very little when it came to investigating the death of a person.

"Sure do. It's over behind the tool shed."

Ralph nodded that he understood, then turned and went to the back of the truck. He got out a stretcher and a heavy canvas tarp about the size of a single bed sheet then started toward the back of the shed.

"Did you get pictures?" Ralph asked.

"I took several of the body from different angles and of the surrounding area before it got dark."

"Good."

Ralph stepped around the shed and saw the body. Bill's spotlight was shining on it. Ralph took a quick look around then knelt down to examine the body.

"You were right," Ralph said as he looked up at Bill. "This guy had taken a pretty good beating before he was shot. It looks like all of his fingers have been broken. From the look of his hands, I'd say all the bones in his hands have been broken as well."

"That's what I thought. Take a good look at his hands," Bill said as he handed a flashlight to Ralph.

"My, what do we have here?" Ralph said as he looked closer at the man's hands with the help of the flashlight. "I think I know how they were broken. It looks like tire marks on his hands. My guess is they drove over his hands."

"That's a bit strange, don't you think?" Bill asked.

"It sure is."

"I have a cast of tire tracks that might be from the vehicle that drove over his hands."

"Great. I'll check it out."

"Who would do that to someone?" Bill asked more to himself than to Ralph.

"Someone who wanted information and was probably mad as hell," Ralph said as he glanced up at Bill.

"That would be my guess."

"Well, let's get him in the truck," Ralph said. "I've done all I can here. It's up to the ME now."

Ralph laid out the heavy canvas tarp as close to the body as possible. Together they rolled the body onto the tarp. They wrapped the body in the tarp, then picked it up and laid it on the stretcher.

They picked the stretcher up and carried it to the back of the coroner's truck and slid it inside. After closing the door, the coroner thanked Bill for his help, got in the truck and drove away.

After the coroner was gone, Bill returned to his patrol car and left the quarry. He went directly home. As he drove to his home, he thought it would be a good idea if he went back up to the quarry and looked around when he had more light to work with. He had no idea what he might find, but he was sure it would be worth the effort. Besides, if he didn't go back and look around, he would always wonder if he might have missed something important.

Once he arrived home, he called in to dispatch and checked out. He then went right to bed.

CHAPTER TWO

Bill had not set his alarm when he went to bed, but woke early even though he had gotten to bed rather late. He dressed in jeans and a shirt then sat down at the kitchen table to eat his breakfast. While eating breakfast, he wrote out his report of everything that had happened last evening, everything he had seen at the quarry, and his contact with Rutledge. He knew he should have written his report last night when everything was still fresh in his mind, but he had worked almost two shifts and was very tired.

When he finished writing the report, he called in to dispatch and asked to talk to the sheriff. He was put through immediately.

"I hear you had a long day," Sheriff Henderson said.

"Yes, sir."

"What's on your mind, Bill?"

"I have my report from my activities last night completed. I can send it in like usual, but I think my investigation of the crime scene is incomplete."

"Oh. How do you figure that? Do you think there's more you can do?"

"Yes, sir. I do. It got pretty dark up there before I had a chance to take a good look around the area. I think it would be a good idea if I went back up there and looked around some more. I have no idea what I might find, but it certainly can't hurt to look around some more."

"I agree. Okay. Check in with dispatch and get on duty before you go up there again. I'll want a complete report when you get done."

"Yes, sir. Do you want me to bring the report to you when I'm done?"

"Yes. Call me if you need help with anything."

"Yes, sir." Bill said then hung up.

Bill tipped back in his chair as he thought about going back up to the old Jasper Quarry. Since he had no idea how long it would take him to search the area, he decided it might be a good idea to take something to eat along with him. He went to the kitchen, made a couple of sandwiches and put them in his lunchbox along with an orange and an apple. He filled his Thermos with the rest of the coffee in the pot then put it in his lunchbox. He finished drinking the coffee left in his cup from his breakfast, then got ready to leave. As soon as he changed into a uniform, he was ready to go.

After checking in with dispatch, Bill drove up to the Jasper Quarry. It took him almost an hour to get there. He drove through the gate, stopped, then took a minute or so to just look around. Bill was not looking for anything in particular; he was just getting familiar with the location of each building in relation to the other buildings in the quarry. He was also looking for anything that didn't seem to belong there or seemed to be out of place. He didn't see anything he didn't expect to find.

He drove on into the quarry and parked his patrol car where Rutledge had been parked yesterday evening. He got out of the patrol car and stood next to it. As he looked off to his left, he could see a small part of the quarry, a part that Mother Nature had not yet reclaimed. It wasn't a very big quarry, but a lot of material had been taken out of it. Since it had not been in operation for many years, there were several small trees and a lot of bushes and weeds growing up in and around the quarry pit. In fact, there were a lot of weeds everywhere.

Off to his right he could see what was left of the office, the large shed that covered the crushing machine, a machine shop, and an elevator that had been used to load the crushed rock into trucks.

The office building had collapsed. There was little left of the office building to even give a hint to what it had been. If there was anything still inside, it would have been crushed when the building collapsed, or had rotted after years of lying under the remains of the roof.

The large shed covering the crushing machine and rock sorter looked like it was in the best shape of all the remaining buildings. That may have been due to the fact it had been one of the stronger buildings. It had a thick concrete floor and heavy steel girders used to hold up the large metal roof. However, the metal roof was made of sheet steel and had rusted through in several places.

Bill walked over to one of the large open doors and looked inside. There were several large pieces of machinery still in the building. Bill could identify only a couple of the pieces of machinery. The rock crusher with its big rollers that crushed the larger rocks into smaller rocks, and the sorting machine used to sort the crushed rock by the size of the rock as they came out of the crusher were the ones he recognized immediately.

Bill went inside the building. He spent some time looking around the large shed. Again, he had no idea what he was looking for, but not to look might mean he would miss a clue, or even some evidence of what had happened at the quarry.

As he walked around behind the large crushing machine, he could see the big wheel used to turn the rollers that crushed the rock. On one of the big wheels, he found several pieces of rope hanging from a couple of the large steel spokes of the wheel. He wondered what they had been used for. He walked toward the wheel to get a better look.

As he approached the wheel, he looked down at the concrete floor at the base of the wheel. It looked as if someone had been shuffling their feet in the dirt right below where the ropes were hanging. It became obvious that someone had been tied to the wheel. He took a few pictures of the area around the wheel including the dirt at the base of the wheel. He continued to look around the crushing machine and the building to see if there was any more evidence or clues before moving any closer to the wheel. He found nothing more.

He moved up closer and took quite a few pictures of the pieces of rope on the wheel. It looked as if there was dried blood on the pieces of rope. After getting the pictures, he cut the pieces of rope from the wheel and put them in a paper sack, being very careful not to disturb the floor near the wheel any more than necessary.

As soon as he had finished, Bill left the large shed and walked over to the machine shop. It was not a very large building compared to the shed with the crushing machine in it. There was not much in the building, but he did find several machines that might have been used to make parts for the crushing machine and for the other equipment needed at the quarry, as well as repair equipment. Everything was rusted and in very poor condition, probably unusable. There were signs that several smaller machines had been removed from the shop, but none appeared to have been removed recently. He was sure Rutledge had probably taken anything usable a long time ago.

Bill knew Rutledge had been a scavenger for many years. He may have even worked at the quarry at one time. That was something Bill might want to ask him.

After going through the machine shop as best he could, and finding nothing of interest, he walked over to the elevator. The elevator was still standing, but didn't look like it was safe to climb up on. Bill looked around the base, but didn't find anything of interest to him. He stepped back away from the elevator and looked up at the storage bin. He could see where the rocks would be dumped out at the bottom of the bin into trucks. Since the gate on the chute was closed, he had no way of knowing if there was anything in the bin.

Bill walked around the elevator, looking at every detail of it. He noticed one of the steel legs used to support the storage bin had cross members that were apparently used to get up to the top of the bin in case the chute got clogged or needed some kind of repair. His first thought was it might be a good idea if he climbed up and got a look inside the bin. He didn't think it looked very safe, but he felt it might be a mistake not to check it out.

He took a minute to look around to see if there was anybody around. Bill didn't see anyone. He slipped the strap of the camera around his neck and over his shoulder, took hold of the steel leg and shook it. Nothing moved. Bill decided it would probably be safe to climb up on it if he was careful. He started to climb the steel leg. When he got to the top, he found a board lying across the opening on the top of the bin. It had apparently been used to stand on while fixing whatever was wrong, or to unclog the chute if it got plugged. It showed signs of being rotten so Bill didn't climb out on it. From where he was standing he could see inside the bin. All he could see was the bin was about half full of crushed rock. He studied it for a minute. He decided the rock in the bin had not been disturbed for a very long time, if at all.

Seeing nothing of importance in the bin, Bill started to climb back down. When he was about halfway down the steel leg, he thought he heard something behind him. He quickly wrapped his arm around the steel leg so he wouldn't fall, then turned around as quickly as he could. It took a couple of seconds before he heard the sound again. It came from behind the building where the crushing machine was located. He watched the part of the area behind the building he could see. If there was anyone behind the building, Bill wouldn't be able to see who it was unless they came out away from the building.

Suddenly, he saw someone run into the woods from directly behind the building. He had only gotten a glimpse of the person, but the person was wearing jeans and a work shirt. He got the impression the person was not very tall. Because he had gotten only a glimpse of the person, he was not sure if it was a male or a female.

"Stop," he yelled. "Stop. Police."

It quickly became clear that yelling for someone to stop when he was halfway up the steel leg of the elevator was really a waste of energy. He was in no position to do anything about it if the person didn't stop and wait for him to climb down, and he was certainly in no position to catch him. Whoever it was would be long gone before he could even get down on the ground. Bill let out a sigh, then continued to climb down.

Once he was back on the ground, he walked around behind the building. He immediately started looking for some sign of who had been there and why. All he found were several footprints in the loose dirt near the back of the building, but they were only partial footprints and not good enough to even get an idea of the size of the shoe that made them. The only thing it told him was someone had been watching him while he searched the buildings for clues to what happened there and who might be involved. He wished he could have caught the person. There was no telling what information he could provide.

Bill took a minute to look around. He still had a lot of ground to cover. The next thing he had to do was to see if he could follow the tire tracks he had made casts of last night. He had no idea where they would lead him.

He walked over to his patrol car and got in. He didn't close the door, but rather just sat there for a few minutes to think. While he was thinking he poured himself a cup of coffee from his Thermos.

While he sat drinking his coffee, he wondered who had been watching him. Was it someone who lived nearby and wondered what the patrol car was doing there? Or was it someone who might know what happened there? The more he thought about the person he saw, the less he felt it was someone who had anything to do with the death of the man. He wasn't really sure why he felt that way, but he did. Even so, he would still like to talk to the person. It was obvious he knew his way around the quarry.

After he finished his coffee, Bill put the Thermos back in his lunchbox, got out of the patrol car and locked it up. He started walking toward the tool shed where he had found the tire tracks yesterday. As soon as he found the one he had made a cast of, he could see a faint trail made by the tires of a vehicle in the grass. With the way the grass had been pushed down by the tires, it was easy to see that the vehicle had gone deeper into the quarry property. It had not gone in the direction that would take it out the main gate. It seemed to be following what had once been a road out to the quarry pit that Mother Nature had not completely reclaimed.

Following the road toward the quarry pit, Bill soon found that the vehicle had turned off the road to the quarry pit, and onto what appeared to have been another road. He could make out where the road had wandered across an open field. It was fairly easy for him to follow the vehicle that had moved across it.

In the field were several old pieces of equipment, most of them didn't look like they were anything more than junk. There was even an old rusted out truck from around the early nineteen twenties.

Bill continued to follow the tracks left by the vehicle. It wasn't long before it came to a wooded area. Once in the wooded area, it was easier to see he was following a road Mother Nature was trying to reclaim, but had not been completely successful. He followed it through the wooded area to a heavy steel tubular gate.

On the other side of the gate, he could see the narrow road turned and ran alongside a plowed field. The road ran between the fence and the plowed field and went away from the road located out in front of the quarry entrance. The field was about eighty acres in size. It looked as if the crops in the field were doing pretty well with the help of the spring rains and some warm sunny days.

Bill went to open the gate to continue on, but found the gate was chained closed and had a heavy lock on it. He looked out across the field and wondered who owned the plowed field.

Since there was nothing more he could do there. A quick look at his watch showed him it was time to turn back. Bill started walking back to his patrol car.

When he got to his patrol car, he got in and headed for the front gate. After driving through the gate, he stopped, got out of the patrol car and closed the gate. He thought about putting a lock on the gate, but didn't have one with him.

Once he was back in the patrol car, he looked both ways. He could turn left and go back to Hill City, write up his report then go into Rapid City to the sheriff's office and meet with the sheriff, or he could turn right to see if he could find out who owned the plowed field. He decided to turn right.

Bill drove down the road keeping an eye out for anyone who might be around. As he came around a corner he could see a plowed field just off to his right. He stopped and looked out over the field. It didn't take him but a minute to know it was the same field he had seen from the quarry where the heavy steel gate was located. He slowly continued on down the road, looking for a house in the hope of finding out who owned the field.

It wasn't long before he came to what looked like a drive back into the woods. It showed signs of having been used fairly regularly. Bill turned up the drive, but only went about a hundred yards before he came to a gate. He stopped and looked around. He could see a small house in among the trees beyond the fence.

Although there was a gate across the drive, there was an opening on one side of the drive between the gate and the fence, wide enough to walk through. Bill got out of his patrol car and began walking toward the house. He was only about fifteen feet from the steps to the front porch that ran across the front of the house when an old man stepped out on the porch.

"There something I can help you with, young fella?"

"I'm Deputy Bill Sparks with the Pennington County Sheriff's Department. I was wondering if you would mind answering a few questions."

"That depends on the questions. Who are you looking for?"

"First of all, I would like to know who you are."

"I'm Wilbur Turnquest. I own this ranch, and I've lived here for almost forty years."

"I've heard of you," Bill said.

"I hope nothing bad," he said with a grin.

"No, sir. Nothing bad."

"Good. In that case you can call me, Wilbur. What are you doing out this way?"

"While I was checking the Jasper Quarry, I saw someone run away from there. He ran in this general direction. I couldn't tell from where I was if it was a young man or woman. I would like to find that person to ask them a few questions about the quarry."

"Well, there aren't too many folks who live around here. If I had to guess, it was probably my granddaughter you saw."

"What makes you think it was her?"

"She's staying with me while she looks for a job. She just graduated from nursing school. She likes to explore the area and hike in the backcountry. She was asking me about the quarry this morning at breakfast. I told her to be careful around all those old buildings. They aren't safe, you know."

"I would like to talk to her, if you don't mind."

"I don't mind, but she isn't here right now. She should be back shortly. She said she would probably be home for lunch, but I wouldn't count on it."

Bill looked at his watch, then looked back at the old man.

"I would like to wait for a little while, if you don't mind."

"Don't mind at all. I don't get much company out this way. Would you like a cup of coffee?"

"That would be nice, but you don't need to go to any trouble."

"No trouble. Have a seat and I'll be back in a minute," the old man said then turned and went inside the house.

Bill stepped up on the porch and sat down on a chair next to a small table, then looked out across the old man's property. He noticed it seemed to have been well kept. The yard was mowed and the buildings looked to be in pretty good shape. There was an old tractor parked in front of the barn door. The tractor looked to be in pretty good shape for its age.

Bill's thoughts turned to the person he had seen in the quarry. He wondered if the man's granddaughter was the person he had seen, but his thoughts were interrupted by Wilbur as he brought coffee out on the porch. He sat down across from Bill and they began to talk.

Time passed slowly while Bill and Wilbur talked. Actually, Wilbur did most of the talking. It became obvious he didn't get a lot of company so far from everyone. However, he did seem to know a lot about the quarry. He also seemed to know a bit about Mr. Rutledge.

"I'll say this much, Rutledge is harmless but you can't trust him. I caught him a couple of times on my ranch," Wilbur said. "I caught him stealing some sweet corn from my garden out behind the barn last year. I think he swiped some of my green beans, and carrots, too, but I couldn't prove it."

"Did you report it?"

"No. I figured he needed it as much or more than I do."

"He's pretty well known for being a scavenger," Bill said. "Would you like me to have a talk with him about it?"

"I doubt it would do any good. Besides, I grow more than I can use. As long as all he steals is some food for himself, I don't really mind."

It was a little past noon and Wilbur's granddaughter had not shown up. Bill was thinking it was time to go. He had other things to do, one of them was to take his report into the sheriff.

"I have a lot to do, so I guess I'll leave for now. I'll stop by later and talk to your granddaughter," Bill said as he stood up.

"You're welcome to stop by anytime," Wilbur said as he stood up.

Bill reached over and shook Wilbur's hand, then turned and walked down the porch steps. Bill returned to his patrol car then drove back to the quarry. He sat in his car and made out his report while he ate his lunch. When he was finished eating and writing his report, he left the quarry and headed for Rapid City and the sheriff's office to fill the sheriff in on what he had found.

CHAPTER THREE

Bill arrived at the sheriff's office in Rapid City shortly after one in the afternoon. He went directly to the sheriff's office and found Mary sitting behind her desk.

"Hi. I was wondering when you would show up. Did you find anything else out at the quarry?"

"Not much that will help, but I did see someone else out there."

"Who was it?"

"I don't know, but I think it might have been Mr. Wilbur Turnquest's granddaughter. At least that's who he seemed to think it might be," Bill said. "Is the sheriff in?"

"Yes. Go right in. He said he wanted to talk to you as soon as you arrived," Mary said with a smile.

Bill nodded slightly, then turned toward the door to the sheriff's office. He knocked lightly on the door then waited for a response.

"Come in."

Bill stepped into the office.

"Did your trip up to the quarry help any?"

"Yes, sir. I believe it did. I found several pieces of rope tied to a couple of spokes of the large wheel used to turn the rock crusher. The ropes look like they had dried blood on them. The dirt on the cement floor just below where I found the ropes looked like feet had been shuffling in it. It looked like it might have been where someone had been tied, and possibly tortured."

"Did you collect any evidence?"

"Yes, sir. I collected the ropes, but I took pictures of the ropes on the wheel and the area around the bottom of the wheel before I cut the ropes off the wheel and bagged them."

"Good."

"There was someone at the quarry while I was there. I didn't get a good look at the person, but I talked to a Mr. Wilbur Turnquest who owns the property bordering one side of the quarry. He thought it was probably his granddaughter I saw."

"Did you get a chance to talk to her?" Sheriff Henderson asked.

"No, sir. She wasn't home at the time I talked to Mr. Turnquest."

"Do you think she might have something to do with it?"

"Not at this time. I'm hoping she might have seen something, though."

"I take it you plan to question her?"

"Yes, sir."

"Okay. Leave your report with me. I'll read it over and talk to you about it later. By the way, let me know what you find out from Turnquest's granddaughter."

"Will do. Do you know Mr. Turnquest?" Bill asked.

"No, but I've heard of him. How about Mr. Rutledge? You arrested him once, didn't you?"

"Yes, almost two years ago. I pulled him in because he gave me a hard time and refused to answer my questions."

"Do you think Rutledge had anything to do with the murder? I noticed he was the one who reported the body at the quarry."

"Not at this point. The only thing I think he's guilty of is being a scavenger. I think he has probably taken a lot of old machinery and small tools, along with a bunch of junk from in and around the quarry over the years."

"I wouldn't be surprised. He's been doing that for years. You think he might have caught someone taking some things from the quarry he wanted. You know, sort of a competitor?"

"I guess it's possible, but I don't see him as the violent type even if he does put up a good show of being tough. When challenged, he backs down pretty easy. Maybe in his younger days he was Mr. Tough Guy, but he's an old man now."

"Even old men can kill if provoked," the sheriff said.

"I know even an old man can kill if he's provoked, especially with a shotgun. I still don't think he is involved in the murder. However, he might know something about what went on up there."

"You might want to have another talk with him. After you jailed him about two years ago, he might figure it would be in his best interest if he cooperates with you, especially if he thinks you might put him in jail again," the sheriff said with a grin.

"I was planning on having another talk with him."

"Okay. What did you do to secure the crime scene?"

"Not much I can do short of sitting there and watching it. Putting a lock on the gate won't stop the kids for using it for their drinking parties."

"I guess you're right," the sheriff said thoughtfully.

Bill sat there and looked at the sheriff, and wondered what he was thinking. He seemed to be looking at his report. He finally looked up at Bill.

"What's your next move?"

"I figured you would probably send an investigator up there."

"I don't have anyone I can spare, and the state can't send out anyone for at least a month, according to the State's Attorney. They told me to do the best I can, and they would send out someone as soon as possible. It seems they have their hands full right now and don't think this murder is a priority.

"Since the murder took place in your area, it looks like you are going to have to do the investigating. It looks like you have a good start, I might add. So, what's your next move?"

Bill just looked at the sheriff and thought about what he was asked for a minute or two before he responded.

"Well, I guess I'll go back to the quarry and look around for something that might let me know what happened there, or why the guy was murdered. And I should start talking to everyone who lives in the area to find out what they might have seen or heard," Bill said, not sure if it was what the sheriff wanted to hear.

"Well, it sounds like a good place to start. I'll do the best I can to cover the routine calls in your area while you work on this case. Keep a detailed record of your activities; who you talk to, what people tell you, and what you find. And keep me posted."

"Yes, sir."

"You're going to be playing detective for a while, so do a good job. If you need anything, let me know. I'll try to get it for you."

"Will you let me know what the ME finds out from the body that might help me?" Bill asked.

"Sure. Call in to check in and out as you usually do, and let me know what you're doing."

"Yes, sir," Bill said, then stood up.

"Oh, one other thing. If you need any warrants, give me a call. I'll make sure you get them."

"Thank you, sir," Bill said, then turned and left the sheriff's office.

Bill stopped off at the dispatcher's desk to tell Mary about his new assignment to work on the murder case, and that he might be working some long hours.

"This could be good for your career. They have been talking about getting a detective in the department," Mary said.

"Even if I solve this case, they wouldn't promote me to detective. I have only two years with the department," Bill said with a disappointed tone in his voice.

"Maybe not, but it sure couldn't hurt your career. You also have four years of experience as a Military Policeman in the U.S. Army, I'm sure they will take that into consideration and that can't hurt any, either."

"That's true enough. Well, I best get going. I have a case to work on," Bill said with a grin.

"Be careful out there," Mary said as Bill turned and started out the door.

Bill waved back at her as he left the building on his way to his patrol car. He almost walked right past the patrol car because his mind was already working on the case. He quickly turned and took the few steps back to his patrol car then got in. Once he was in the car, he immediately began to make a list of some of the things he wanted to do and who he wanted to question. The first on his list of people he wanted to talk to was Wilbur Turnquest's granddaughter.

Bill reached down, turned the key and started his patrol car. He headed out of town and back up into the Black Hills. He drove through Hill City, without stopping at his home, and headed deeper into the mountains toward Jasper Quarry.

As he approached the Jasper Quarry, he slowed down and turned in. When he got to the gate, he discovered it was still closed. He wished he had brought with him a heavy lock so he could secure the gate when he left, even if he was sure a lock was not likely to keep anyone out who wanted in.

Bill got out of his patrol car and checked for tracks going in the gate. He didn't see any fresh tracks. With the narrow gate, only wide enough for one vehicle at a time to pass through, he didn't see any vehicle tracks over his from the morning.

He didn't open the gate. Instead, he backed down to the road then drove to the Turnquest farm. He again drove up to the gate, parked his patrol car and walked toward the house. Bill was only about halfway to the house when Wilbur Turnquest stepped out on the porch. Wilbur watched him as he walked toward the house.

"Good afternoon, Deputy. I guess you are here to talk to my granddaughter."

"Yes, sir. Is she home?"

Just as he asked if she was home, a young woman stepped out on the porch. Bill was a bit surprised. It turned out that Wilbur's granddaughter was a very striking young woman. She had dark brown hair that hung down onto her shoulders and the deepest brown eyes Bill had ever seen, and they seemed to be smiling at him. The red plaid blouse and tight jeans showed her figure very nicely. She was almost as tall as Bill in her cowboy boots. Even in work clothes she was a beautiful young woman.

"This is my granddaughter, Julie," Wilbur said with a slight grin when he noticed Bill's expression.

"Ah, nice to meet you, Miss Turnquest."

"Nice to meet you, Deputy – ah," she said as she waited for him to tell her his name.

"Bill, Bill Sparks."

"Deputy Sparks. You can call me, Julie. I understand you would like to talk to me."

"Yes."

"Why don't we sit here on the porch to talk," Julie suggested.

Bill stepped up on the porch then waited for her to sit down. He sat in a chair while Wilbur sat down beside his granddaughter on a padded bench.

"Were you the one I saw behind the building where the crushing machine is located in the quarry this morning?"

"Yes," she replied as she looked at him, but offered no additional information.

"Do you mind telling me what you were doing over there?"

"I don't mind at all. I was just looking around. I happen to find the old quarry an interesting place. My father worked there years ago. In fact, he died in the quarry in an accident only a short time before it closed down. I was pretty young when he died."

"I'm sorry to hear that. Do you often go over there?"

"I wouldn't say often, but I do wander around the place from time to time."

"Did you notice anything unusual the last time you were there?"

"Why, yes, I did," she said with a grin.

"Would you tell me about it?"

"I saw a sheriff's deputy hanging on one of the legs to the tall storage bin and yelling for me to stop," she said with a wide grin.

Bill looked at her. He was feeling a little embarrassed at the moment, but then he probably did look a little ridiculous hanging onto one of the legs while yelling for her to stop.

"I was hoping you might have seen something a bit more interesting," he said, "at least more interesting to me."

"I'm sorry," she said with a slight giggle. "To answer your question, no. I didn't see anything you might think was unusual or even interesting."

"Were you over there yesterday or the day before?"

"No. Today was the first time I've been there for several weeks."

"There was a body found over by the tool shed. He had been beaten and then shot."

Julie's face turned pale and her jaw dropped. From the look on her face, Bill was sure she didn't know anything about it.

"When was he killed?" Wilbur asked.

"We're not sure at this time, but at least a couple of days ago. Did either of you see or hear anything unusual in the past two or three days?"

Wilbur and Julie looked at each other, then turned and looked at Bill. They shook their heads to indicate they had not heard anything unusual. It seemed Julie was taken aback by the fact someone had been murdered just across the fence from their farm. It took a moment for her to compose herself.

"I'm sorry if I have upset you. I should be going. If you think of anything, would you please call the sheriff's office and let them know you would like to talk to me?" he said as he looked first at Wilbur, then at Julie.

"Do you have to go?" Julie said, her eyes showing she hoped he would stay a little longer. "It's almost dinner time. Would you like to stay for dinner? It won't be anything fancy."

Bill looked at Julie, then at Wilbur. He noticed Wilbur was smiling then nodded his head slightly.

"Well, I guess I could stay for a little while," he said with a smile.

"Good," Julie said.

Julie smiled then turned and went back into the house. Wilbur and Bill sat down at a table on the porch.

"I'm sorry if I upset Julie," Bill said.

"Don't worry about her. She'll be fine."

"I understand she just graduated from nursing school when I first talked to you. Where did she go to school?"

"She just graduated from the University of South Dakota. She has her degree in nursing."

"I believe you said she was looking for a job. Where is she looking to go to work?" Bill asked.

"She is looking for a job close to here. I think she feels I need looking after," Wilbur said with a grin.

That last bit of information set well with Bill. If she lived not too far from Hill City, he might like to get to know her.

The conversation between Wilbur and Bill turned to the Jasper Quarry. He found out it had closed down because they had trouble getting people who would work there. It seems there had been a number "accidents" in a relatively short time. The workers accused the owners of causing the "accidents", and the owners accused the workers of sabotaging the quarry. The relationship between the owners and the employees deteriorated rather quickly. According to Wilbur, things got so bad between the workers and the owners, that the owners just closed the quarry and walked away.

It wasn't long and the conversation turned to activities at the quarry since it closed. Bill, of course, knew that kids gathered there to drink and smoke on weekends when the weather was nice. It had become a hangout for some of the rowdy, nonconformist kids who spent a good deal of time there causing trouble. They ran in gangs. Bill was well aware of the partying because he had been called up to the quarry a couple of times to run them out of there.

"Have you seen or heard any activity at the quarry lately," Bill asked Wilbur.

"I'll have to think on it, but there was some noise from over that way, but I'm not sure what day it was," he said thoughtfully. "It was two, or maybe three days ago that I thought I heard something from over there, but I was working on my tractor in my hayfield. It's on the opposite side of the farm from the quarry, so I couldn't be sure.

"What time of day was it?"

"I was getting the first cutting of hay from that field. I worked a bit after it was dark. It would have been sometime close to seven, maybe a little later."

"Do you usually work that late?" Bill asked.

"No, but it had been wet in the morning from a short rain. I waited until the field dried before I went out to cut."

Julie stepped out on the porch with a tray in her hands, interrupting the conversation. Bill pushed back away from the table to allow Julie room to set the tray on the table. On the tray were three bowls filled to the brim with a thick meat and vegetable stew, a plate with crackers and three glasses of milk. To Bill, it looked like a meal fit for a king. It didn't hurt any that it smelled as good as it looked. She set the food on the table then sat down.

"Dig in while it's still hot," Julie said.

Bill wasted no time. He scooted up to the table and began eating. He found it as delicious as it looked and smelled. It had been a long time since he had had a home cooked meal, other than what he made for himself.

"This is delicious," he said with a smile.

"I take it you don't get home cooking very often," Julie said as she watched him take another spoonful from the bowl.

"I live alone and get tired of my own cooking. The only break I get from my own cooking is eating in cafés, and that gets old in a hurry," Bill said as he took another spoonful.

Julie just smiled at him then began to eat. Bill had a second helping of the stew and enjoyed it as much as he had the first bowl.

When dinner was done, Julie took the dishes into the house leaving Bill on the porch with her grandfather. She could hear them talking. Their conversation picked up where they had left off.

"What did you hear or see?" Bill asked.

"I'm not really sure what it was I heard. It almost sounded like a wounded animal. I figured that was what it was, but I did see lights over toward the quarry."

"Could you tell what kind of lights you saw?"

"No. They could have been from a car or a truck. My best guess would be a truck. Whatever it was, it needed a new muffler."

"Then it was fairly loud?" Bill asked.

"Oh, yes. It would have had to be loud for me to hear it over my tractor, and being so far from the quarry."

"Do you know of anyone around here who has a vehicle that needs a muffler?" Bill asked, thinking there were probably dozens of vehicles in need of new mufflers.

"One I can think of right off hand would be Rutledge's old pickup. That old bucket of bolts needs just about everything new on it," Wilbur said with a chuckle.

Bill remembered hearing Rutledge's pickup when he started it and left the quarry the other night. It was possible Wilbur had heard his pickup, but Bill remembered the tire tracks didn't match the tires on Rutledge's truck. There was also the fact Wilbur would hear Rutledge's pickup fairly often as he lived just down the road from Wilbur's place. In fact, he might have heard Rutledge's pickup, but not because it was in the quarry, but simply because he drove by at about the same time.

It wasn't much to go on, but he would have to check it out. Rutledge was often scrounging around in the quarry. Bill also knew him to be a bit of a hothead, but he couldn't see him killing anyone, especially like the man in the quarry who had been beaten and then shot. It was violent, brutal and messy. The man in the quarry was killed by someone who was very angry, in fact, down right mad.

"I guess I better be going. It's been a long day and I still have reports to write."

"You're leaving?" Julie asked as she stepped out on the porch.

"I certainly wasn't going to leave before thanking you for a very good and delicious meal, and without saying goodbye."

"Oh, thank you." she said as she looked at him. "I'll walk you to your car."

Bill said goodnight to Wilbur, then stepped off the porch with Julie. She walked with him to his patrol car down at the gate.

"I'm glad you stayed for dinner," she said softly as she looked him in the eyes.

"So am I. I was wondering if I might call on you some time."

She smiled and said, "I would like that."

"Goodnight," he said then reached out and opened the patrol car door.

Julie stood at the gate and watched him as he got in his patrol car and shut the door. He started the engine, turned on the lights, then began to back down the drive. He lost sight of her when he turned out onto the road and his lights no longer shined down the drive.

Bill had a lot on his mind as he drove back to his house in Hill City. He had to admit his thoughts of Julie were pleasant thoughts.

When he arrived at his house, he immediately sat down at the kitchen table and wrote out his report of the day's activities, at least those that were part of his investigation. He didn't think it was any of the sheriff's business that he had dinner with Julie and Wilbur Turnquest. However, he did add to his report his questioning of Wilbur and his granddaughter.

When he was finished with the report, he took a shower and turned in for the night.

CHAPTER FOUR

Bill woke to the annoying sound of his alarm clock next to his bed. He reached over and shut off the alarm then swung his legs off the side of the bed and sat up. He rubbed the sleep from his eyes, then went into the bathroom.

After he was finished in the bathroom, he put on his uniform. Bill had no desire to fix his own breakfast. Instead, he got in his patrol car and went to the Hill City Café on Main Street.

The café had the usual run of regular early morning customers. Almost everyone in the café turned and looked at Bill when he came in the door. It seemed they had a real interest in him this morning. It was as if they were waiting to see who he was there to question. He looked around the café until he found an empty booth. He walked over to it and sat down.

Sandy, a short, stocky, middle aged woman with tired eyes who was wearing a white apron over her jeans and blue blouse, approached him. She was carrying a cup of black coffee that she put down on the table in front of him.

"What'll it be, Bill?" she asked with a smile.

"What's with all the interest in me this morning?" Bill asked softly.

"You know there aren't any secrets in this town. They've heard about the killin' up at the old Jasper Quarry, and they're wonderin' what you're going to do about it."

"Oh, is that all. I thought maybe I forgot to zip up my fly," Bill said with a grin.

Sandy smiled, then asked him again, "What'll it be?"

"I'll have the morning special, two eggs, hash browns and ham."

"Eggs over easy?" Sandy asked.

"Yes, please."

As soon as Sandy left to put in his order, Bill leaned back in the booth, picked up the cup of coffee and took a sip from it as he looked around the room. Everyone looked away when he looked toward them. When he saw Rutledge, he immediately knew who had spread the word about the murder at the Jasper Quarry. Rutledge was not only known as scavenger, he was also well known for spreading rumors and gossip, but rarely did he ever get the facts right.

Bill had already decided to talk to Rutledge again, but he didn't want to do it here. The last thing he wanted was to get more rumors started. He would wait until he could see Rutledge at his home. Talking to him on his own turf might make Rutledge feel a little more comfortable, and more willing to talk. He also wanted to see what

Rutledge's place looked like, since he had never had a reason to go there before.

Bill planned to visit the quarry again and do a slow walk around in the hope of finding more evidence, anything that would help him with the case. His time spent checking out the quarry would give Rutledge time to finish his breakfast, and any other business he might have in town, and get back home.

It wasn't long before Sandy brought Bill's breakfast and set it on the table in front of him. She refilled his coffee cup then went to another table to refill the coffee cups at that table. Bill glanced around the room before he began to eat his breakfast. He had not said anything to anyone in the café, except Sandy; but as he ate, he got the impression that Mr. Keaton might want to talk to him, but not there.

The reason he felt that way, was Keaton kept glancing in his direction, and then he would look away as if he was hoping no one had seen him look toward Bill. He wasn't really sure Keaton wanted to talk to him, but it didn't matter since he planned to talk to Keaton anyway.

Keaton was in his late fifties or early sixties. He had a full head of hair with a good deal of gray. He wasn't very tall, had a potbelly, a thick gray beard and mustache, and was wearing bib overalls and a plaid work shirt with the sleeves rolled up to his elbows. He would have been in his late thirties or early forties, when the Jasper Quarry closed down. Keaton walked with a very noticeable limp as if his right leg had been injured some years ago.

Keaton had a small place about a mile down the road from the front gate of the quarry. Bill had been there only once, and that was at least a year ago. He remembered there was a small house set back in the woods that could not be seen from the road. There was also a barn, if he remembered correctly, and a lot of junk around the place.

As far as Bill knew, he had a small garden near the barn. He had no idea how Keaton made his living now or in the past. Keaton was a quiet man. No one seemed to know much about him, or talked about him. Bill decided he would stop by Keaton's place to have a talk with him.

Bill suddenly remembered what kind of vehicle Keaton drove. It was a beat up old one-ton stake truck, probably about a 1921 or '22 Ford. It had some writing on the side door that had faded to the point it was almost impossible to read. Bill wondered where the stake truck had come from.

Remembering he had been told there had been several "accidents" at the Jasper Quarry prior to its closing; Bill began to wonder if Keaton's limp was a result of one of those "accidents". His next thought was maybe the stake truck had once been owned by the quarry. He wondered if Keaton had worked in the quarry at sometime. It was just some of the things he hoped to find out.

Since Bill didn't want to throw suspicion on anyone, especially on Keaton, he would finish his breakfast then head out to the quarry. He would spend sometime at the quarry doing a walk around the crime scene, then drive over to Keaton's place to have a talk with him. If he had time, he would pay a visit to Rutledge and have a talk with him, too.

Bill finished his breakfast and left a tip on the table for Sandy. He then paid his bill then left the café. He walked to his patrol car and got on the radio. He called in and told Mary that he was headed to the Jasper Quarry and to log him on duty.

"Is there anything I need to tell the sheriff?"

"No. Not at this time. I have a couple of people I plan to question today, but nothing new yet," Bill said.

"Okay. You be careful out there."

"I will," Bill said then signed off.

Bill left Hill City and headed toward the Jasper Quarry. It took him close to an hour to get to the front gate. The gate was still closed. He got out of his patrol car to go open the gate, but stopped suddenly when he looked down and saw fresh tire tracks over the tracks his patrol car had made yesterday. He knelt down and looked at the tracks closely.

After studying the tracks carefully, he looked toward the quarry. He wasn't looking at anything special, he was just thinking. The tracks he had seen reminded him of the tread pattern on Rutledge's pickup. There had been very little in the way of tread marks in the dirt, and the tires on Rutledge's pickup were almost bald. He wondered if Rutledge had returned to the quarry even after he had been told not to come back there.

It occurred to Bill there could be other vehicles in the area that had bald, or almost bald, tires on them. It was not uncommon to see bald tires on vehicles belonging to some of the poorer people who lived back in the hills. Bill decided he should make plaster casts of the tire tracks and compare them to the tires on Rutledge's pickup. He knew Rutledge's pickup had not made the tracks he had found when he took the first plaster cast of tire tracks where the body was found.

Bill took the time to make casts of the new set of tracks and photos of where he found the tracks before he opened the gate and drove in. He parked where he had parked before and got out of his patrol car. Even though it was light outside, he checked his flashlight before he started searching the area. He then walked to the tool shed and went around behind it.

He first started looking for clues where the body had been, starting at the large reddish brown spot on the ground. He carefully studied the area. He discovered several shotgun pellets in the boards of the tool shed, which made sense. A shotgun had been used to shoot the victim. From the looks of the body last night and size of the shot pattern, the victim had been shot at fairly close range.

Bill had a little experience with the pattern a shotgun makes depending on the choke used and the size of the shot. He knew he was guessing, but based on his experience, he guessed the victim had been shot from a distance of eight to ten feet, but no further than twelve feet. It was also clear that the victim was sitting on the ground with his back to the tool shed when he was shot.

Bill took his knife and carefully dug out a few of the shotgun pellets from the boards of the tool shed. He didn't know what value they would be other than to tell him what size shot was used.

Bill also discovered something he had not expected to find. He found a single bullet hole in the side of the tool shed right where the victim had been sitting. He only noticed it because blood from the victim had not filled in the hole. From the size of the hole, Bill was pretty sure it was from a .38 caliber pistol, although he couldn't be one hundred percent sure without the slug. He shined his flashlight into the bullet hole to see if the bullet was still in the board, or if it had gone through. He couldn't tell for sure, but it looked like it might have gone through the board.

Since it seemed important, Bill went around to the front of the shed. With the way the shed was leaning he wasn't sure he wanted to go inside, but it would be the only way to find out if the bullet was inside the shed. He slowly pulled the door off the single hinge that was still holding the door on the shed and set it aside. He looked again at the shed. Being as careful as he could, he bent down and moved into the shed. With the shed leaning so sharply to one side, Bill was unable to stand up inside. He worked his way into the shed being very careful not to disturb anything for fear it would fall down on him.

It didn't take him long to find where the bullet had come through the board. It had come through splintering the backside of the board. That meant the bullet had passed through the board from the outside and was probably somewhere inside the shed. Bill began looking around, slowly covering every inch of the floor of the shed, being very careful when moving the loose boards on the floor. A couple of times it felt as if the shed was about to collapse. He had every desire to get out of the shed, but he wanted the bullet even though he had no idea if it was important.

Suddenly, he heard what sounded like someone coming. He had no idea who it was, and he didn't want to be caught in the shed. He was sure that almost anything would cause the shed to collapse on him. Just as he was ready to bail out of the shed, he saw the bullet. It was between two boards that had once been part of the floor of the shed. He reached down and quickly picked it up. He slipped it into his shirt pocket, then scrambled out of the shed. In his effort to get out quickly, he hit the door frame with his foot. He was able to jerk his foot out of the tool shed before the shed collapsed with a crash and a cloud of dust and dirt.

He looked around as he stood up and saw Julie looking at him. Her eyes were big and she looked like she had been scared half to death.

"What are you doing here?" Bill asked.

She just looked at him for a moment before she spoke, "What are you doing? Were you trying to kill yourself going into that shed?" Julie said with a hint of panic mixed with a little anger in her voice.

"No. I was looking for evidence," he said as he turned and looked at the flattened shed, then turned back to look at her. "I'm sorry if I frightened you."

Julie stood there looking at him while she tried to catch her breath. Bill walked up to her then reached out and took her by the hand. She was as pale as a ghost.

"Are you all right?" Bill asked.

She looked up at him and could see in his face his concern for her. She could also see his face was smudged with dirt, and he was covered with dust. The frightened look slowly left her face. It was slowly replaced with a smile.

"You need a bath," she said as she stepped away from him.

He looked down at the front of his uniform, then looked back at her.

"Yes, I do," he said with a sheepish grin as he tried to brush some of the dirt off the front of his shirt and pants with his hands.

"What are you doing here?" he asked.

"I saw your car turn in here. I thought I would come over to see what you were doing and invite you to lunch."

"It isn't even close to lunchtime."

"I know, but I wanted to catch you before you left. I had no idea how long you planned to be here," she said.

"I will probably be here for some time."

"What are you doing, besides trying to get yourself killed," she asked.

"I'm looking for evidence and clues."

"In a dilapidated old tool shed?"

"Yes. The body was found on the backside of the tool shed."

"Oh," she said as she looked at the place where the tool shed once stood. "I better go back home and let you do your job."

"Would it be all right if I stop by later?" Bill asked.

"The offer for lunch still stands, but you will have to eat out on the porch if you look like that."

"You never know, I might just look a lot better by lunchtime," he said with a grin.

"I hope so," she said then turned and walked away.

Bill stood there watching her walk away. He couldn't help but notice how nice she looked in jeans.

He let out a deep breath as she disappeared into the woods. He then looked around to see if anyone was around. He saw no one. He hoped he had not destroyed any evidence by knocking over the tool shed, but he had gotten the bullet.

He turned and started his slow and methodical search of the area. He made a pattern in his head to help him make sure he checked every inch of a twenty-foot area around the location the body was found. The only other thing he found was a twelve-gauge shotgun shell. He picked it up by sticking his pen in the end of the shell so he wouldn't smudge any fingerprints that might be on it, then carefully dropped it into a small paper evidence bag then put the bag in his pocket. He didn't find anything else he thought might have anything to do with the death of the victim.

When he was reasonably sure he had covered the ground around the tool shed, he took a quick look at his watch. He decided he had time to return to Hill City, take a shower, change into a clean uniform and return in time for lunch with Julie.

He went to his patrol car and drove back to Hill City. He took a quick shower, put on a clean uniform, then headed back toward Jasper Quarry.

As he drove through Hill City, he saw Rutledge's pickup parked in front of the café. He didn't know if Rutledge was in the café or not, but decided it didn't really matter. He doubted Rutledge was going very far, and he could find him when he was ready to question him.

He also saw John Keaton's old stake truck. It was at the gas station. It looked like it was having new tires put on it. Bill immediately pulled into the gas station. He got out of his patrol car and walked into the garage.

"Hi, Bill. How's it going? I hear you got a murder case on your hands," Jim Anderson said.

Jim Anderson was the owner of Anderson's Service Station. He was tall and lanky, but well muscled. His clothes were stained with grease and oil spots, especially the front of his pant legs were he would often wipe his hands while working on cars. Anderson ran the station by himself and was well liked by almost everyone in town.

"Yeah. Say is that Keaton's truck?"

"You kidding? You know that's his truck."

"What are you doing to it?"

"I'm replacing the tires on it."

"He is getting new tires?" Bill asked thinking that Keaton didn't have enough money to replace all four tires at once.

"Nah. I'm replacing the old ones with some newer ones. He can't afford new tires."

"What do you do with the old tires?"

"It depends. If there's any good tread left on them and there's nothing else wrong, I put them on that rack over there and resell them," he said as he pointed to a rack of used tires. "If they're as bad as Keaton's here, I put them out back to be taken back to the distributor. I get a little money for them if I send them back."

"Do me a favor. Put the tires off Keaton's truck some place where I can see them later."

"Sure, but they ain't no good for anything," he said, looking at Bill as if he were crazy.

"Don't tell anyone. I want to use them as examples of worn-out tires. I'm working up a class for the other officers on identifying tire tracks."

"Oh, sure thing. I'll save 'um for you, but they don't have hardly any tread left on 'um," he said.

"There is still a little tread left in spots. I'll stop by and get them later," Bill said.

"Okay," Jim said.

As Bill turned to leave the garage, he walked by Keaton's truck. He took a moment to look at the old sign on the side of the truck. It was badly faded, but he could make out the logo for the Jasper Quarry. He had no idea what that bit of information meant to the case he was working on, but it gave him something to talk to Keaton about when he went to question him.

Bill got back in the patrol car and drove out to Turnquest's place. He got there just in time to have lunch with Julie.

CHAPTER FIVE

Julie and Bill were sitting at the kitchen table, just getting ready to eat, when Wilbur came in the backdoor. He hung his hat on a peg next to the door then stepped into the kitchen.

"You're just in time for lunch," Julie said as she stood up.

She got a glass and plate for her grandfather and put them on the table for him, then sat back down.

"I see you have company. It looks like you survived the collapse of that old tool shed," he said while grinning at Bill.

"Yeah. It was close."

"I'll say," Julie said.

"How are things coming with your investigation," Wilbur asked.

"Slow," Bill replied without further comment.

"I think there has been enough talk about that for now," Julie said. "Bill is off duty and on his lunch break. He should be able to eat in peace without everyone asking him questions."

Wilbur smiled at his granddaughter, then looked at Bill. He winked at Bill then sat down.

"Since we can't talk about the murder at the table, what do we talk about?" Wilbur asked.

"We could talk about what you found in your oat field this morning," Julie said.

"Oh, I guess," Wilbur said.

"What did you find?" Bill asked.

"Well, I found a wooden box at the edge of my oat field. It had a label on it reading 'Jasper Quarry'. It looked old, but the strange thing was it was setting right out in the open, and it wasn't there two or three days ago. I'm sure of that," Wilbur said.

"Was there anything in the wooden box?" Bill asked.

"Yes, and that's the interesting part. There wasn't anything in the wooden box but packing sawdust. It was about half full of it."

Bill sat there looking at Wilbur for a minute. He was thinking about the box, and what might have been in it. The only things he could think of that might have been in a wooden box packed with sawdust were explosives, such as dynamite or nitroglycerin.

"Are you sure there wasn't anything in the wooden box?" Bill asked, his face looking serious.

"Yeah. Nothing but sawdust, at least that's all I saw in it."

"Do you still have the wooden box?"

"Yeah. It looked like it was in good condition. I can always use a good sturdy wooden box to put things in."

"I would like to see the wooden box," Bill said.

"I think you can wait until you have finished your lunch. Then we will all go look at the wooden box," Julie said.

Bill looked from Julie to Wilbur. He noticed Wilbur was grinning. He also noticed Wilbur began to eat again.

The three of them finished eating lunch before anything else was said about the wooden box. When they were done, they all got up and went outside.

"Where did you find the wooden box?" Bill asked as they walked toward Wilbur's workshop.

"I found it next to the fence that runs between my property and the quarry's property. It was ah – maybe ten or fifteen feet from the gate that goes into the quarry."

"Was there any chance it had been there for years?"

"No. No. I certainly would have seen it long before now. I'm sure it wasn't there a couple of days ago," Wilbur said as they walked into his workshop.

Bill saw the wooden box immediately. It was setting on the workbench just inside the workshop. Bill walked up to it and looked it over without touching it.

It was obvious that the wooden box had not been setting out in the weather for any extended period of time. The wooden box was in good condition and the name on the box was fairly easy to read. It had apparently belonged to the Jasper Quarry. The wooden box measured about eighteen inches high, two feet wide and two feet long; and it had the top which was still on it.

"What do you think it was used for?" Wilbur asked.

"I take it you have had it open," Bill asked, ignoring his question for the moment.

"Yeah, sure. That's how I know it had sawdust inside."

"Is the sawdust still in it?"

"Yeah. I opened it when I found it. I didn't do anything with it except close it up and bring it back here and set it on the bench. Say, what's going on here?" Wilbur asked as he looked at Bill, wondering why he was so interested in the box.

"It would be my guess this wooden box was used to transport explosives of some kind, most likely dynamite or nitroglycerin."

"You're not kidding are you?" Julie asked, a worried look on her face.

"No. It was used to carry dynamite or nitroglycerin. Both would have been packed in a solid wooden box with sawdust as a cushion, and both would have been used in the quarry."

"Do you think there might be some of the explosives still in the box?" Wilbur asked.

"Did you check to see if there was anything buried in the sawdust?"

"No. I just brought it here and set it right where it is," he said looking a little nervous.

"Do you think there might still be explosives in the box?" Julie asked.

"I don't know, but I would rather be safe than sorry. I think I should find out." Bill said.

"How do you propose to do that?" Julie asked, her voice showing her concern.

"What do you want us to do?" Wilbur asked.

"I want both of you to go around to the other side of the house and wait there."

"What are you going to do?" Julie said, afraid of what he was going to say.

"I'm going to find out if there is anything under the sawdust. Now, kindly do as I said."

"Come on, Honey." Wilbur said as he grabbed Julie by the arm. "Bill knows what he's doing. He doesn't need us here to distract him."

Bill looked at Julie and watched as Wilbur led her out of the workshop. As soon as they went around the corner of the house, he turned and looked at the wooden box. Bill had no idea how old the wooden box was, but something he had heard a long time ago was that dynamite becomes more unstable with age. He didn't know if nitroglycerin became more unstable with time, but he knew it was very unstable to begin with.

Although he had no experience with explosives, except for hand grenades while in the Army, he thought he had to do something to make sure the wooden box was safe.

Slowly, and very carefully, Bill reached out and lifted the top off the wooden box. He noticed the wooden box seemed to wobble slightly as if on an uneven surface. The last thing he wanted was for some slight motion to set it off. As he stared at the wooden box trying to think of a way to steady it, he remembered that Wilbur had brought the wooden box to his workshop from the field. He certainly must have wiggled it around a little and it didn't blow up.

Being as cautious as he could, Bill set the top on the bench then looked over the edge of the wooden box to see if he could detect anything inside other than the sawdust. He could see nothing but sawdust. After taking a deep breath, he slowly and carefully reached inside. When his fingers touched the sawdust, he hesitated for a second, took a deep breath, then very gently pushed his fingers down into the sawdust at one end of the wooden box. Moving slowly, he dragged his fingers through the sawdust feeling for anything that might not be sawdust.

Sweat ran down Bill's face as he cautiously moved his fingers through the sawdust. After running his fingers from end to end, he took a deep breath in order to relax his tense muscles. He then ran his fingers through the sawdust from side to side in an effort make sure there was nothing in the box but sawdust. He let out a sigh of relief when he had finished checking the entire inside of the wooden box for anything other than sawdust, and found nothing.

Bill pulled his hand out of the wooden box, turned around and leaned back against the work bench. He took a handkerchief from his back pocket and wiped the sweat from his face, took a deep breath, then turned back around and smiled as he looked again at the wooden box.

His thoughts soon turned to Julie and her grandfather. He was sure they were waiting impatiently and praying there was nothing dangerous in the wooden box. He turned and walked out of the workshop toward the corner of the house.

When he walked around the corner, he could see Julie and Wilbur leaning up against the house. The expressions on their faces showed they had been worried, in fact, down right scared.

"All is well," Bill said. "There was nothing but sawdust in the wooden box."

"You took an awful chance," Julie said.

She stepped in front of him and put her arms around him, then laid her head on his chest. He was a little surprised by her actions, but he certainly didn't mind.

Bill held her for a few minutes then looked down at her and said, "I could really use a cup of coffee."

"Me, too," Wilbur said with a smile.

The three of them went into the house. Julie made a pot of coffee while Bill and Wilbur sat down at the table.

"I'm sure glad the wooden box was empty," Wilbur said.

"So am I," Julie added.

"Well, I sure am, but I wonder what was in the wooden box and where the contents of the box are now."

"What do you mean?" Wilbur said.

"The wooden box was designed to carry dynamite or nitroglycerin. The wooden box doesn't appear to be very old, or it was stored in one of the buildings, or some place else to keep it out of the weather. The wooden box was just too clean to have been stored at the quarry since it closed. That makes me wonder what was in it and who has the contents now."

"I see what you mean, but it had the Jasper Quarry name on it," Wilbur said.

"True, but I saw a stencil of the Jasper Quarry in the tool shed before it collapsed. It didn't look like it had been lying around there very long."

"Did the stencil look like it had been used?" Julie asked.

"I really can't say. I was a little too busy finding what I was looking for and getting out of there. Since the tool shed collapsed on it, there's no way to tell if it had been used recently or not."

"You know, the wooden box did seem to be pretty clean to have been the property of Jasper Quarry," Wilbur said, thoughtfully. "You think someone might have put the Jasper Quarry logo on the box or over someone else's logo?"

"It's possible. Wilbur, I'm going to need the wooden box."

"It's all yours, and if I don't get it back, I won't mind at all."

"Good," Bill said, then looked at Julie. "I have to be going. I still have a lot to do before I can call it a day."

"When will I see you again," she asked.

"I'm not sure, but I'll call you," he said. "Walk me to my car?"

"Sure."

Bill walked out to the workshop and picked up the wooden box. He joined Julie at the backdoor of the house. Julie took his arm and walked with him around to the front of the house and down the drive to the gate where he had left his patrol car. He put the wooden box in the back seat.

He turned around and leaned back against his patrol car as Julie stepped up in front of him. He reached out and put his hands on her narrow waist, while she put her hands on his broad shoulders.

"Will you stop by and see me when you're out this way again," she said softly.

"Yes. I might just come out to see you anyway."

"I'd like that."

"So would I. Would you be upset with me if I kiss you?" he asked looking into her blue eyes."

"I might be very upset with you if you don't," she said as she leaned into him.

Bill's lips met hers. It was not a real passionate kiss, but it was one that let them know there was something between them, something that might be lost if they didn't help it along.

"That was nice," Julie said as she pushed herself back a little. "I wouldn't mind if you did that again."

Bill didn't say anything. He simply drew her to him and kissed her again. It was a much more passionate kiss with a much deeper meaning for both of them, and it lasted longer. After the kiss, Julie straightened up and looked him in the eyes, but didn't say anything.

"I better go before I decide to stay right here," he said, the expression on his face showing her he meant what he said.

"I think that would be a good idea," she replied, "but don't stay away too long."

"I won't, that much I can assure you," he said as he let go of her.

Julie stepped back away from the patrol car and watched him as he got in. She waited for him to start his patrol car and back down the drive before she reached up and touched her lips. She could still feel his kiss, and she liked it. As soon as he disappeared out onto the road, she turned around and walked back to the house.

Bill drove down the road toward Rutledge's place. With his thoughts so completely focused on Julie, he almost missed the drive to Rutledge's house. He had to slam on the brakes in order to make the turn. Once he turned onto the drive to Rutledge's house, he quickly turned his focus to Rutledge and what he wanted to talk to him about.

As he pulled into the yard, he noticed Rutledge's small farm looked more like a junk yard than a farm. There were all kinds of machinery, from farm machinery to machinery that looked like it might have come from the quarry. There were several old trucks, pickups and cars along a hedgerow with two and a half to three feet high weeds growing around them. All the buildings, including the house, looked in need of repair, to say nothing of all the junk lying around them. He was sure the inside of the buildings, as well as the house, were as full of junk as the yard.

Bill pulled up in front of the house and stopped his patrol car. He sat behind the wheel and looked around. It was hard for him to imagine living with all that junk.

His attention was brought to the front porch door when he saw movement. The door swung open and Rutledge stepped out carrying a double barrel shotgun held firmly in both hands. The look on his face was anything but friendly. Since the two of them had not gotten along very well, Bill had no idea what would happen when Rutledge saw a sheriff's patrol car in front of his house.

Bill reached down and unhooked his gun, then opened the patrol car's door. The way he was parked hc had his patrol car between him and Rutledge, which made Bill feel a little better about getting out of it. He stepped out of the car and stood beside it.

"Mr. Rutledge, put down the shotgun," Bill ordered while keeping his hand on his gun where Rutledge could not see it.

"You're on my property," he said without even lowering the shotgun.

"Mr. Rutledge, I'm here to talk to you."

"You got a warrant?"

"No. I'm just here to simply talk. It doesn't have to be anything more than that unless you want to make it more," Bill said with a voice of authority.

"I don't have to talk to you."

"No, you don't. But if you decide not to talk to me, I will get a warrant and take you all the way into Rapid City where you will either talk to me and the sheriff, or sit in jail until you do. Now which is it going to be?"

Bill just stood there keeping his hand on his gun while waiting for Rutledge to make up his mind.

"Well, what's it going to be? I don't have all day."

"Okay. I'll talk to you," he said then set his shotgun on the porch, leaning it against the door frame.

"Step away from the shotgun," Bill ordered.

"You can't come in my house."

"Okay. You come out here and we'll talk at my car. You can lean against it if you want."

Rutledge looked at Bill for a moment or so before he walked down his porch steps toward the patrol car, leaving the shotgun on the porch. As he walked up to it, Bill stepped around in front of the car.

"What do you want to talk about?" Rutledge said as he leaned against the patrol car.

"First of all, what gauge is your shotgun?"

"You come all the way out here to ask me that?"

"No, but I want to know."

"It's a sixteen-gauge Browning double barrel. Why?"

"Do you have any other shotguns?"

"No. I got a couple of rifles though."

"What about pistols?"

"I got two. One's a .45 caliber auto I got after the war. It was war surplus. And I got a 9mm German Luger my younger brother took off a German officer after he kilt him during the war in Europe. Why?"

Do you have a .38 caliber pistol?"

"No, and I ain't never had one."

"Were you in the Jasper Quarry since you and I talked in the quarry the night you found the body?" Bill asked, then watched his face for some kind of reaction.

"You ain't tryin' to pin that on me?"

"No. I just want to know if you've been back there since that night."

"No. I ain't been back there. You told me to stay away and that's just what I done."

"Okay. That's all I wanted to know. See, it wasn't so hard, was it?"

"No," Rutledge admitted. "You comin' back again?"

"I don't know. I might have to talk to you again, but right now I don't know if I'll be back."

"Okay."

Bill turned around, got back in his patrol car and started it. Rutledge moved away from the car. Bill glanced over at Rutledge, then started toward the road. He watched Rutledge in his rearview mirror. Rutledge just stood there and watched Bill until he turned out onto the road.

When Bill got back to the road, he headed toward Hill City. It was getting on toward dinnertime. Needless to say, it had been a busy and interesting day. He was beginning to think it was time to call it a day.

As he drove into Hill City, he remembered that he had asked Jim to keep Keaton's tires from his old truck for him. He noticed Jim had closed up for the night. Getting the tires in the morning would be okay. He could pick them up and do his tests on them at his house in the morning.

He called in and checked out, then fixed his dinner. After dinner, he sat down at his desk and wrote out a report for the sheriff. He also made a few notes on what he planned to do the next day. After listening to the news on the radio, he turned in for the night.

CHAPTER SIX

Bill was lying in his bed with his eyes closed when his alarm went off. He reached over and shut it off. He had been thinking about the wooden box Wilbur Turnquest found at the edge of his field bordering the Jasper Quarry. What concerned him about it most was the fact it was empty. If it had had anything in it, who had the contents now and where were they? He thought it would be a good idea to let the sheriff know about it, even though there was no proof, or no indication the wooden box had had anything in it, other than the sawdust.

He got up, took a shower then ate his breakfast. As soon as he was done, he called the sheriff's office and asked to talk to the sheriff. His call was quickly transferred to the sheriff.

"Do you have something for me, Bill?" the sheriff asked.

"Yes, sir. A wooden box, the same kind used for transporting explosives, was found on Wilbur Turnquest's property. The box was empty except for the sawdust used as a packing material. The box had the Jasper Quarry's name on the side, but didn't look old enough to have been around the quarry for very many years," Bill explained.

"Do you think you have someone running around with some explosives?"

"I can't say for sure, but it is certainly a possibility. The condition of the box may be the result of it having been stored in someone's house and was just an empty box one of the former employees saved but never used for anything. However, the fact it was found in a place it had not been three days earlier makes me wonder. It's also possible the Jasper Quarry logo was put on it over some other logo to give the impression it was old."

"Okay," the sheriff said thoughtfully. "I don't think there's much we can do with so little information about the box, things like who had it, and where has it been all these years. If you come up with more information on it, follow up on it."

"Yes, sir," Bill said.

"Is there anything new on the murder at the quarry?"

"No, not at this time. However, I'm following up on a few things. I did find a bullet hole in the tool shed where the victim was shot with the shotgun. It was located directly behind where he was sitting when he was shot. You might check with the ME to find out if the victim was shot with a .38 caliber gun as well as with the shotgun. I've got the bullet. It was inside the tool shed.

"I also found a shotgun shell in the weeds about twelve feet from where the victim was found. I don't know what it will show, but it might have fingerprints on it. I've been careful not to touch it with my hands."

"I want you to get it into the lab as soon as possible," the sheriff said.

"I'll bring it in now, and my report of yesterday's activities. By the way, I found some more tire tracks at the quarry. I may have found who made them, but I will have to get the tires from the local gas station here in Hill City. My report will explain it all."

"Okay. Secure those tires before you come in. I don't want anything to happen to them. They may be important, they may not be, just make sure they are the right tires."

"Yes, sir. I'll take care of it," Bill said.

"Good. You're doing good work, keep it up. I won't be here when you get here, so drop off your report. Drop off the bullet and shotgun shell at the lab, and tell them all you can about them, then head on back. I'll call you if I have any questions about your report."

"Okay," Bill said then the phone went dead.

Bill left his house and went directly to Anderson's gas station. He found Jim under a car on his lube-rack. He was changing the oil in the car.

"Morning Jim."

"Mornin' Bill. How's it goin'?"

"Okay. I came to pick up the tires I asked you to save for me."

"Sure. They're right out back," Jim said as he wiped his hands on his pants, then turned and walked out of the garage.

Bill followed him around behind the gas station where he saw a pile of used tires stacked up against the back of the station. His first thought was he hoped Jim had not put the tires in that pile. It would be hard to prove which tires were the ones off Keaton's truck.

"Which ones came off Keaton's truck?" Bill asked as he looked at the pile of worn-out tires.

"Ain't none of them. I set them aside so they didn't get mixed up with the others. They're over here," Jim said as he pointed to four tires leaning up against a small storage shed.

Bill walked over and looked at the tires. He noticed each one of them had the word "save" written on them. Bill let out a sigh of relief when he saw the tires. He walked over and looked at them.

"Are you sure these are the tires you took off Keaton's truck yesterday?"

"Yup," Jim said with an air of confidence.

"Good."

"It seems important that the tires are off Keaton's truck. Is Keaton in any kind of trouble?"

"Not that I know of," Bill replied while looking at Jim. "Like I said yesterday, I want to use them to make casts of tire tracks. It really didn't matter where the tires came from, I just wanted some tires with almost no tread in order to show that casts of tires that are almost bald can still be useful in identifying the tire."

"I see."

"It might be a good idea if you say nothing about whose tires they are, but rather they were just some old tires. We wouldn't want to start rumors about Keaton, would we?"

"Right. I know how the people are around here. Not a word," Jim assured him.

"Thanks. It might be best if you say nothing at all about the tires."

"Mum's the word. I won't say a word to anyone about them."

"Thanks, Jim."

Bill reached down and picked up two of the tires and started back to his patrol car. Jim picked up the other two and followed him. Bill put the tires in the trunk then turned to Jim.

"I know you get some money for tires you send back, so I'll get them back to you as soon as I'm finished with them."

"That would be great. I've got of lot of old tires out back waiting to be picked up."

"Thanks again for the use of the tires," Bill said.

"No problem," Jim said then watched as Bill drove away.

Bill left town for the sheriff's office to leave his report. After he left his report, he took the bullet and the shotgun shell to the lab and told them that they had come from the quarry and where in the quarry he had found them. As soon as he was done, he drove back to his house in Hill City.

Bill pulled into the driveway, opened his trunk and took the tires out. He set them up against his garage, opened the garage door, then backed his own car out.

Once his car was out of the way, he raked the dirt floor of the garage until it was smooth. He took the tires, one at a time, and rolled them across the smooth dirt floor, then leaned each tire up against the wall of the garage at the end of the track made by the tire.

Bill went inside the house, got a bucket of water, a bag of Plaster of Paris and a stick to mix it, then returned to the garage and made up the mixture. He carefully poured the mixture over the tire tracks he had made on the garage floor. When he was finished in the garage, he went into his house and made his lunch then sat down and ate it while he waited for the plaster to dry and harden.

Once he finished his lunch, he took a piece of chalk and went into the garage where he labeled each cast and the tire matching the cast. He then carefully laid out the casts in the sun next to the driveway. He went to his patrol car and took out the cast he had made of tire tracks at the gate to the quarry. He compared the cast from the quarry with each new cast he had just made. None of them matched. It was clear that Keaton had not been the one with the bald tires who had gone into the quarry after he left.

However, not finding a match was no excuse not to talk to Keaton. He might have seen something that would give Bill a lead since he lived just down the road from the quarry entrance. It was time to go have a talk with him.

Bill made sure each cast had been marked with where he made it, and when he made it, along with any information that would clearly identify the cast. He stacked them in the garage then closed and locked the door. It was a little after two o'clock when he left his house for Keaton's place just down the road from the quarry entrance.

It was almost three in the afternoon when he turned into the drive to Keaton's farm. He drove back in among the trees, but couldn't see the house until he drove out of the trees into a large clearing. In the center of the clearing was a small house that looked like it could use a good coat of paint and some repairs. The steps on the porch needed fixing and the screen door needed the screen replaced.

Bill stopped in front of the house, shut off the engine and got out of his patrol car. He took a minute to look around. He didn't see Keaton, but his old truck was parked in front of the barn.

"Can I help you, Deputy?"

Bill swung around to see Keaton coming out of the house. He smiled then walked toward the front door.

"I thought I would come out and have a talk with you."

"Why?"

"I'm sure you know I'm investigating the murder at the Jasper Quarry. I was ----," Bill said, but was interrupted.

"What's that got to do with me?" Keaton asked angrily.

"Nothing I know of. I just wanted to ask you a few questions."

"Like what?"

"Well, I would like to know if you heard anything, or saw anything, either during the day or at night last week, especially anything coming from the Jasper Quarry."

"I mind my own business."

"I'm sure you do, Mr. Keaton. It would be a great help if you could tell me if you heard anything."

"Like what?"

"Like cars or trucks going in and out of the quarry, the sound of gunshots, anything, someone screaming or yelling."

"There's cars and pickups going in and out of that place at all hours of the day and night. I even hear the sound of gunshots being fired sometime over there. People from town use the quarry pit for target practice and to hunt coons, squirrels and who knows what else. Like I said, I mind my own business."

"Yes, you did say that," Bill said with a hint of frustration. "Have you driven over to the quarry lately?"

"Why would I do that?"

Bill was beginning to think he had made a mistake when he thought Keaton might want to talk to him.

"Mr. Keaton, do you own a .38 caliber pistol?"

"Why do you want to know that?"

"Just answer the question, please," Bill said getting a little frustrated with Keaton's answers.

"Yeah, I have one. Why?"

"Have you used it lately?"

"No."

"You never did answer my question, have you been over to the quarry lately?"

"No. I don't have a reason to go over there."

"I have one more question for you, how did you injure your leg?"

Keaton looked down at his leg, then looked at Bill. Bill wasn't sure he was going to answer him.

"I don't think that's any of your business. I've answered all the questions I'm goin' to. You can get off my property, now," he said the sound of anger in his voice.

Bill looked at Keaton for a moment before he turned and walked back to his patrol car. Before he got in the car, he took a minute to look up at the house. He was a little surprised to see the curtain in the window moving since the window was closed. It certainly wasn't the wind as it was dead still.

Bill opened the door and slipped into the driver's seat. He looked at Keaton through the windshield while he started the patrol car. Bill put the car in gear and drove on down the long drive to the road. The thought passed through his mind that there was someone else in the house. He was sure Keaton was not married, however, he didn't know if he had any children. Who was in the house, Bill wondered. It was obvious Keaton didn't want him to know there was someone else around, but why?

When Bill reached the road, he stopped and looked both ways. His thoughts were about the person in the window. He was trying to decide if he should go back to town and see if he could find out a little more about Keaton's life, or should he go see Julie and her grandfather to see if they knew anything about Keaton's personal life.

The thought of seeing Julie helped him make the decision to turn left to go see if Julie was home. He turned left and started down the road. As he passed the front of the Jasper quarry, he slowed down and looked toward the gate to see if anyone might be there. He didn't see anyone and the gate was still closed, so he continued on down the road.

It was less than five minutes from the time he left Keaton's to the time he turned into the Turnquest farm. For the first time, the gate was open. He drove through and parked in front of the house.

Just as the patrol car stopped, Julie came out on the porch. He was glad to see she was smiling at him. He got out of his patrol car and walked up to the house then stepped up on the porch.

"I didn't expect to see you so soon," Julie said with a smile.

"I was in the neighborhood," he said with a grin.

"In other words, you were at the quarry."

"Actually, I was visiting Mr. Keaton at his home. What can you tell me about him? It seems he was not too friendly toward me."

"Not much. I can tell you that he ran me off his property about a month ago."

"What were you doing on his property?"

"I didn't think I was, but he sure thought I was. I was hiking around the rim of the quarry pit. It's actually kind of pretty back in there. The rim comes close to his property line. His fence is about a hundred yards from the edge of the quarry pit at the closest place to his property. I was still on the quarry property, but I guess he thought I was on his property."

"Can you see his house from there?"

"You might if you worked your way through the trees and got real close to his fence. Are you thinking about going over there?"

"No, not at the moment. Could you see his house from where you were when he told you that you were trespassing?"

"No. There's no way you can see it from there. That's why it surprised me so. I was still a good sixty yards from the fence line. He was so angry with me being there that he scared me, and I haven't been back in that area since. I have no idea what he would do," Julie said.

"What makes you say that, is he a violent man?"

"Not that I know of, but I didn't want to find out."

"Do you know if anyone lives with him?"

"As far as I know, he lives alone. Grandpa said he was married once, but after the accident at the quarry, his wife left him. I don't think anyone has seen her since. I don't remember ever seeing her. I think it all happened before I was born, or when I was very little."

"Did they have any children?" Bill asked.

"I remember hearing rumors a long time ago that he had a son, but nothing to make me believe it was true."

"Does he have any friends?"

"If he does, I wouldn't have any idea who it might be. Keaton and Rutledge are two of a kind. Neither one of them seems to like anyone. Neither of them are very friendly. Do you think one of them had something to do with the murder at the quarry?" Julie asked.

"No. I have nothing to indicate they had anything to do with it. But I will agree they are not very friendly."

"Do you have time for a cup of coffee?"

"I always have time for a cup of coffee," Bill said with a grin.

Bill followed her into the kitchen. He sat down at the kitchen table and watched her while she put the coffee pot on the stove.

While the coffee was brewing, Julie turned around and sat down at the table.

"How is your investigation going," Julie asked.

"Slow is about the best answer I can give you. I don't even have a good suspect," Bill said.

"All I've got is a body without a name to go with it, a shotgun shell that may or may not have fingerprints on it, a wooden box for explosives I doubt has anything to do with the murder and a bunch of casts of tire tracks that may or may not have anything to do with anything," he said with a hint of frustration.

"What are you going to do next?" she asked then stood up.

Julie got them each a cup of coffee, put them on the table then sat back down.

"At this point, I'm not sure," he said as he picked up the coffee cup and took a sip. "I'm thinking I should do a complete search of the quarry, every foot of it."

"That could take a bit of time."

"Yes, it could, but right now I don't have anything to go on. So far all I've really done was walk around the immediate area where the body was found, and check out the buildings that are still standing. I did find something that might be evidence, but I still don't know if it means anything."

"What did you find?"

"I found a bullet inside the tool shed just before it fell over. I took it into the lab along with the shotgun shell I found just outside the tool shed. Who knows if they will mean anything. There has got to be a lot of people who use the quarry for target practice and shooting squirrels, rabbits and birds. I'd be willing to bet your grandfather has hunted in the quarry at one time or another," Bill said.

"He has hunted rabbits over there just like he has hunted them in the woods around here. He's even hunted turkeys around here, including in the quarry," Julie said as she looked at Bill.

"You can see how difficult that can make it. If I search the entire quarry, I would be willing to bet I'd find dozens of shotgun shells, some old and some fairly new. I will probably find shell casings for rifles and pistols, too."

"Does that mean you are not going to search the quarry?"

"No. I have to search it, if for no other reason than to make sure I didn't miss something important to the case."

"When are you going to do that?"

"It's a little late to start tonight. It should be a nice day tomorrow. It would be a good time to do it. I'll get an early start."

"Would you like to have me bring over something for you to eat around noon?" she said with a smile.

"I would like that as long as you bring enough so you can eat with me," Bill said hopefully.

"Oh, I think I could do that," she said with a big smile.

"I best be going," Bill said as he got up from the table. "I have a couple of reports to write about who I saw, what was said, and what I found out. I'll see you about noon tomorrow then?"

"Yes. I'll walk you to your car," she said as she stood up.

Bill drank the rest of the coffee in his cup, then set it on the table. She followed him out of the house to the porch. He turned in front of her and looked down at her. Reaching out to her, he drew her close then leaned down and kissed her lightly on the lips.

"See you tomorrow," he said, then let go of her and walked down the porch steps.

"Drive careful," Julie said as she watched him get in the patrol car.

Julie stood on the porch and watched him as he drove away. She smiled to herself with the idea she would see him again tomorrow. It was not hard for her to admit she liked him a lot. And it looked like he liked her, she thought.

Bill had a lot on his mind as he headed back to Hill City. Most of it had to do with Julie. She was pretty, smart, and he was pretty sure she liked him. With Julie on his mind, it didn't seem to take as long to get back to Hill City as it had taken him to get to the quarry, but his thoughts were disturbed by the thought that he still had a lot to do before he could call it a day.

Once he was home, he got busy and completed his reports for the day. When he was done, he fixed dinner, listened to a little radio, then went to bed. He quickly fell asleep with thoughts of Julie on his mind.

CHAPTER SEVEN

When morning came, Bill got up and dressed in his uniform. Since he would be on official business at the quarry, he wanted anyone who saw him to know he was a deputy sheriff, not just some guy nosing around the place. After breakfast, he made extra coffee and put it in his Thermos then got in his patrol car and started for the quarry.

As he turned onto Main Street in Hill City, Bill saw Keaton sitting in his truck talking to someone who was standing outside the truck leaning against the door. He could not make out who it was until he turned at the corner and glanced back down the street. He saw it was Rutledge who had been talking to Keaton, and it seemed they were having a rather pleasant conversation as Rutledge was smiling. Bill noticed Rutledge's smile quickly left his face, and he turned away when he saw Bill looking toward him.

The only other time Bill could remember seeing those two together was when he was first assigned to Hill City over a year and a half ago. They got into a verbal argument just outside the Hill City Café. Bill ended up having to break it up when it looked like they were going to get physical. The one thing he couldn't remember was what the fight was about.

All the rumors he had heard indicated Keaton and Rutledge didn't get along at all, and their feud had been going on for years. Bill couldn't help but think it might be a good idea if he tried to find out a little more about them and what had caused the feud in the first place.

Bill continued to drive toward the Jasper Quarry, but his mind was on Keaton and Rutledge. Although he had only gotten a glimpse of the two of them, they didn't look like they were having an argument. Actually, it looked more like they were just talking like old friends. In fact, it looked like they were laughing about something.

As he drove along the road, he tried to remember the times when he had seen them in the same place at the same time. He remembered seeing Rutledge cross the street in order to avoid Keaton who was coming toward him, then cross back across the street after Keaton had gone by. The few times he had seen them in the café, they had always sat on different sides of the room and never talked to each other.

Just as Bill arrived at the quarry, he decided he would put what he had seen in the back of his mind until later when he would have a chance to think about it some more. For now, he needed to concentrate on the quarry and what he might find there.

Bill turned into the quarry and found the gate still closed. He stopped, got out of his patrol car and walked toward the gate. As he approached the gate, he looked at the ground to see if there were any new tracks. He didn't see any new ones.

After opening the gate, he returned to his patrol car and drove it onto the quarry grounds. Bill stopped, got out and closed the gate before driving to where he had parked before. He spent the first hour or so looking around the area where the buildings were located, but found nothing else of interest to him, as least for now.

Leaving the patrol car, he started walking toward the quarry itself. He spent well over an hour walking around inside the quarry pit looking for anything that didn't seem to belong there. He found a number of shotgun shells, most of them old and weathered indicating they had been there for a very long time. He didn't find any that were fairly new, except the one he had found behind the tool shed.

Bill found several cartridge casings from .30 caliber rifles, but they seemed to be in groups or several casings within a small area as if someone had been shooting from the same place. When he looked around, it became easy to see why the cartridge casings were in groups. About two hundred yards away, there were three wooden frames in front of a rock cliff. The cliff had been used as a backstop and the wooden frames would have been used to hold targets. It had been a place where some individual or individuals had sighted in their hunting rifles, probably in preparation for deer or elk hunting.

After spending some time in the quarry pit, he also found several places where people had practiced shooting pistols. The only thing of interest was the twenty-five spent .38 caliber cartridge casings he found, several of them had not been there for very long. Since they were of the same caliber as the bullet he found in the tool shed, he carefully gathered them up and put them in a bag. His hope was the lab could connect them to the bullet. He also took pictures of all the places he found casings as well as the target area.

When he was finished in the quarry pit, he decided he would take a walk around the outside perimeter of the quarry pit. He wanted to find out how close it came to Keaton's property, and if he could see Keaton's house or barn from the quarry rim.

He was just walking out of the quarry pit when he heard the sound of a horn. It sounded several times before he was out of the quarry pit. When he was out of the pit, he could see Julie standing next to her grandfather's pickup truck. Bill glanced at his watch and realized it was very close to noon. He smiled as he walked over to Julie.

"How are things going?" she asked as he approached her.

"Not too bad. I guess I lost track of time."

"It's okay. I know you have a lot to do. Are you ready for lunch?

"Sure. Where would you like to eat?"

"I have grandpa's truck. I thought we could drive back in a ways and have a picnic at the edge of the woods," she said with a smile.

"I guess we could do that. I still have to walk the rim of the quarry pit, but I can do that after we eat."

"Okay. Do you want to take your car or the truck?"

"Let's take your truck," Bill suggested. "You drive."

She smiled, opened the door, and got back in the truck. Bill walked around to the other side and got in.

"I would like you to drive slowly so I can look around," Bill said."

"We could walk back to the woods, if you prefer."

"I don't think that will be necessary. If I see anything of interest, I'll ask you to stop."

"Okay."

Julie started the truck and began to drive along the same trail Bill had followed that led to the gate to her grandfather's field. As they approached the woods, before the trail continued on to the gate, Julie pulled off to the side and stopped.

"Did you see anything?"

"No," Bill replied. "Is this where you would like to have lunch?"

"It's a nice place here. We can lay out the blanket on the grass in the shade of the trees."

"Sounds good to me," he said as he opened the door and got out.

Julie got out of the truck and handed a blanket to Bill then picked up the lunch basket. They walked over to a shady spot near the trees and spread out the blanket. As Bill sat down on the blanket, Julie knelt down and began getting their lunch out of the basket. It wasn't long and they were enjoying a lunch of roast beef sandwiches, sodas and apples. When they were done, Julie packed up the leftovers and closed the basket.

"That was good," Bill said. "Thank you for coming out here and bringing lunch."

"You're welcome. I'm glad you liked it," Julie said as she sat down and moved next to him.

"I was wondering if you might like to go to Rapid City for dinner and a movie sometime."

"I would like that."

"As much as I would like to spend time with you right now, I still have a lot to do. It could be almost dark by the time I get done."

"Are you trying to get rid of me?" she asked with the hint of grin.

"Yes, but only temporarily. You are a distraction. If we spend much longer in this nice secluded spot, I might not let you go."

"That sounds like an interesting idea," she said with a grin. "But the way I see it, if you give me kiss, I'll let you go back to work."

"That's sound fair," Bill said.

Bill stood up, reached out a hand to Julie and helped her to her feet. They gathered up everything then walked back to the truck together. After putting everything in the truck, Julie turned toward him. She stepped up in front of him then reached up and put her hands on his shoulders. Bill reached around her and pulled her up against him as he leaned down until his lips met hers.

As they kissed, Julie slid her hands around behind his head and held him close. It was a long and passionate kiss, leaving both of them a little short of breath. They reluctantly pulled back a little and took a deep breath as they looked into each other's eyes. A smile slowly came over Julie's face as she looked into his eyes.

"I hope that will keep you thinking of me," she said.

"I didn't need that to keep me thinking of you. I think of you often."

"That's nice. I better be going," Julie said. "I don't want you out here after dark."

"Okay," Bill said as he leaned down and kissed her lightly on the lips.

Julie turned and got in the truck. Bill didn't make a move to get into the truck.

"Aren't you riding back to your car with me?"

"No. I'm going to walk back to the quarry pit, then walk around it."

"Will I see you later?"

"I don't know. It will depend on when I get done here and what I find. I might have to go into the sheriff's office when I finish here. If I don't, would you like me to stop by when I'm finished?"

"Yes. I hope you are done by dinner time. If you are, you can have dinner with us."

"I doubt I will be if you don't get a move on and let me get back to work," Bill said with a grin.

"I'm going. I'm going," she said then started the truck.

"Love you," Bill said.

"Love you, too," she said then put the truck in gear.

As she drove away, Bill watched her and thought about her last words. As soon as she was out of sight, Bill looked around for a moment, then started walking back toward the quarry pit. His mind was not on his work, but on Julie.

Bill walked along the road toward the entrance to the quarry pit. Even though his mind was on Julie, his eyes continually moved as he looked around. He suddenly stopped at the sight of something almost hidden by the tall grass in a shallow ravine. Off to the side of the road was some kind of container that looked like it didn't belong there. It looked a little too new to be something from the days when the quarry was in operation. It showed no signs of rust or faded paint, but it was painted in an olive drab green typical of U.S. Army containers he had seen in Europe during the war.

Bill worked his way through the tall grass and weeds toward the container. When he got fairly close to it, he quickly recognized it as a World War II heavy steel military container used primarily to haul explosives. It still had some of the military markings on the side and didn't appear to have been there very long.

On closer examination of the container, he discovered it had a new padlock on it, but the lock was not typical of the locks used by the military. It was a hardware store brand of lock. He quickly wrote down the brand name of the lock so he could possibly find out where it had come from, and hopefully who purchased it.

He stepped back and looked at where the container was located. It was in among a lot of steel junk that had probably been used in the quarry, most of it rusty and not good for anything. If he hadn't been looking for things that didn't belong there, he would have missed it. There was also the fact that very little of it was visible from the road. He was also on the wrong side of the truck to have seen it when he went with Julie to the woods for their picnic.

Bill began by taking several pictures of the steel container. He took pictures from all sides, of the lock, of the markings on the container, and several back away from it so it would show how well it had been hidden. He also looked around for tracks. Bill knew it was not the kind of container that could easily be moved even if it was empty. It was about six foot long, four foot wide, and four foot tall and made of heavy gage steel. He quickly found tire tracks in the grass that appeared to be from a truck that had backed into the grass. The tire tracks stopped short of where the container was, indicating the truck that had brought the container there was probably a one ton or larger stake truck.

Bill was curious about what might be in the container. He hoped it did not contain what it was designed to carry. Explosives in the hands of someone who didn't know how to use them could be very dangerous. They were also dangerous in the hands of someone who knew how to use them, if they had a mind to do so.

The one thing he knew for sure was the type of container he discovered was not in use prior to WWII. He was also aware of the fact that the quarry had closed long before WWII. From the tracks, it was clear the container had not been there very long, not more than a few days at the most.

The container was something very important, something he should report quickly. As soon as he was sure he had all the information on the container, and had taken all the pictures of it he needed, he started back to his patrol car. It was some distance from the container.

He hadn't gone very far when he heard two very distinct pistol shots. It sounded like they came from the area where his patrol car was parked. The only person Bill could think of who would fire a gun to get his attention was one of the deputies, but why would he shoot a gun? If it was a fellow officer, he would probably have given a couple of short blasts of the siren on his patrol car to not only get Bill's attention, but to let him know who was there.

Bill started running toward where he had left his patrol car. As he ran, he drew his gun from his holster. Since he had no idea what was going on, he wanted to be ready.

As he came around the corner where he could see his patrol car, he slowed down and stepped off the road. He didn't see anyone around and there was no patrol car other than his. Being very cautious, he moved slowly toward his patrol car keeping close to cover. When he got closer, he could see the driver's side window had been shot out.

Bill quickly drew back behind some old quarry equipment and began looking around. He had no idea what was going on, but it was obvious someone didn't want him snooping around the quarry. After scanning the area as best he could from where he was, he again looked at his patrol car. There didn't seem to be any bullet holes in it. The only damage seemed to be to the driver's side window. He had heard two shots. Carefully looking over the patrol car from his hiding place, he was sure they had not shot any windows out on the passenger's side, and the patrol car was sitting level so there was little likelihood they had shot any tires.

There was no way for him to tell if they had shot the motor through the grill so the patrol car wouldn't run, putting him on foot. He couldn't see any fluids under the patrol car, but from his location it would have been very difficult to see them anyway.

As Bill began looking around for where the shots might have come from, it suddenly became clear what was going on. Whoever shot the patrol car was probably shooting at the radio, and possibly the engine, or something that would make the car unusable. Without the radio and being unable to drive the car, he would not be able to call for help, and he would have to walk to get help. That thought caused him to hunker down. The only question was why?

As he hid behind the heavy equipment while listening and looking around, he began to think of other possibilities. Was it possible they had disabled his radio and the patrol car so he would have to leave the area on foot in order to call for help? If he had to leave to call for help, it would give someone the chance to remove the container. He knew if he left to place a call for help, he would be gone for at least twenty minutes, probably more, just to get to a phone. That would give someone plenty of time to remove the container, or its contents. The last thing he wanted was to give anyone time to remove the container before he knew what was in it.

A look at the sky told Bill it would be at least four hours before it would start getting dark, and almost five hours before it would be dark enough that he would not be able to see. He had a decision to make. Should he leave the area and hope no one moved the steel container or its contents, or should he find himself a place to hide where he could watch the container to make sure it was not moved? If he stayed around, how long would it take before someone missed him and came looking for him? It would probably be hours before anyone would miss him.

Bill looked around. He decided to work his way closer to his patrol car in order to see what the damage was to it. If it was out of commission, he would retrieve what he could use to spend the night. Hopefully, his shotgun was still in the car. Maybe the siren still worked, and he could use it to get someone's attention and possibly some help.

He began working his way closer to his patrol car. Bill picked his way from one bit of cover to the next. His patrol car was parked on the other side of the road. It meant he would have to run across the open space to get to the other side. He was able to see there was no glass on the ground on the driver's side of the car. That meant the shot had been fired from the same side of the road he was on, or from someone in the road. He quickly turned around to see if there was anyone behind him, but didn't see anyone.

After checking for someone behind him as best he could, he looked back at the patrol car and the road. He couldn't tell from his location if the bullet went straight into the patrol car, or if it hit the patrol car at an angle. If it was at an angle, it would mean that it was shot at by someone on the road or standing next to the patrol car.

Looking at the road, there were only a few places in the road where he would be able to see footprints. He saw what might have been footprints in one area where there was some sand, but he couldn't tell if they were from him or someone else. Since it had been quiet for some time, he decided to rush across the road to his patrol car. With his gun held tightly in his hand, he crouched down and quickly ran across the road and around to the other side of the patrol car. He opened the door and looked inside. The military style radio had two holes in it. There was little doubt it was out of commission. It didn't look like anything else had been damaged other than the driver's side window.

Bill looked around as he thought about what he should do next. He wasn't on foot, but he didn't have any way to communicate with the sheriff's office to get help. In order to get in touch with the sheriff's office, he would have to leave the scene and find a phone. The closest phone was at Turnquest's place. If he drove over there, whoever had shot at him would be able to get what was in the container out and disappear before he could get back.

As Bill thought about what he should do, he remembered something he had seen the first time he was there. He remembered the vehicle tracks from where the body had been found led away from the entrance he had used to get into the quarry. He had followed it to a steel gate which was locked. The road continued on the other side of the fence by running along the edge of the field going away from the road out in front of the quarry and deeper into the forest. Bill began to wonder where the road went, and who had the key to the gate.

Bill got to thinking about the container and the disabling of his radio. It was obvious someone had seen him looking around. Whoever it was, they probably thought he would discover the container. They also probably figured he would know what it was, since it was general knowledge he had been in the Army during the war. He would at least know what the markings on it meant. If that was the case, they would feel the need to get the container out of there, or at least remove its contents as quickly as possible.

While crouched down beside his patrol car, Bill reached up and opened the door. Just as he was reaching for his shotgun, he thought he heard the sound of a vehicle. The sound came from up the road near where the container was located.

Bill quickly jumped in the driver's seat, reached down, put his key in the ignition and started the patrol car. The engine jumped to life. Bill put it in gear and stepped on the gas. The tires spun as it started to move. He raced up the road toward where the container was located. As he came around a fairly sharp curve, he saw a large piece of steel angle iron lying across the road. He slammed on the brakes and turned in an effort to miss the obstacle in the road, but it was laid all the way across the road, and he wasn't quick enough to stop his patrol car before he hit it. He immediately heard a front tire blow out. When his patrol car came to a stop, it was just in time for him to get a glimpse of a pickup truck through the windshield as it disappeared around a corner. It was headed toward the steel gate that allowed access to Mr. Turnquest's farm from the quarry.

Out of frustration, Bill hit the steering wheel with his fists. After taking a deep breath, he got out of the patrol car and looked at the front tires. He quickly discovered both front tires were flat. A quick examination of the patrol car indicated the only thing preventing the car from going were the two flat tires. There didn't appear to be anything else wrong with the car.

Bill looked around, but didn't see anyone. He wondered if the container had been emptied. Taking his shotgun with him, he started walking up the road toward where the container had been. It wasn't long and he found the container, but it was open and very empty. He had no idea what it had contained, but it must have been something very important to someone.

He walked up to the container and looked around. There appeared to be several sets of footprints in the grass, but none of them would help identify who they belong to. The one thing he did notice was a shiny piece of metal lying in the grass near the open door of the container. He had not noticed it when he had first looked around the container. He reached down and picked it up. The side he saw first looked like a small round piece of copper that had a pin with a clasp on it, and the clasp was open. When he turned it over and looked at the front of the pin, his eyes got big as he stared at it.

On the front of the pin was the logo of a black swastika on a white background surrounded by a red circular border with the words, "Nazi Political Party" in white within the red border. His first thought was he had fought them in Europe, he didn't think he would have to fight them here. It was hard for him to believe there were any of them in the Black Hills. He knew there were still a few Nazis in the east, but he didn't think he was going to have to deal with them here.

It suddenly occurred to him that the steel container probably contained some kind of weapons or explosives. The only questions he had was who had them, what did they plan to do with them, and where did they get them.

Bill slipped the pin into his shirt pocket, buttoned it down, then looked around. It was becoming clear to him that the location had been used as a supply depot and/or a distribution location for stolen weapons. It would probably not be one any longer, since the authorities now knew about it.

It crossed his mind that the body found behind the old tool shed might have something to do with the container, the lapel pin, and destruction of his radio. He just wasn't sure how.

Bill returned to his car, locked it up, then started walking. The closest place to find a phone was at the Turnquest Farm. He headed there.

CHAPTER EIGHT

It took Bill a good twenty minutes to get to the gate leading up to the Turnquest's farm. As he approached the house, Julie stepped out onto the porch and smiled. The smile faded from her face when she saw the look on Bill's face. She knew something had happened. She looked down the drive toward the road and didn't see his patrol car.

"Where's your car?"

"It's over at the quarry. It wouldn't start so my radio doesn't work. I would like to use your phone to call for a tow truck," Bill said.

"Sure. Come on in. If you have to wait for a tow truck, you can have dinner with us."

"That would be nice. It will take the tow truck over an hour to get here," Bill said as he followed her into the house.

Julie pointed at the phone then stepped back. Bill picked up the phone and called the sheriff's office. As the phone rang, he looked over at Julie. She smiled at him then went outside.

"Pennington County Sheriff's Office. May I help you?"

"Yeah, Mary. This is Bill. Is the sheriff in?"

"Sure. How's it going?"

"Not well," he said with a hint of frustration in his voice.

"I'll put you through," Mary said without further comment.

"How's it going, Bill? Have you got a problem?"

"Yes, sir. First of all, I need to report my patrol car is currently disabled at the Jasper Quarry. My radio is also disabled. I'm calling from the Turnquest farm just down the road."

"What happened?"

Bill looked around the room to make sure no one could hear his conversation with the sheriff. He then explained what had happened at the quarry and about the damage to his car and the radio.

"I'll get someone out there with tires, but it might take over an hour. You'll have to bring the car in for a new radio, and to fix the door window. We have a car in the shop you can use while they repair your car. What are your plans now?"

"By the time I get another car, it will be too late to track the truck I saw leaving the quarry out the back way. I have no idea where the road goes, do you?

"No, but there are several fire roads in that area. It could lead almost anywhere."

"Tomorrow I'm hoping to get some casts of tire tracks from the truck so we can identify it if we find it. I also plan to find out where the road goes."

"Okay. That sounds like a good plan," the sheriff said. "Then what do you plan to do?"

"I'm not sure at this point. I did find something that concerns me a little."

"What is that?"

"I found a Nazi Political Party lapel pin on the ground next to the container."

"You found what?" the sheriff asked, his voice showing his surprise.

"I found a Nazi Political Party lapel pin. It doesn't look like it had been there very long, probably no longer than the container. It is still shiny, without a bit of tarnish on it. I was careful to pick it up by the pin. I don't know if they can get fingerprints from the front of it or not."

"The lab might be able to. Do you think the container and the lapel pin might have some connection?"

"I don't know, but there could be a connection. I have heard the Nazi Political Party is still active in some places on the east coast, but they operate secretly. I was thinking there could be some members who live around here who might use the quarry to hide things since it is out of the way.

"As for the container, it was back in where hardly anyone goes. It was only by chance that I saw it. The kids that use the quarry for a place to smoke and drink rarely, if ever, go back past the buildings near the front entrance. I don't think any of the kids would even know what the container was used for or even be able to see it where it was hidden. I only found it by accident."

"Where are you going to be?"

"I've been invited to have dinner with Mr. Turnquest and his granddaughter while I wait for a tow truck."

"Do they know why your car is disabled?"

"No, sir. I just told them it was disabled causing my radio not to work so I couldn't call for a tow truck."

"Good. When you go back to the quarry to wait for the tow truck, go alone," the sheriff said."

"Yes, sir. I will probably get to the gate before the tow truck gets there, but if I'm not, tell the driver to wait for me at the gate."

"Okay. Be careful out there. Call in before you go out to the quarry in the morning."

"Yes, sir," Bill said then hung up.

As soon as Bill hung up, he went out on the porch to find Julie. She was sitting in a chair near the end of the porch.

"Did you get someone to come out to get your car?"

"Yes. It will be a little over an hour before he gets here. I'll meet him at the gate."

"Well, it seems you will have time to have dinner with us," Julie said with a smile.

"That would be nice."

Julie got up and walked into the house. Bill followed her to the kitchen. He could smell something that smelled very good.

"Sit down. Grandpa should be in shortly. He's out in his workshop working on the tractor.

Bill sat down and watched her as she set plates on the table.

"Have you had trouble with your car before? I thought it was brand new," Julie asked.

"It is brand new, and I have not had any trouble with it before today. It's probably some wire that came loose or something simple like that. You know how new things often have some little bugs in them that have to be fixed. It is usually nothing serious."

"I hope you don't have problems with it when you have to get some place in a hurry."

"I'm sure they'll fix it."

Julie and Bill looked toward the door when they heard the sound of someone coming up onto the porch. It was Julie's grandfather.

"Oh, hi. I didn't know you were here. I didn't see your car," Wilbur said.

"His car wouldn't start. He was over at the quarry. He came over here to call for a tow truck," Julie said.

"Oh. Is there something I can do to help you with it? Maybe we could jump the battery."

"No. I appreciate your offer, but we are required to call in and have one of the shop people come out and fix it. It's policy, I guess. I don't think they want anyone other than our own people working on any of our equipment, including patrol cars."

"I guess I can understand that. How long will it take before someone will get out here?"

"About an hour. After dinner, I'll walk back over there and meet the tow truck driver."

"Dinner's ready," Julie said interrupting Bill and Wilbur's conversation.

Julie set the hot dish on the table. Wilbur poured milk for everyone while Julie put a plate of corn bread next to Bill.

"Dig in," Julie said with a smile.

"I can drive you over there after dinner," Wilbur said as he passed the hot dish to Bill.

"I was thinking I'll walk back. I've got a few things to think about. It'll give me a chance to think and hopefully get a handle on things."

"Okay, but don't say I didn't offer," Wilbur said with a smile.

"I won't," Bill said as he smiled at Wilbur.

"Did you get your walk around the outer edge of the quarry pit?" Julie asked.

"No. I'll have to do that tomorrow. I think I'm pretty well done for today. I'll have to go back with the car unless they bring me a different one."

"Do you think they will bring you another car?"

"I hope so, but I doubt it. If they don't I'll have to go back to Rapid City with the tow truck driver and get another patrol car," Bill said.

Talk around the dinner table turned to things other than Bill's patrol car. When dinner was over, Bill helped Julie clear the table and do up the dishes. As soon as everything was done, Julie and Bill walked out to the front porch. Bill did not sit down.

"I think I should start heading on over to the quarry," he said as he held her hand.

"Are you sure you wouldn't like company. I could drive you over there and wait with you until the tow truck arrives," Julie said hopefully.

"I don't think I'll have to wait very long. Besides, I really do need to spend sometime thinking about the quarry and what happened over there."

"I understand," Julie said reluctantly.

Bill leaned down to her as she looked up at him. Their lips met in a soft and tender kiss. As soon as the kiss ended, he looked down at her and smiled."

"When will I see you again?" she asked.

"I'm not sure. I may have to spend sometime in Rapid City. I want to find out what the lab found out from the evidence I gave them to analyze. There may be something there that will point me in the right direction. Right now I'm not sure what is going on."

"Okay. Will you call me?"

"Sure. If I don't come out here tomorrow, I'll call you in the evening."

"I'd like that," she said as she slipped her arms around his neck.

Bill leaned down and kissed her again before he let go of her, then turned and walked down the porch steps. As he got close to the gate, he turned around and waved at her as she stood on the porch watching him leave. She waved back just before Bill disappeared around the corner.

As Bill walked along the road toward the front gate of the Jasper Quarry, his thoughts turned to what had happened at the quarry today. He knew there was no way for him to know what had been in the Army explosives container, but he was sure it had contained something important to whoever it was who went to all the trouble to get it out of there. What other reason would anyone have to open it and race away from the scene so quickly?

By the time Bill arrived at the front gate, the sun was beginning to set below the trees on a nearby ridge. It would not be long before it would be getting dark. He leaned against the gate and looked down the road while he listened to the sounds of a quiet evening.

It wasn't long before he thought he could hear a vehicle coming up the road from the direction of town. A quick glance at his watch showed him it seemed a little early for the tow truck. He straightened up and stepped back behind a tree while he waited to see who was coming. Bill slipped his hand over his gun while he waited. It was only a moment or so before an old pickup truck went on by the entrance. He didn't recognize the truck or the driver. The only thing he was sure of was that it was not the same truck he had seen in the quarry only a little over an hour ago.

A few minutes later, a Pennington County tow truck came and turned into the quarry. It stopped at the gate and the driver looked around. Bill stepped out from behind the tree and walked over to the gate.

"I'll get the gate," Bill said then swung open the gate.

The driver of the tow truck drove through the gate then stopped. Bill closed the gate and jumped into the truck.

"My car is down this road a little way," Bill said as he pointed in the direction he wanted the driver to go.

"What's the damages to the car?"

"Both front tires are flat. I hit a piece of angle iron that was laid across the road. I was after someone and didn't see it until it was too late."

"It must have been a pretty good size piece of angle iron for it to flatten both tires," the driver said as he drove toward the car.

"Yeah. It's right around this next corner."

The driver slowed down and stopped as soon as his headlights lit up the patrol car. Bill and the driver got out of the tow truck and walked up to the patrol car. The driver of the tow truck looked at the damage and at the angle iron, then turned and looked at Bill.

"No wonder the tires are flat. The edge of this angle iron has been filed to a razor sharp edge. It cut right through the tires. I'd say it was intended to stop any vehicle," the driver said. "Does the car run?"

"Yeah."

"First of all we need to get it off the angle iron and back here where we can lift it up. I have tires for it, but I understand you have problems with the radio, too."

"Yeah. It has two very nice neat holes in it," Bill said. "Someone shot it, twice, right through the driver's side door window."

"Well, I guess I can't do anything about that out here. Get in and back it off the angle iron very slowly. We don't want to do any more damage than has been done already."

Bill got in the patrol car and started it. He put it in reverse then slowly backed it off the angle iron.

Once he had it where the tow truck driver could hook up to it, he stopped and shut off the engine.

The tow truck driver hooked up the patrol car and lifted the front of it off the ground. He took a flashlight and checked the underside of the car for any damage.

"I don't see any damage to the car except for the flat tires. I'll take it into the shop and change the tires there. We'll have to take it in anyway to replace the door window and the radio, and I'll have to look it over before we can put it back in service. I want to make sure there's no damage to the undercarriage before I'll know if it's okay to drive."

Bill nodded that he understood and got in the tow truck with the driver. They towed the car back to Rapid City. It was getting close to ten o'clock by the time they got the car to the county garage.

"The sheriff told me to give you another car until we could go over this one and make sure nothing else is wrong with it. That car over there is the only one we have available at the moment," he said as he pointed to a three year old patrol car. "It's old for a patrol car, but it runs real good. We should have your car ready for you in a couple of days."

Bill walked over to the patrol car and looked inside. It had a radio in it and looked to be in pretty good shape. The keys were in it. Bill turned and looked at the tow truck driver.

"You want to check this out to me?" Bill said.

"It's already checked out to you."

"Is there anything else you need from me," Bill asked.

"No. The sheriff said you had already reported what happened to him."

"In that case, I'll head for home. It's been a long day."

"Take care of that car. It's the only extra one we have at the moment," the tow truck driver said with a grin.

"I'll do my best," Bill replied.

Bill took his personal things from his patrol car and put them into the loaner, got in the car, started it and drove back to Hill City. He went right to his house. It had been a long day and he was tired. He took a quick shower, then turned in. It didn't take but a few minutes before he was sound asleep.

CHAPTER NINE

Bill was still sleeping when his alarm clock went off. He reached over and shut it off, then laid there for a few minutes looking up at the ceiling. The first thing that came into his mind was the Army explosives container, and the first questions were what had been in it and where were the contents of the container now.

He knew his questions were not going to get answered while he lay in bed. He swung his legs over the side of the bed and sat up. He stretched, then stood up and went into the bathroom for a quick shower.

As soon as Bill was dressed and ready to go to work, he left his house and walked out to the patrol car. He drove to the café on Main Street for breakfast. When he walked into the café, he saw Keaton sitting in a booth with three other men. Bill recognized two of the men as locals, but didn't really know them, the third man he didn't recognize. They had been talking very quietly when he arrived, but stopped talking as soon as they saw him.

Bill took a seat in a small booth in the corner. He sat on the side of the booth that would allow him to see almost everyone else in the café. He had just sat down when Sandy came over to his booth with a cup of coffee.

"Good morning, Bill. What will it be this morning?"

"I think I'll have a couple of pancakes with two eggs over easy, and a glass of orange juice. You might add a sausage patty to that, please."

"Okay," she said as she wrote it down on her pad.

"There's one other thing. Without looking over at the table where Keaton is sitting, can you tell me who the man in the suit is?"

Sandy looked at Bill for a second before answering him.

"I've never heard his name mentioned, but I have heard that he is an insurance salesman of some kind, but I've never seen him sell anything in here. I don't think any of the men at the table could afford any insurance," she said.

"Thanks," Bill said then Sandy nodded, turned and went toward the kitchen.

Bill watched the four of them in the booth out of the corner of his eye. The only thing he was sure of was they were talking about him. He also glanced around the room to see who else might be around. He saw Jim Anderson sitting with a young man Bill had seen a number of times around town, but didn't know his name.

In another booth, he could see Rutledge sitting with a woman who looked to be about his age, maybe a little younger. Bill knew the woman to be Mrs. Howard, the owner of a small campground located just a little west of town. They seemed to be enjoying themselves. Bill knew the woman was a widow. He wondered if Rutledge and Mrs. Howard were sweet on each other. It crossed Bill's mind that Mrs. Howard could be good for Rutledge, maybe cool his temper down a little.

Just as Bill's breakfast was brought to the table, Bill saw the man in the suit get up and leave the café while the other three men stayed in the booth. Bill noticed he didn't have a briefcase or any kind of folder or papers. He couldn't remember ever seeing an insurance salesman without a briefcase, or at least a folder of some kind. The man sparked Bill's interest, but there was little he could do about it without even knowing the guy's name.

As Bill ate his breakfast, he continued to watch the three men who had stayed behind. It wasn't long before two of the remaining men got up and left the table. Once outside the café, they both headed down the street in the same direction the "insurance salesman" had gone.

Bill had just finished his breakfast when Keaton got up, paid his bill and left the café. Bill stood up, left a tip on the table, then walked up to the counter to pay for his meal. As he was paying for it, he watched Keaton turn and go down the sidewalk in the same direction the others had gone. Bill had no idea what was going on, but there was a chance they broke up because he came into the café. His gut feeling was they were going to meet again as soon as he left town.

Bill had no idea if there was anything going on that should concern him and the law. If there was, there was nothing he could do about it without actual knowledge of it. The only thing he could do was to continue his search for whoever had killed the man at the quarry, and see if it might lead back to one or more of those he saw in the café. Even so, he couldn't help but think there was something going on.

Bill returned to his patrol car, got in and started to leave town. As he drove by the end of the alley that ran behind the café, he got a glimpse of several men standing in the alley. With just a glimpse, he wasn't sure who he had seen, but he thought one of them was wearing a suit. There were not too many men wearing suits around town. He thought about going around the block and checking it out, but he had no real reason to go back. As far as he knew, Keaton and the others had not done anything against the law. If that was the case, it was none of his business.

Bill continued on toward the quarry. When he arrived at the quarry, he found the gate was wide open. He checked for tracks at the gate, but found all the tracks, including those from his car and the tow truck from last night, had been wiped away. There were no tracks at all. No tracks from any kind of vehicle, and no tracks from people walking through the gate. It appeared as if a large broom similar to the kind used to sweep concrete floors had been used to brush away the tracks. Bill found that interesting. Why would someone go to the trouble of brushing out the tracks? Had some sort of vehicle that could easily be identified by its tracks been driven in or out of the quarry?

With no tracks, Bill reasoned something had either been brought into the quarry, or something had been taken out. It was Bill's guess something had probably been taken out. He reasoned that whoever had been keeping things in the quarry as a place to hide them was getting a little concerned about the amount of activity in the quarry by the police, namely the Sheriff's Department, making it no longer a safe place to hide things.

Bill got back in the patrol car and drove into the quarry. He parked the patrol car where he had parked his other patrol car, then got out. Bill immediately began to look around. He was looking for what was missing. He decided he would not let the patrol car out of his sight, if he could help it. He did not want anything to happen to the car.

Slowly, Bill took his time looking for any signs of something that had been moved from the area, as well as tracks that might have been left while removing it. When he finished searching an area, he moved the patrol car a little way down the road then got out and searched that area. As he worked each side of the road, he continued to check for tire tracks on the road as well as off the road.

It wasn't until he got to the area where the Army explosives container had been that he found anything of interest. He found the empty explosives container was gone. He also discovered a place where some kind of vehicle had driven through the grass. The grass had been pushed down by a vehicle much heavier than those of the tracks he had seen late yesterday afternoon when he found the explosives container empty. From the looks of the tracks, the truck had double rear wheels, probably a two or three-ton truck of some kind, probably a covered stake truck.

He stood close to where the explosives container had been and looked along the trail through the tall grass left by the truck. It looked as if it was going around the rim of the quarry pit. However, the truck that had left the area in such a hurry late last evening had gone down the road and through the gate onto Turnquest's farm, then on into the woods behind the farm; but the new set of tracks had gone toward the rim of the pit.

The questions that came to Bill's mind were what did they want with the empty container, and where had they taken it. The only answer he could come up with was they wanted the container to put what they had taken out of it back into it. For some reason, it was important for them to keep the contents in the container. But why didn't they just take the container with the contents in it the first time? The answer was simple in Bill's mind, they didn't have a big enough truck to take it all at once, but the contents had to be moved quickly.

It was time to find out where the tracks went, but he didn't want to leave the patrol car in the quarry where it could be damaged like his last car. It occurred to Bill that Turnquest had horses. If he could get Wilbur Turnquest to loan him one of his horses, he could leave the patrol car at Turnquest's place and ride back into the woods on horseback following the tracks from where the container had been.

Bill got into the patrol car and drove over to the Turnquest's farm. When he pulled up in front of the house, Wilbur stepped out onto the porch. He waited for Bill to get out of the patrol car and walk toward him before he spoke.

"Didn't expect to see you so soon. You got a problem?"

"Yeah. I stopped by to see if you would loan me a horse for a few hours."

"I think I could do that. You ride a lot?"

"Not a lot lately, but I was raised on a ranch and used a horse most of my life."

"Well, in that case, I'll let you take one of mine. Come on out to the barn."

Bill walked out to the barn with Wilbur. In the small paddock behind the barn were three horses. They all looked like they had been well taken care of, and were in good health.

"The chestnut gelding is a good steady horse. He's fast, and he takes commands well."

"He looks good," Bill said as he walked up to the horse.

Bill stroked the horse on his neck and rubbed his forehead. The horse seemed to like it.

"This one will do nicely."

"I'll get a saddle and bridle for you," Wilbur said then turned and went into the barn.

Bill followed him into the barn and picked up a saddle while Wilbur got a bridle and saddle blanket. Bill set the saddle down on the ground then took the saddle blanket from Wilbur, swung it up on the horse's back and smoothed it out. He then saddled the horse and got him ready to ride while Wilbur put the bridle on the horse.

"Would you like me to go with you?" Wilbur asked.

"No. I think it is best if I go alone. There could be trouble."

"Okay. Take care of my horse, and be sure to take care of yourself," Wilbur said as he watched Bill swing into the saddle.

"How long do you expect to be gone?" Wilbur asked.

"I'm not sure. I should be back by five or six at the latest," Bill said.

"Okay. I'll get the gate for you," Wilbur said, then walked to the gate and opened it.

Bill rode the horse out of the gate then trotted the horse on toward the quarry. He rode along the fence that ran between the quarry property and the Turnquest farm. When he got to the gate, he found the gate was closed, but the lock was hanging open on the gate. Bill reached down from the horse and pushed open the gate. After crossing onto the quarry property, he closed the gate.

Bill rode down the road to where the Army explosives container had been, from there he picked up the tracks made by the heavy truck. He then followed the tracks toward the rim of the quarry pit. He cautiously followed the tracks only to discover they followed the rim of the quarry pit for some distance before the tracks turned and went away from the quarry pit. It wasn't long before he came to a place where he could see the fence line of Keaton's property.

He was a good seventy or eighty yards from the fence, but he could still see where the truck had crushed the grass as it moved further away from the quarry pit. In fact, the trail left by the truck slowly turned again, and ran about twenty to thirty yards from the fence, but parallel to the fence.

Staying back about twenty yards away from the tracks, Bill rode parallel to the tracks. He continued to follow the tracks until he came to another fence line. There appeared to be a sign on the fence. He rode up to it and looked at the fence to see what the sign said. It was faded and hard to read, but it said "No Trespassing, Jasper Quarry". It was clear he had found the back boarder of the quarry property. It was also clear the quarry pit only took up a small part of the land belonging to the Jasper Quarry.

Bill looked down the fence line. About fifty yards down the fence line, he could see a gate. He knew who owned the property on each side of the quarry, Keaton on one side and Turnquest on the other, but he didn't know who owned the property on the backside of the quarry. He would have to find that out.

He sat on the horse and thought for a minute. Bill decided it might be best if he found out who owned the property in front of him before he went onto the property. He also decided to turn back and ride around the side of the quarry closest to Keaton's place. He wanted to know if Keaton's house could be seen from the quarry.

Bill turned the horse around and started back to the quarry pit. When he got to the rim of the pit he turned and followed the rim of the pit along Keaton's side of the quarry property. He found one place where he could see Keaton's barn and a good part of his house, but not the entire house.

He stepped down off the horse, tied it to a tree then made his way among the trees to where he could get a better look at the house. Just as he found a better spot to see the house, a man in a suit came out of the Keaton's house, the same man he had seen with Keaton and two other men in the café earlier. He saw Keaton shake the man's hand. If the man was an insurance salesman, it appeared that Keaton might have just bought a policy from him. But again, the man didn't have a briefcase or any kind of folder or papers.

He watched as the man got in a car and drove away. Bill took note of the car. It was a fairly new top-of-the-line Oldsmobile four door sedan, a fairly expensive car.

Seeing the man leaving Keaton's place left Bill with more questions than answers. He decided he would return the horse to Wilbur and head back to town. There were a few questions he wanted answers to, and he couldn't get the answers out there.

Bill returned to the horse, mounted, then turned the horse around and headed back to Turnquest's farm. When he got back to the farm, he unsaddled the horse and rubbed it down, then turned it out in the corral.

Wilbur told him that Julie was in Rapid City and wouldn't be home until late. Bill thanked Wilbur for the horse. He got in the patrol car and drove back to Hill City.

Once he arrived at his home, he took some time to write out a report of his day's activities. He thought about sending it in, but decided he would go into Rapid City in the morning and take his report to the sheriff. He would also go over to the lab and talk to the ME to see what he might have found from the body of the man killed in the quarry, and from any of the other evidence he had sent in.

After he had finished his report, he fixed himself some dinner, then listened to a baseball game on the radio. When the game was over, he went to bed.

CHAPTER TEN

Bill was up before his alarm clock went off. He reached over and shut off the alarm, then swung his legs over the side of the bed. He had gone to bed thinking about what was going on at the quarry and found himself thinking about it when he woke up.

After a quick shower and putting on his uniform, he sat down for a breakfast of coffee, orange juice, and a bowl of corn flakes with a banana. While he ate his breakfast, he made out a list of questions he wanted to ask the ME and the lab personnel. He was hoping they would have come up with something that would help him figure out what was going on, and hopefully point him toward the person or persons who had killed the man in the quarry.

He knew his first stop would be at the sheriff's office to turn in his report. Bill hoped the sheriff would be in. He wanted to talk to him as well as give him his report. Maybe, the sheriff could give him some ideas that would help him in his investigation. It was his first time investigating a murder.

After he finished eating and making his list, Bill went out to the patrol car and headed to Rapid City. The drive into Rapid City was uneventful, arriving about ten minutes after eight. The sheriff was in his office, and Bill requested time to talk to him which was immediately granted.

"How's it going out there?" Sheriff Henderson asked.

"Slow. Here's my report," Bill said as he handed the report to the sheriff.

"Why don't you tell me what's been happening. I'll read your report later."

Bill told him what he had done, what he saw and what he planned to do today. The sheriff thought about what Bill had said, then nodded his approval of what he had done so far and what he planned to do.

"The problem I have at the moment is how do I get in touch with someone in the Army who might know where the explosives container came from. It might help. If they can tell us were the container came from, they might be able to give us a list of names of those who had some access to the container," Bill said.

"What do you hope to gain from that inquiry?"

"Well, sir, if the container was sold as war surplus, we might be able to track it and find out who purchased it. If it was stolen from military supply, I might be able to learn where it was stolen from, what base; and I might be able to get a list of names of those who had access to the container. The list of names might lead us to someone who is in this area. If nothing else, it would give us a suspect, something we don't have now."

"I see your point, but don't you think it's stretching it a bit?" the sheriff said looking skeptical.

Well, sir, ah - - I think it's worth a try. I have all the numbers and identifying information from the container which should make it fairly easy to track. Even so, I have to agree with you, it is a long shot; but if it was stolen, it would be nice to know what was in it when it was stolen. Don't you think?"

"I have to agree with you on that," the sheriff said. "I don't have any idea who to contact in the Army, but you might go out to the Rapid City Air Force Base and see if they can help you. It was not that long ago the base was part of the Army."

"I'll do that as soon as I get done talking to the lab personnel and the medical examiner."

"Is there anything else?"

"Yes. Could you find out who owns the property around the Jasper Quarry? I'm especially interested in the property directly behind the quarry."

"Sure. Give me a call after you've done what you can at the Rapid City Air Force Base. I'll have the names of those who own all the land around the Jasper Quarry. By the way, you're doing a good job. Keep up the good work."

"Thank you, sir. I'll stop in before I head back to Hill City," Bill said as he stood up.

The sheriff nodded his approval, then watched as Bill left the office.

Bill left the sheriff's office and went directly to the lab. As he walked in the door, he was greeted by a nice looking young woman who smiled up at him.

"What can I do for you, Deputy?"

"I would like to talk to the medical examiner about the autopsy he did on the man murdered at the Jasper Quarry."

"Oh," she said sounding a little disappointed. "One moment."

The woman pressed the button on the intercom and asked for the ME to come to the office. She explained that there was a deputy from the sheriff's office seeking information.

"I'll be there in a moment," he heard the ME say over the intercom.

It only took a few minutes before a man in his mid-fifties came out to the office. He saw Bill and walked over to him.

"How can I help you, Deputy? I'm Doctor Harrison, the medical examiner."

"The coroner brought in a body from the Jasper Quarry. I'm interested in what you might be able tell me about the man who was killed in the quarry."

"Come back to my office. We'll talk there," Doctor Harrison said.

Bill followed the doctor to his office. Once inside, the ME pointed to a chair for Bill. Bill sat down and watched the doctor as he looked through several files on his desk.

"Here it is," Doctor Harrison said as he opened the file. "First of all, I can tell you it was not the shotgun blast to his chest that killed him. It was a nine millimeter slug from a German Luger that killed him. My best guess is he was shot with the shotgun in the hope of covering up the single bullet hole that passed through his heart."

"Then the slug I found in the tool shed was not a .32 caliber slug, but a nine millimeter slug?"

"No. It was a .32 caliber. You were right about that, but it was not the slug that killed the man. I found the nine millimeter slug in the body. I think it probably would have gone completely through him if it hadn't been for the fact it hit several bones and had been fired downward into the body. Whoever shot him was standing almost over him."

"I found signs around the quarry that he might have been tortured before he was shot."

"There is little doubt he was tortured before he was killed. The ropes you sent in showed blood and skin tissue of the same type as the victim's, plus the rope burns on the victim's wrists matched up with the ropes indicating he had been hung up on something. From the pictures you sent in, I'm almost a hundred percent sure he was hung on that big wheel. It was very likely he sustained the burn marks on his back while tied to the wheel. The marks showed it was probably a running iron that was used on him."

"I take it you are talking about a running iron like cowboys use for branding?" Bill said.

"That's right."

"I didn't see any signs of a fire that would be needed to heat up the running iron."

"My guess would be they used a charcoal grill or something else like a torch to heat up the running iron and took it with them when they left."

"I take it from what you are saying, the victim was tortured for sometime," Bill said.

"I'm sure he was. By the way, you were right when you said it looked like someone had driven over his hands, and not just once but several times."

"Were you able to identify the victim?" Bill asked.

"No, not yet. I have not gotten back any results on his fingerprints from the FBI, but we did find something of interest."

"What was that?" Bill asked, impatient to hear what he had to say.

"We found a small mark on his left shoulder. At first we thought it was a birthmark in a shape similar to an irregular circle, but when we took a closer look at it there was a darker shape inside the circle. The darker shape was that of a swastika."

"Are you sure?" Bill asked with surprise.

"There was no doubt about it. It looked like the circle was an attempt to make the swastika almost invisible so anyone seeing it would think it was an almost round birthmark."

"You knew I found a lapel pin for the Nazi Political Party?"

"Yes. The sheriff told me about it. That, along with the tattoo on the victim's left shoulder, might suggest the victim was probably a Nazi," Doctor Harrison said.

"You might be right, but there's also the possibility the pin belonged to someone else. The lapel pin was not found anywhere near where the victim was found, or near any known place he might have been. And since it was a lapel pin, the kind usually worn on the lapel of a suit coat or sport coat, it might not have been the victim's. I know he was not wearing a coat of any kind, at least when I found him," Bill said.

"I guess that's your job to find out if it was the victim's pin or not. I can only tell you what I found on the victim."

"You have told me a lot. My problem is I still don't know what it all means," Bill said with a grin. "So, I guess it is time for me to find out what

I can about the now missing Army explosives container I found in the quarry," Bill said thoughtfully.

"How do you plan to do that?"

"I'm going to start by going out to the Rapid City Air Force Base. It was the Army Air Corp before it broke off from the Army and became the Air Force. There's a good chance that the explosives container came from there. If not, I'm hoping I can find out where it came from."

"Sounds like a good place to start. You might want to contact Captain Simon Walker. He's the guy in charge of supply for most of the base. If he can't help you, he might know who can," Doctor Harrison said.

"Thanks. I'll go talk to him," Bill said as he stood up.

After thanking the ME, Bill left the medical examiner's office and walked out to his patrol car. His mind was going a mile a minute trying to figure out why the victim had been tortured. What was it he knew that was so important to whoever killed him? Was the dark circle over the tattoo on the victim's shoulder there to just make it harder to see, or was it an attempt to cover up the swastika? If it was an attempt to cover it up, why? Was he trying to get out of the Nazi organization, and others thought he knew too much to let him go? Certainly a possibility, Bill thought. The fact the victim had been shot with a German Luger caused Bill to think the victim might have been shot by a member of the Nazi Political Party.

As Bill got in his patrol car and started out to the Rapid City Air Force Base, he realized he had more questions than answers about the murder. He also realized, during his talk with Doctor Harrison, he had not found out how old the murder victim was. Bill remembered he didn't think he was very old, maybe in his mid-to-late twenties.

The drive out to the Rapid City Air Force Base didn't take much more than about twenty minutes. When he drove up to the main gate, he was stopped by a sentry.

"How may I help you," the sentry asked.

"I'm Pennington County Deputy Sheriff Bill Sparks. I'm here to see Captain Simon Walker."

"Is the captain expecting you?"

"No, I don't think so," Bill said not knowing if the ME had called ahead.

"Just a moment, please," the sentry said then stepped into the guardhouse.

Bill could see him pick up a phone and place a call. He couldn't see the sentry's face as he had his back to him, but he was sure he was calling Captain Walker. It was just a moment or two before the sentry hung up the phone and returned to the side of the patrol car.

"Captain Walker will see you. Drive straight down this street to C Street," the sentry said as he pointed in the direction Bill was to go. "Turn left and park in front of the second building on your left. Captain Walker will have someone waiting for you."

"Thank you," Bill said as the sentry stepped back away from the patrol car.

Bill followed the sentry's instructions. When he came to C Street, he turned left and quickly saw the second building on the left. He pulled into an empty parking space just as a young airman stepped out of the door. Bill got out of the patrol car and walked up to the airman.

"Right this way, Officer," the airman said without introducing himself.

Bill followed the airman into the building. The building was obviously a supply building with long rows and rows of large heavy shelving. As he followed the young airman, he looked down one of the rows and saw several large crates at the end of the row. He had no idea what was in them, but they were large enough to be aircraft engines.

As he walked by another row, a large explosives container at the end of the row caught his attention. It caused him to stop and look down the row. He stood there looking at a large explosives container similar to the one he had seen at the Jasper Quarry.

"Excuse me, sir," the airman said startling Bill. "The captain is waiting for you."

"Yes," Bill said then quickly caught up with the airman.

Bill followed the airman until he stopped in front of a door with a name on it. The name was Captain S. Walker. The airman knocked on the door.

"Come in."

The airman opened the door and stepped back so Bill could enter.

"I understand you wish to talk to me, deputy," the captain said as he stood up. "What can I help you with?"

The captain sat back down and pointed to a chair. Bill sat down.

"I'm investigating the murder of a man in the Jasper Quarry. During my investigation, I discovered an Army explosives container, one of those large ones."

"I know what you are talking about. There are a number of them that were sold off after the war as surplus. What is your interest in the container?"

"I understand a number of them were sold off after the war, but this one was fairly new and still had identification numbers on it. I was wondering if you could tell me who might have bought one within the past six months or so," Bill said.

"I'm afraid I wouldn't have that information. If it was sold as surplus, it would be under surplus supplies. I don't handle surplus supplies."

"Can you tell me who does?"

"That would be handled by the supply sergeant in charge of surplus stock. He is located in the building next door."

"Who makes the determination that something should be sold as surplus?" Bill asked.

"If it comes from this building, from the inventory in this building, I would recommend it be sold off as surplus. The recommendation would go to Colonel Shaw. He would check to see if anyone has requested the item. If no one wanted the item, he would put it on a list of items to be sold off, then the item would be sent to the building next door," Captain Walker explained.

"How long does it take to get it listed as surplus?"

"Usually close to a year. He puts it out on an available list that goes out to other bases. It stays on the list for at least six months. If no one requests it, it is then listed as 'surplus' and sold. In the case of an explosives container, it would be emptied, of course, before it was put out as surplus."

"I noticed on my way to your office there are several containers in this building similar to the one I found in the quarry. Is it possible that the one I saw in the quarry came from here?"

"I guess it's possible, but I have not sent any to surplus since I've been here."

"How long have you been here?"

"Almost three years."

"Could you check and see if all of the explosives containers you have in your inventory are actually here?" Bill asked hoping his question would not upset the captain.

"Are you suggesting someone might have stolen one of those containers from here?" the captain asked as he looked at Bill.

The question came across as if the captain was angry with Bill for even thinking of such a thing. The captain looked at Bill while waiting for him to reply. The look on the captain's face was not a pleasant one.

"No, sir. What I'm really asking is would you take a moment to check your inventory to see if one of the containers might be missing. I guess I need to eliminate any possibility the container was from here," Bill said with an apologetic tone to his statement.

The captain sat across his desk just looking at Bill. It was clear he was thinking about what Bill had asked him. He suddenly turned and picked up the phone. It was almost immediately answered.

"Sergeant Miller, come in here."

It was only a matter of seconds before Sergeant Miller came into the captain's office.

"Sergeant, I want the list of all the explosives containers we have on hand."

"Yes, sir," the sergeant said, then glanced at Bill before he turned and left the office.

Bill could feel the tension in the room while they waited for the sergeant to return with the inventory sheet. Bill was beginning to think he was not going to get a real answer, that he was being stonewalled. Just when he was about to get up and go over to the base commander in an effort to get some cooperation, the door opened and the sergeant walked in with a clipboard with several sheets of paper on it.

"I take it you will not be satisfied until you see for yourself that we have the same number of explosives containers in our inventory records we say we have on hand," the captain said as he stood up. "Follow me."

Bill stood up and followed the captain and sergeant out into the storage area. They hadn't gone very far when they turned down the row to where the explosives containers Bill had seen when he first came into the building were kept.

"All the explosives containers we have are at the end of this row," the captain said.

"How many containers do you have?" Bill asked.

"Sergeant?"

"The inventory sheet shows we have nine, sir," the sergeant said.

They walked up to the containers. The captain looked at the containers, then turned and looked at Bill.

"As you can see, they are three in a row across the front and three in the second row across the back and three in the row on top of the back row. That puts six on the floor and three on top of the back row for a total of nine."

"Yes sir," Bill said as he looked at the containers.

Bill moved over to the left side of the containers and looked down the end of the row. What he saw caused him to take a second look. Everything he had seen in the supply building was stacked perfectly, except that back row of containers on the floor. The container on the left side, in the back row on the floor, was inset toward the center from the front row and the top row by almost a foot.

"Are you satisfied, Deputy?" the captain asked.

Bill looked at him, but didn't answer him. Instead he walked over to the right side of the containers and looked toward the back of the stack. The container in the back row, on the floor, on that side was also inset almost a foot from the front row and the top row, too. With the containers setting tightly together in the front row, the back row should have been even on both ends with the front row, if there were three containers all the same size. Bill turned and looked at the captain.

"Excuse me for asking, sir, but are all nine of these containers the same size?"

"Yes, of course," the captain answered, looking a little surprised at Bill's question.

"If that is correct, then you might be missing one container. It appears there are only two containers in the back row on the floor."

The expression on the captain's face was that of disbelief. He quickly looked at the ends of the back row, first on one side then the other, and saw the same thing Bill had seen.

"Sergeant, get a forklift in here and take the center container off the top row, NOW! And give me that inventory list."

The sergeant handed the inventory list to the captain, then quickly ran down the aisle to where a forklift was parked. The sergeant returned and drove the forklift up in front of the stack of containers.

"Lift the center one on the top row off the stack," the captain ordered.

The sergeant did as he was ordered. He drove the forklift's forks under the center container on the top, lifted it up, then backed away with it. He set the container down on the floor off to the side.

They quickly discovered there was a large hole where a container should have been. The top center container had been held in place by moving the two outside containers just close enough together to support the container on the top, covering the hole left by the missing container.

"Well, I guess you were right. We have one missing container," the captain said.

"What was in the container?" Bill asked.

"I'll have to check all the numbers to find out which one is missing before I can tell you what was in it."

"I have the numbers from the one I found in the quarry. I'll give them to you so you can see if it is the one you are missing," Bill said.

"I appreciate that. In return, I'll find out what was in it and let you know. I can tell you this much, in the wrong hands it could prove dangerous."

"I've already figured it would. It might help if you can figure out how long it has been missing and who had access to it."

"I'll do what I can. You said you saw it in the Jasper Quarry, is it still there?"

"I'm afraid not. It had been moved by the time I was able to get back there. If I find it again, I'll let you know," Bill assured him.

"Thank you," the captain said, then turned to the sergeant. "Call security and have them get over here on the double, and don't touch anything."

"Yes, sir," the sergeant said, then turned and ran toward the office.

The captain turned back and looked at Bill and said, "You can go."

"Shouldn't I wait until security gets here?" Bill asked.

"No. There's no reason for you to hang around here. Besides, I know where to get in touch with you if I should need to. I hope you will stay in touch with me," the captain said.

"I will," Bill said then returned to his patrol car and left the air base.

Bill wondered why the captain seemed to be anxious to have him leave the base. Maybe it was because it would be embarrassing for the captain to have to face a lot of questions from the security officers, and he didn't want any outsider there when he was questioned.

Bill stopped by the sheriff's office to get the information on who owned the property around the Jasper Quarry, and to tell him what happened at the Rapid City Air Force Base. The sheriff was not in the office, so Bill picked up the information he had requested, and left a short report of his contact with Captain Walker on the sheriff's desk.

After leaving the report, he headed back to Hill City. He went directly to his home and called it a day. He would look at the information he got from the sheriff's office in the morning and plan his day. It had been a long day.

CHAPTER ELEVEN

Bill had not set his alarm clock before going to bed, but he was up early just the same. His mind was filled with questions he couldn't answer, the most important one was what had been in the explosives container he had found in the quarry. As he laid in bed thinking, he wondered if Captain Walker would call and tell him what was in the container they were missing. He had his doubts. He knew how secretive the military can get, especially when they had to deal with civilian authorities.

His thoughts were suddenly disturbed by the ringing of his phone. He quickly got out of bed and went to his phone, then picked up the receiver.

"Hello."

"Hi. Did I wake you?" a pleasant female voice asked.

"As a matter of fact, no," he said as he recognized Julie's voice. "What's on your mind?"

"I'm going to be in town in a little less than an hour. I was thinking if you haven't had breakfast, you might like to have breakfast with me."

"That sounds good. I would like to have breakfast with you. Where did you have in mind?"

"How about the Hill City Café? It's the best place in town to get a good breakfast."

"Okay. How about I meet you at the café?"

"I'll see you there," she said with a smile in her voice then hung up.

Bill took a second to look at the phone while he hung it up. He smiled to himself at the thought of having breakfast with Julie. He walked back to his bedroom and got out a pair of jeans and a nice looking shirt. He decided since it was a date, sort of, he would not wear his uniform. Besides, it was Wednesday, his day off. Maybe after breakfast they could do something together.

He took a shower, shaved, and got dressed. When he was ready, he found he still had time enough for a cup of coffee. He made a cup, sat down at his kitchen table to enjoy it, and thought of seeing Julie again.

Bill's pleasant thoughts of having breakfast with Julie were suddenly shattered by the sound of his phone ringing. He got up, walked across the room and answered the phone.

"Hello."

"Bill, this is Mary. I know this is your day off, but the sheriff wants to talk to you."

"Put him on."

"He wants to talk to you here in the office at one o'clock this afternoon. He said it was very important that you be here."

"Well, that shoots my day off," Bill said with a disgusted tone in his voice. "What's it about?"

"He is meeting with a Captain Walker from the Rapid City Air Force Base at one. He didn't say what it was about, only that he wanted you here. He knows it's your day off. He told me to tell you that you can have tomorrow off," Mary explained.

"Okay. Tell him I'll be there."

"Okay. Talk to you later," Mary said then hung up.

Bill hung up his phone and returned to the table. As he sat down, he wondered why Captain Walker had requested a meeting with the sheriff. Had the captain found the missing explosives container from his supply building was the one Bill had found? If it wasn't, there didn't seem to be any reason for him to want to talk to Sheriff Henderson about the missing explosives container. Had he found out there was something dangerous in the missing explosives container? His last question seemed to make some sense.

There were a lot of questions going through Bill's mind; none of them were going to get answered until the meeting in the afternoon. All he could do now was to speculate, which for the most part, was a waste of time and energy.

There was one other thing he could do, and that was to make the best of what time he would be able to spend with Julie. That thought improved his outlook on the day. A quick check of his watch showed him it would not be too early to go to the Hill City Café to meet her.

He poured the remaining coffee in his cup into the sink then rinsed out the cup. He left his house and went to his car parked in the garage. He drove downtown and found a parking space across the street from the café. He parked his car, then walked across the street to the café and went inside. He found a booth and sat down.

It was only a matter of a couple of minutes before Sandy came over to his booth with a cup of coffee. She set the coffee down in front of Bill, then took her order pad out of the pocket of her apron.

"What would you like this morning?"

"Just the coffee for now. I'm waiting for someone. She should be here shortly."

"Okay. I'll come over when she comes in."

"Thanks, Sandy," Bill said then Sandy turned and walk over to another table.

Bill took a minute or so to look around the café to see who was there. Rutledge was there. He was sitting in a booth by himself. He had obviously been watching Bill, but quickly turned away when Bill looked at him.

He did see the man in the suit in the café. He was sitting by himself in a corner booth reading a paper. He turned slightly so that the paper blocked part of his face from where Bill was sitting. Bill had seen the man in Hill City only once before, and wondered who he was. He thought about asking someone who the man was, but didn't think it was a good idea to ask anyone in the café. He didn't want to show any interest in the man, just yet.

There were two local men sitting at a table talking and eating. Bill recognized them as local businessmen. Over in the corner were three women Bill also recognized as locals. They appeared to be just having coffee and chatting, about what he had no idea and certainly had no real interest in finding out.

Bill's attention was drawn to the front of the café when he heard the door open. He smiled when he saw Julie walk into the café and look around. A smile came over her face when she saw Bill. He took notice of her as she walked toward him. She was wearing jeans and a blouse that showed off her nice figure. He couldn't help but think she was a very nice looking young woman.

"Hi. I hope I didn't make you wait too long," she said as she slipped into the booth across from him.

"No. I've only been here for about ten minutes."

"You're not in uniform. Is this your day off?"

"It was until I got a phone call from the sheriff's office shortly after you called. I have to go into the office for a meeting at one," he said with a hint of disappointment.

"I was hoping we could spend the day together."

"So was I," he said just as Sandy walked up to the end of the table.

"What can I get for you?"

Julie and Bill ordered breakfast, then waited for Sandy to head toward the kitchen.

"I was told I would have tomorrow off since I have to go into the meeting. Will you be free to spend tomorrow with me?" Bill said hopefully.

"I would like that. What would you like to do?"

"How about we go into Rapid City. I have a few things to get in Rapid City. We could take in a movie and have dinner together. Maybe visit the museum," Bill suggested.

"That sounds good. I'll meet you at your house in the morning and we can leave from there," Julie suggested.

"I'll fix you breakfast before we go to Rapid City."

"Great," Julie said.

While they waited for their breakfast, they talked about some of the things they might do while in Rapid City. Just then, Sandy brought over their breakfast. There was very little talk about

Bill's investigation. It seemed neither one of them wanted to talk about it.

After breakfast, Julie and Bill decided to take a walk around Hill City. Since Julie didn't know where Bill lived, they walked by his house, but didn't go in. Time had passed quickly and it was getting close to the time Bill would have to get ready to go to Rapid City for the meeting at the sheriff's office. Since Bill's car was parked across the street from the Hill City Café, he walked Julie back to her grandfather's pickup truck which was also parked near the café. She got in and he closed the door for her. She looked up at him.

"I'll see you for breakfast tomorrow at your house," Julie said with a smile.

"Drive careful," Bill said as he leaned in and kissed her lightly on the lips.

Julie smiled up at him, then started the truck. Bill stepped back and watched her as she drove away. He then walked back to his car and drove home to get ready to go to Rapid City.

It wasn't long and he was in uniform and on his way to Rapid City in his patrol car. He stopped off for lunch in Rapid City before driving over to the sheriff's office for the meeting.

Bill arrived at the sheriff's office at about quarter to one. He checked in with Mary so she could tell the sheriff he was there.

"Hi, Mary. Is the sheriff in?"

"Yes. He's in the conference room with Captain Walker from the Rapid City Air Force Base, and some other guy. They are waiting for you. He said you are to go in as soon as you got here."

"I guess I'd better get in there."

Bill turned and walked down the hall to the conference room. He was wondering what the captain had to tell them. He also wondered who the "other guy" might be.

He took a deep breath as he opened the door to the conference room. As he stepped inside, he saw Captain Walker, Sheriff Henderson, and another man Bill did not recognize sitting around a large table. The third man was wearing the uniform of an Army Sergeant. The pin on his uniform collar, which Bill recognized immediately, indicated the sergeant was an Ordnance Technician. The pin indicated the man probably knew a lot about explosives.

"Sit down, Bill. You know Captain Walker," Sheriff Henderson said. "This gentleman is Sergeant David Johnson from the Army Ordnance Depot."

"Call me, Dave," the sergeant said as he stood up and shook Bill's hand.

"Bill," he said as he shook Dave's hand then sat down.

"As you may have guessed, the explosives container you saw at the Jasper Quarry contained at one time some rather nasty explosives," Sheriff Henderson said. "I want you to fill these gentlemen in on everything you saw in relation to the container."

Bill spent the next few minutes telling them how he found the explosives container with the lock on it and that he had left it for a short time; but it was empty when he returned. He told them the container had been hauled away by the next time he was in the area again, which was the very next day.

"Do you have any idea where it is now?" Dave asked.

"No. All I know is it was taken out the back of the quarry property on a fairly heavy stake truck, probably a two or three ton stake truck from the looks of the tracks."

"Any idea why they took the container after it was empty?"

"Not really, but my guess would be they knew what they had and wanted to keep it in a safe place. It was probably safer for them to keep whatever had been in the container in it, since it was built for that purpose. It would keep prying eyes from seeing what they had, and it was probably easier for them to transport the contents in the container than to transport them separately."

"It's my understanding you knew what the container was used for. That being the case, why is it you didn't stay with the container until someone could come there, when you first found it?" Captain Walker asked, his demeanor was less than pleasant when asking the question.

"I can answer that," Sheriff Henderson said when he looked at Bill and saw him looking at the captain as if the captain was thinking Bill had been negligent in not staying with the container to protect it.

"First of all, Deputy Sparks did not know what was in it. In point of fact, he still doesn't know what was in it. Secondly, it had a lock on it which was not a military style lock. It was a common hardware store padlock. For all he knew, it could have been an Army surplus container someone had bought to store almost anything in. Third, his car and radio had been disabled. Since he was alone, there was no way for him to get in contact with anyone to help him without leaving the area; and it could have been hours before anyone knew he needed help, or where he was at. Does that satisfy your question, captain?" the sheriff said with a firm tone in his voice.

"Yes," Captain Walker replied softly, looking at the sheriff.

"Since you have such a great deal of interest in the explosives container I found, I take it it is the one you are missing. Is that correct?" Bill asked.

Bill watched as Captain Walker and Sergeant Johnson looked at each other. It was clear they didn't really want to discuss the loss of an explosives container from a military supply depot with a local law officer, but what choice did they have? The container was already off the base, and the local sheriff's office knew it.

"That would be correct," Captain Walker admitted.

"I think it would be wise for you to tell us what was in the explosives container when it was in your custody, since my men are likely to be the ones who will find it," Sheriff Henderson said rather sharply.

Again, Captain Walker looked at Sergeant Johnson. He was reluctant to tell civilians what was in the container, but it again appeared they had little or no choice.

"I think we should tell them," Sergeant Johnson said. "They need to know what they are dealing with, if for no other reason than to protect themselves."

"What the hell was in that container when it was stolen from your depot?" Sheriff Henderson asked, demanding an answer.

Sergeant Johnson looked at Captain Walker. When Captain Walker didn't say anything, Johnson spoke up.

"There were four cases of hand grenades, several boxes of .30 caliber small arms ammo, namely 30.06 ammo, and two mortars with twenty rounds," Sergeant Johnson said.

"In the hands of someone who knows how to use them, they are very dangerous and very effective. In the hands of the wrong people, they could cause a lot of damage. They could be used for any number of things."

"I don't think you need to tell us what they could be used for," Sheriff Henderson said, interrupting the sergeant. "I can think of a lot of things they could use that kind of weaponry for, and none of it pleasant. The only question is what are they planning on doing with it?

"Bill, I want you to get with Jess. Have him get several deputies together and find out where that container is," Sheriff Henderson said.

"I think it would be better if I go up to the quarry and find out where the tracks lead alone."

"I don't think that's a good idea," Sheriff Henderson said, wondering what Bill had on his mind.

"If I'm alone, I will be harder to spot. I've been on missions like this when I was in the Army. The more people involved, the better the chance of being spotted before I get close enough to find it."

"He might have a point there," Sergeant Johnson said. "We can supply him with the latest walkie-talkie radio, and have someone in the area he can radio information to. Once he locates the container, we can move in."

"You would have to be far enough away from him that you wouldn't tip them off you're there," the sheriff said.

"That would be no problem. We could put a man up on top of one of the hills up to a couple of miles away. He would be able to pick up Bill's walkie-talkie radio transmission," Sergeant Johnson said.

"What do you think, Bill?" Sheriff Henderson asked. "It's your butt on the line."

"I think it might work," Bill said.

"I think it's time to leave Sergeant Johnson and Bill to work out the details. I have a Forest Service map of the area," Sheriff Henderson said as he set the map on the table in front of Bill.

"It shows the area very well," Sheriff Henderson added.

"I think we are done here," Captain Walker said. "Sergeant, since you drove here in your own car, I'll head back to the base. I'll want to talk to you when you get done here."

"Fine, sir. I'll let you know what our plans are when we get done."

The captain nodded he agreed then stood up and left the conference room. Sheriff Henderson followed the captain out leaving Bill and Dave to work out a plan to find the explosives container.

Bill and Dave laid out the Forest Service map on the conference table. Once they found where the Jasper Quarry was on the map, they looked for possible places where the container could have been taken. There were a number of Forest Service roads in the area, but only two came near the back of the quarry property.

"If I take a two-way radio up on this hilltop, I can only pick up a walkie-talkie radio communication from you on this road," Johnson said as he pointed to one of the two Forest Service roads.

"I take it you and I are doing this," Bill said.

"I think it's best that way. Don't you?" Dave asked.

"Yes, I think so," Bill said.

"This other one would put you behind this hill," Dave said. "I would not be able to pick up any communications from you in several areas."

"What about here?" Bill said as he pointed to a different hill.

"It looks like it might be better, but there would be places on both roads where I would not be able to hear you. However, there would be more places where I could hear you."

"Let's use this last place. I will make it a point of getting to higher ground to talk to you, if at all possible," Bill said.

Dave studied the map to see if there was a better place, but didn't seem to be able to find one. He looked up at Bill.

"The last hill seems to give us the largest area where we should be able to keep in touch, but it also puts you out of touch in several places. That could prove to be a problem. What do you think?" Dave asked.

"I agree," Bill said looking at Dave and wondering if he should share his concerns. "I have a question for you."

"Sure."

"Do you know Captain Walker very well?"

"No. He seems all right," Dave said wondering what Bill was getting at.

"Have you worked with him before?"

"No. Today was the first time I've seen him. He called in to have me at the meeting because I'm an expert on explosives."

"Do you know for a fact what was in the container?"

"Well, no, not from actually seeing it before it was stolen. I've seen the packing list. What are you getting at?"

"Who provided you with the packing list for the container?"

"An airman who works in the supply depot. I didn't get his name."

"When I was in the supply depot and discovered the missing container, I got the impression Captain Walker didn't seem as surprised about the missing container as I would have expected. By the way, I was the one who found it was missing.

"You found it was missing?"

"Yes. I spotted the attempt to cover up the space where the container had been stored. It wasn't hard to see."

"He didn't tell me that."

"When there's something containing the kind of explosives he claims it contained is missing, you would think it would have been reported immediately to his commanding officer. Once that was done, they would have been all over the place in seconds. They would be asking questions, and looking for evidence as to how and when it was removed without anyone knowing."

"I agree," Dave said.

"His reaction to the missing container was not what I would have expected. He seemed more upset that I found it missing than the fact it was missing. He didn't report it while I was there, which I found interesting. He dismissed me when he knew that I could have told the investigators how I happened to discover it missing, and what they might want to look for in an effort to find out if anything else was missing."

"I agree. That does seem a little strange," Dave said thoughtfully.

"I don't mean to say that I think Captain Walker had anything to do with the missing container, but there are too many things that just don't seem to add up, at least to my way of thinking. If I'm going into the hills looking for the container alone, I want people I can trust backing me up. I don't feel comfortable trusting Captain Walker. I would like where I'm going to be, and where you are going to be, kept between us."

Dave looked at Bill for a minute. It was clear he was thinking. It was also clear he didn't like the thought Captain Walker might have something to do with the missing container.

"I sure understand that. I take it you have something on your mind," Dave said.

"Yes. I would like our locations kept between us. You and I are the only ones who have a need to know, except for the sheriff. Someone needs to know where we are in case something goes wrong."

"I agree. If I'm pressed for our locations by the captain, I'll give him different locations. If the captain gets upset when he finds out, I'll tell him I must have gotten the positions wrong, and that I'm not familiar with the backcountry of the Black Hills," Dave said with a grin.

Bill shook Dave's hand, then they planned out where they were going and how they would stay in contact with each other. In order to make it more difficult for anyone to figure out who it was, they chose code names when talking on the two-way radio. Dave would be Bow, and Bill would be Arrow. As soon as they had it figured out, they set the time when they would be at their positions tomorrow. They would make contact at ten in the morning and keep in contact every twenty minutes with five minutes extra before sending in help.

Bill walked out with Dave to his car and got a walky-talky radio from Dave. He was shown how to use it, and they were ready for tomorrow. Bill said goodbye to Dave then went to the sheriff's office to talk with the sheriff.

After a brief discussion on what Bill and Dave had worked out, Bill left and drove home. He arrived home about dinner time. He decided to call Julie and tell her things had changed, again, and he wouldn't have tomorrow off after all. Her phone rang about three times before it was answered.

"Hello," Julie said.

"Hi."

"Hi. How did things go at the sheriff's office?"

"Not well, I'm afraid. I have to work tomorrow."

"I'm sorry. What happened?"

"I can't really talk about it now, but maybe we can get together when this investigation is over."

"You mean I won't be seeing you until you're done with it?" Julie asked, her voice showing her disappointment.

"No. I will see you again, it's just that I don't know when I'll be able to get away to spend some time with you. I'll still find time to see you and call you. It's just we can't really plan anything for a while. I won't know when I will have any time off. We're shorthanded."

"I understand," Julie said, but with little conviction in her voice. "I guess if that's the way it has to be."

"I'm sorry, Honey. Does it help any that I love you?"

"It sure doesn't hurt," she replied with a little more enthusiasm in her voice. "I love you, too."

Bill and Julie spent the next half hour or so talking about nothing of any real importance. They shared thoughts about what they would like to do and things they might do when Bill was done with the investigation. It wasn't long and they decided to call it a night.

"It has been a long day. I'll try to call you tomorrow, but it may be late."

"That's okay. You can call me anytime, even if it's late."

"Your grandpa won't mind?"

"No. He won't mind. I think he likes you," Julie said.

"I like him. I better get some rest. I have a busy day tomorrow. I love you. Goodnight."

"I love you, too. Goodnight," Julie said then hung up the phone.

Bill hung up his phone, then went to the kitchen to make his dinner. He ate, then got ready for bed, but didn't go right to bed. Instead, he went over his plans for tomorrow. Once he was sure he had it all worked out, and had gotten what he was going to need for his trip into the hills, he turned in for the night.

CHAPTER TWELVE

Bill woke early and got dressed in brown pants and shirt that would make it harder for anyone to see him in the woods. He put on his hunting boots, then sat down for breakfast. After breakfast, he grabbed his brown cowboy hat that would not only help make it harder for anyone to see him, but would help keep the sun from shining on his face. He used an old brown leather holster instead of his shiny black holster and belt he wore with his uniform. As soon as he had his deputy's badge pinned to the inside of his left breast pocket so it wouldn't shine in the sun, he looked in the mirror. He was ready to go into the woods to look for the explosives container.

Bill went to the patrol car and got out the walkie-talkie radio Sergeant Johnson had loaned him and put it in his personal car. He then got in his own car and headed for one of the Forest Service roads located a little way from the quarry. He found a road about a mile before he would come to the drive to Keaton's place. He didn't want to drive by his place, or Rutledge's place for that matter, because he didn't want them to accidently see him. He didn't want them to know he was in the area. He also didn't want Turnquest to know he was in the area, either. He didn't want

Turnquest to accidentally tell someone that he had seen Bill in the backcountry.

He turned off the main road onto the Forest Service fire road after making sure there was no one around who might see him make the turn. He drove back in for almost a mile before he found a place where he could hide his car. Bill parked his car off the fire road, then got out taking his binoculars and the walkie-talkie radio with him.

Before Bill began walking along the fire road, he took a few minutes to check the road to see if it had been used lately. There were no signs that there had been anything on the road except for a few deer that had left tracks in the dirt.

Bill stepped off the road, moving in among the trees. Keeping to the side of the fire road and in among the trees, Bill began walking parallel to the fire road. From what he could see, he was sure he was well away from the quarry and probably several hundred yards from Keaton's place.

He had been walking alongside the road for some distance when he came to a place where another Forest Service fire road intersected with the fire road he had been walking beside. Bill looked around then slowly moved out onto the intersecting road to check for tire tracks. He quickly found a set of tire tracks that looked like the ones he had seen near the explosives container when it was still on Jasper Quarry property.

Looking at the tracks, Bill could see that the rear wheels of the truck crossed over the tracks made by the front wheels. It indicated to him the truck had come from the direction of the quarry, then turned onto the fire road he had been walking beside. Bill looked up the fire road that the tire tracks had indicated the truck had gone. He had no idea where the road went, or where it came out to a county road or a state road.

A quick look at his watch showed him it was about time to call in to "Bow" and see if he was in position. At exactly ten in the morning, he put the walkie-talkie radio up to his mouth and ear, then pressed the button allowing him to talk to "Bow".

"Arrow to Bow. Do you read me?"

"Loud and clear," Dave said. "I'm at MM. Have good position."

Bill knew Dave was on top of Medicine Mountain. From that location, he would have good reception from Bill's walkie-talkie radio as long as he had a direct line of sight to Dave's location.

"I'm ready. Have found good dirt, will proceed," Bill said.

"Continue to shift through the dirt."

Bill continued to follow the tracks from the truck. It was slow going, but he had good cover alongside the fire road and was still able to see the tracks clearly. As he moved alongside the fire road, he continued to check his back trail to see if there might be someone coming up the road behind him. He didn't see anyone, but he noticed the fire road curved ever so slowly. He began to think if it continued to curve around in the direction it was going, he could end up on the other side of the quarry, maybe to the road running alongside Turnquest's farm.

Keeping an eye out for anyone in the area, while watching the tracks in the fire road, was keeping him busy. He had traveled a long way when it was time to call in again. He had just put the walkie-talkie radio up to his mouth when he heard a branch of a tree only a foot or so from his head explode, followed almost immediately by the sound of a shot. Bill dove to the ground and drew his pistol. He had heard enough shots during his time in the military to know he had been shot at by someone using a rifle, and it had been close.

Bill looked at the tree. He could see where the slug had hit the tree, which made it possible for Bill to figure out the direction the shot had come from. He looked around for a better place to take cover. He saw a dead tree that had fallen a number of years ago. It would provide better cover for him than lying on the ground. He crawled behind the downed tree, staying as low as possible. He listened carefully for some sound that would indicate where the person might be who had shot at him. He also kept looking around to see if the person had moved and was possibly trying to get behind him.

Looking around the end of the downed tree, he thought he saw movement off to the left of where he thought the shot had come from. It looked as if whoever had fired at him was trying to work his way around in order to get a better shot at him. Bill was not about to let that happen.

Bill waited and watched. He kept an eye on the man who was slowly moving around, while keeping an eye out for someone who might be working his way around to the other side of him.

Suddenly, there was another rifle shot which hit a tree close to where he had been, but Bill had seen where it had come from. He took careful aim at the bush next to the large tree where the shot had come from. He slowly squeezed the trigger until his gun fired. He heard the sound of someone who had either been surprised that Bill's shot had come so close, or the shooter had been hit by the bullet from Bill's gun.

It was only seconds later Bill heard the sound of someone running through the woods. Whoever it was, they were running away from him as fast as they could go. Bill's first thought was to take off after the shooter, but decided against it. He had no idea if there was a second shooter who would be waiting to shoot him when he got up and exposed himself.

Bill waited behind the downed tree and listened. After a few minutes, he slowly got up while keeping his eyes moving as he looked for any movement that would indicate someone might still be around. When he was sure it was safe, he picked up his walkie-talkie radio and called in.

"Arrow to Bow."

"Go ahead, Arrow."

"I was just shot at,"

"I heard. You okay?"

"Yeah. I think I might have hit the shooter."

"What now?"

"I'm going to check out his location. There may be something there to tell me if I actually hit him," Bill said.

"Be careful. They know you are in the area and might know who you are."

"I will," Bill said then took a minute to look around.

Bill was trying to make sure there was no one in the area. When he was satisfied there was no one who presented a danger to him, he began working his way toward where the shot had come from. Bill slowly moved from tree to tree moving ever closer to where the shooter had been. It took him almost twenty minutes to find the spot. When he got to the spot where the shooter had been, he found a small amount of blood splatter on one side of the tree next to the bush. It was fresh blood. He knew he had hit the shooter, but didn't know how badly he was injured. It was probably a minor wound since the shooter had run away.

Bill also found a brass casing from a .30 caliber rifle cartridge. The cartridge was a 30.06, the same kind of ammo used by the military in many of their service rifles like the M1 Grand and the Springfield rifle, the two most common rifles used by the military. It was also a fairly common caliber for hunting rifles. The end of the brass casing was stamped in letters and numbers showing it was the casing from U.S Government issued ammunition. Bill knew from the report of the contents of the explosives container there had been several boxes of government issued .30 caliber small arms ammo in the container. The only question was did the casing he found come from one of the boxes of .30 caliber small arms ammo that had been in the missing explosives container. The casing itself was not enough to confirm it.

He picked up the casing with his handkerchief and carefully put it in his pocket. If he was lucky, it might have fingerprints on it. He also gathered up a couple of leaves with blood on them for evidence. The blood could be tested for blood type.

Bill could see where the shooter had run off. There were tracks in the grass as he ran to get away. He decided he would follow the tracks as best he could in the hope of finding out where the shooter went, but it was not to be. He lost the shooter's tracks in the pine needle covered forest floor. It had become apparent the shooter had not sustained a very serious injury as he had not left a blood trail.

Since Bill had lost the trail of the shooter, he returned to the place where he had been shot at and pick up the tire tracks he had been following. Still keeping off the road and in the trees, he continued to follow the tire tracks. It wasn't long before he found the fire road ran into another fire road. The tire tracks turned and went further away from the quarry.

"Bow to Arrow."

"Come in Bow," Bill said.

"I saw a ribbon of dust being kicked up by something moving very fast. It was headed away from your area. It would be my guess it was who shot at you," Dave reported.

"Could you get anything that might help us identify the vehicle?"

"All I can tell you is it was a black pickup, possibly an International or a Dodge, but I can't be sure. It was too far away and kicking up too much dust to get a really good look at."

"Could you tell if the explosives container was on the truck?"

"No. I couldn't tell if there was anything in the truck. I only saw it for a second."

"Okay. You might keep an eye out just in case it comes back," Bill said, a little disappointed.

Bill looked down the road. He was a little disappointed at how things had worked out. He decided that since he had been seen, there was little likelihood anyone would stick around. It was time to call it a day. If the explosives container was still on the truck, it would have been moved away from the area as quickly as possible.

"Arrow to Bow."

"Go ahead Arrow."

"I think we should call it a day. I don't think we will find our target now. It would have been moved to some other location."

"I agree. How about we meet in Hill City for lunch?"

"I think we should meet somewhere else. How about Custer?"

"Okay. See you there. Out."

Bill swung the strap of the walkie-talkie radio over his shoulder, then looked back the way he had come. He thought about taking the road leading to the gate between the quarry and Turnquest's farm, but thought better of it. Instead, he decided he would go back the way he had come.

By going back, the way he came, he could get back to his car without walking down the main road in front of Keaton's place. He wasn't sure if Keaton was involved in moving the explosives container, but Bill didn't want to risk being seen by Keaton just in case he was involved.

It took Bill over an hour to get back to his car. He got in and headed for Custer to meet Dave.

When Bill arrived in Custer, he quickly found Dave's car parked in front of one of the local cafés. He parked, got out of his car and went into the café. It didn't take him but a moment to find Dave. He walked over to the booth where Dave was sitting and slid into the booth across from him.

"Well, that didn't work out very well," Dave said, the sound of disappointment in his voice.

"I don't know. I found a - - -," Bill said, but was interrupted by the waitress.

The waitress set two glasses of water on the table and two menus. She then turned and walked away.

They picked up the menus and scanned them quickly. It was only a couple of minutes before the waitress returned.

"What would you like?" she asked.

Bill and Dave ordered lunch then waited for the waitress to leave before continuing their conversation.

"As I was saying, I found a .30 caliber casing from the gun that was used to shoot at me. The casing was from a military 30.06 cartridge. It was shiny, so my guess is that it was new ammunition."

"You think it was from the missing container?"

"I doubt we can prove it, but there is a very good chance it was," Bill said.

Just then, Bill saw the waitress coming toward them with their order. He leaned back while she set their order on the table.

As soon as the waitress left the table, they started to eat. By the way they ate, it was obvious they were hungry. It wasn't until they were almost halfway through with their lunch that either of them spoke.

"What are your plans now?" Dave asked. "Are you going to try again to see if we can find the container?"

"I'm not sure, but I think I should stop off at the Forest Service Office and see if I can find out where those fire roads go. I'm sure someone will know."

"That sounds like a good idea. They probably have a map showing them. If you go back in there, you might want to take someone with you," Dave suggested.

"I'm sure you're right," Bill said thoughtfully.

"Did you get the idea someone knew we were going to be snooping around behind the Jasper Quarry this morning?" Bill asked as he picked up his cup of coffee and leaned back.

"I hadn't really thought about it, but with what happened I wouldn't be surprised."

After looking around the café, Bill leaned forward and said, "The only people in the meeting were Sheriff Henderson, Captain Walker, and, of course, you and me. I didn't tell anyone except Sheriff Henderson, that we were going to be snooping around in the backcountry behind the quarry. I'm sure Sheriff Henderson didn't tell anybody."

"I didn't tell anybody. I didn't even tell my Lieutenant. I came out here on my own time so I wouldn't have to tell anyone where I was going, or what I would be doing."

"Did you have to tell someone when you got the walkie-talkie radios?"

"No. I already had them in my car."

"Then that leaves Captain Walker."

"Do you think he might be involved?" Dave asked.

"I don't know, but I get the feeling whoever shot at me, knew we would be out there. Of course, there's always the possibility the person who shot at me was simply there to make sure no one got close to the explosives container, or whatever they are hiding in the woods."

"I sure hope we don't have an officer involved."

"It wouldn't be the first time an officer was involved in stealing government property. I think we just might have someone of rank involved, or at least someone who could arrange to get the explosives container out of the supply building and off the base without anyone seeing it," Bill said.

"There are probably several non-coms who could do it." Dave said. "They would have to work in supply and, at the very least, know what was in the containers in order to get what they wanted."

"I'm sure you're right. Do you know how many people work in the supply building at the air base where the container had been?"

"Let me think. There are four airmen, all with ranks of sergeant or above. There are two airmen with a rank below sergeant. There are two officers, Walker of course, and Second Lieutenant Simon."

"What can you tell me about Lieutenant Simon?"

"He's fresh out of Officer's Training School. The air base is his first real duty station. I don't think he knows enough about the workings in supply to be able to get something as big as an explosives container out of the building and off the base without anyone knowing it."

"Do you work at that supply building?"

"You don't think I had anything to do with it?" Dave asked, not sure what Bill was getting at.

"No. I don't think you had anything to do with it. I was just asking to find out if you work there and if you might know something about the men who work in the supply building."

"I don't work on the air base. I work at the South Dakota National Guard Base. I don't have much to do with the air base except for assistance to Captain Walker when he needs something. He called me shortly after the explosives container was discovered missing. He wanted to know what to do about it."

"What did you tell him?"

"I told him to tell his Commanding Officer, Colonel Bennett, immediately."

"Do you know if he did that?"

"I would think so, because my base commander called me and told me to get over there and see what was going on. I was instructed to help in any way I could. He obviously thought that Captain Walker knew little about procedures in a case of missing weapons or ammo, and would need help."

"So that's how you got involved," Bill said thoughtfully.

"Right."

Bill and Dave finished their lunch, paid the waitress then walked outside. Standing next to Dave's car, they talked for a little while longer. It was decided Dave would not say anything about what they had been doing, or what they talked about, or about the shooting.

Bill returned the walkie-talkie radio to Dave before shaking hands and saying "Goodbye". Dave said he would be glad to help in any way he could, and Bill was to call him if he could help.

Bill thanked him for his help and his offer to help him again, then stood next to the curb and watched as Dave drove away. He was thinking over what had happened and what they had talked about. Bill couldn't help but think there had to be someone inside the supply building who was involved. There was little doubt there had to be an order to get a container as big as the explosives container off the base without someone seeing or knowing it.

Bill walked to his car, got in and headed back to Hill City. He went directly to his house and called the sheriff. He told the sheriff what had happened and what he had talked to Sergeant Johnson about. The sheriff seemed to agree with what Bill was telling him.

"What's your next move?" Sheriff Henderson asked.

"I don't know. The one thing I think I need to do is find out where those fire roads behind the quarry go."

"I would think it would be good to know."

"I'm going to go to the Forest Service Office tomorrow to find out if they know where those roads go. Hopefully, they will have a map. I have serious doubts the explosives container is still in the immediate area. At least, I doubt it is hidden in the forest or at the quarry, although, it might be. It would be just like them to think it was safe to put it back in the quarry since we know it has been moved."

"You might have something there," the sheriff said. "However, I would bet they won't have it setting out in the open again.

"That gives me an idea. I might want to go back up to the quarry for a look around again."

"Okay, but you be careful."

"I will, sir," Bill said. "By the way, did you find out who owns the land directly behind the quarry?"

"Yes. A good part of the land belongs to Keaton, about a hundred acres of it. It is part of his land that runs from the road up alongside the quarry, then sort of wraps around behind the quarry for a little ways. The land behind the quarry that runs between Keaton's property and Turnquest's fence line on the other side of the quarry is Forest Service land."

"So, all the land directly behind the quarry belongs to Keaton and the Forest Service."

"That's right."

Bill thought about that for a moment. He couldn't see what difference it made, but he would think about it.

"Is there anything else?" the sheriff asked.

"Ah – no."

"Is there something on your mind you would like to talk to me about?" the sheriff asked thinking Bill was keeping something from him.

"No, not at this time."

"What's on your mind?" the sheriff asked.

"I was just thinking about Mr. Keaton," Bill said.

"You think he is involved?"

"I'm not sure, but there are a few little things that don't seem to add up."

"Do you think you have enough evidence to get a search warrant for Keaton's property?"

"No, but I don't think it will hurt any to have another talk with Mr. Keaton."

"Okay, if you think it might help, but be careful. You don't want to scare him off. If he runs, we may never find him again."

"I'll be careful, sir," Bill said then hung up the phone.

Bill sat down at his kitchen table after he made himself a cup of coffee. As he sipped at the coffee, he thought about what little he knew about Keaton. He decided it might be a good idea if he could get some information on the closing of the quarry. The local paper might have some information on the quarry, things like accidents, injuries at the quarry, and why it closed down, and precisely when it closed.

Bill had made up his mind to spend a little time in the local newspaper office going over any articles they had on the quarry, especially anything having to do with Keaton and any others in the area who had worked there. He knew he would have to be careful not to mention any names to anyone working in the newspaper office.

Bill took a look at his watch and saw it was time to think about what he wanted for dinner. He had just gotten up from the table and was reaching for the refrigerator door when there was a knock on his front door. He went to the door and opened it. Julie was standing on his front porch smiling at him.

"Hi," Bill said as he smiled at her.

"Hi. I saw your car and your police car were here, so I took the chance you might be home."

"I guess you were right. Come in," he said as he held the door for her.

Julie walked into his house and looked around. She found his place to be a lot cleaner than she had expected. She also noticed there were not a lot of pictures on the walls, and there were very few pieces of furniture. As he closed the door, she turned and looked at him.

"Well, what do you think?' he said as he looked at her.

"About what?"

"About my place? Was it what you expected?"

"Yes, and no."

"You want to explain that, or would you rather not put your foot in your mouth," he said with a grin.

"Okay. Your home has very little furniture, but what you have is what you would use most of the time. There are very few pictures on the walls, but what you have are pictures of things or people who are important to you. And, your home looks very clean, but I haven't seen your kitchen, yet."

"In other words, you expected my house to be sort of a mess, and my kitchen would have dirty dishes in the sink, and there would be mold on the food in the refrigerator. Is that about it?"

"Well, sort of," she said a little embarrassed by what she had said.

"That being the case, come with me," he said as he walked to the kitchen.

Julie followed him. When they got to the kitchen, he walked over to the refrigerator and opened the door.

"Tell me, do you see any mold on any of the food in here? Are there any dirty dishes in the sink?"

"No," she admitted. "I'm sorry."

"In other words, the only thing you found that fits your image of what a single guy's place should look like was the fact it lacks a woman's touch in decorating?"

"I guess so. I'm sorry," Julie said as she walked up in front of him.

She looked up at him for a moment then put her arms around his neck and tipped her face up to him. She gently pulled him down toward her until their lips met. After a very soft and tender kiss, she looked up at his face again.

"Apology accepted," he said with a grin then kissed her again.

"I was hoping you might not have had dinner yet," she said as she looked up at him.

"I was just about to fix myself something. Would you like to have dinner here with me?"

"Sure. What were you planning on having?"

"I have a ham, and a few potatoes, and some corn on the cob."

"That sounds good. Would you like me to help you fix dinner?"

"Since this is the first time you've been here; I'll fix dinner for you. It only seems fair since I have eaten at your place twice without helping you. The coffee's fresh. You can pour yourself a cup of coffee and sit at the table to keep me company while I fix dinner.

Julie got a cup of coffee, then sat down at the table. She liked to watch Bill as he worked in the kitchen. In fact, she liked to watch him anytime. She quickly discovered he seemed very comfortable working in a kitchen.

When dinner was ready, they sat down and enjoyed a meal together. Most of their talk had little to do with the investigation Bill had been working on. In fact, he directed the conversation more to what she had been doing. She had found a job in Rapid City at the hospital. She explained it was not what she had wanted, but it was a place to start.

After dinner was over, she helped him clean up the kitchen. When they were done, they went into the living room and sat down on the sofa together. It wasn't long before Julie was curled up with Bill, and they were doing a little necking.

Time seemed to pass rather quickly. It was close to nine-thirty when either of them bothered to look at a clock.

"It's getting kind of late," Bill said. "You still have almost an hour of driving to get home."

"I could stay here tonight," she said as she looked into his eyes.

"As much as I would like that, I don't think it's a good idea. I have a couple of nosey neighbors who would like nothing more than to start rumors about us."

"So, you're tossing me out?"

"No. I'm suggesting you go before I decide you aren't getting out of here until the sun comes up in the morning."

"That sounds like an invitation for me to spend the night with you," she said playfully.

"I would like that very much, but do you think it's a good idea?"

Julie looked into his eyes. She was sure he would really like to have her spend the night with him, but his earlier comment told her that he was concerned about what people would say and what kind of rumors they would spread. She was sure he was trying to protect her from any nasty rumors.

"No, I think you're right. I should go, but under one condition."

"What's that?"

"That you give me a goodnight kiss, and, think about me."

"I don't see any problem with your request. After all, I think of you a lot already."

"You do?" she said with a big grin.

"Yes."

"I love you," she said as she threw her arms around his neck and kissed him.

It was a long hard kiss showing him that she really did love him. He found no problem with kissing her back with as much passion as she had shown him. When they finally let go of each other,

Julie looked at him. Her eyes sparkled with her love for him. She took a deep breath, then stood up.

"I have to go. One more kiss like that, and you'll never get me to leave," she said as she stood up and looked down at him still sitting on the sofa.

Bill didn't know what to say. He felt the same way at that moment, but he couldn't expose her to the rumors that were sure to come from some of the people who lived near him.

Bill stood up, took her hand then walked her to her grandfather's pickup truck. He opened the pickup truck's door for her and waited for her to get in. She leaned over and kissed him, then got into the pickup. As soon as she was seated behind the wheel, she looked up at him.

"I have to work tomorrow. Would you like me to stop by on my way home?"

"Sure. What time do you think you will be here?"

"About the same time as today, around five-thirty."

"I should be here by then. If I'm not, then something came up."

"I hope nothing comes up. I'll see you tomorrow," she said then smiled as she started the pickup.

Bill closed the door, then stepped back. He watched her as she backed out of the drive and turned down the street.

As soon as she was gone, he returned to the house and went into the bathroom to get ready for bed. As he climbed into bed, his thoughts turned to Julie and how nice it would have been if she had stayed the night. It wasn't very long and he was sleeping soundly.

CHAPTER THIRTEEN

It was almost eight o'clock when Bill woke, but he was in no real hurry to get up. He knew he had things to do, but none of them were going to take him very far from town. Bill got up and went out into the kitchen to fix his breakfast. Just as he was about to sit down and eat, his phone began to ring. He got up and walked over to the phone and picked up the receiver.

"Hello."

"Is this Deputy Sparks?" a deep, rather scratchy male voice asked.

"Yes, it is. Who are you?" Bill asked not recognizing the voice.

"Who I am is not important. I called to tell you that you might want to take a look at the hay piles near the back of Keaton's property. You might find it rather interesting," the voice said, then the phone went dead.

Bill stood and looked at the phone for a moment before he hung it up. He thought about what had been said in an effort to try to remember if he had heard the voice before, but he didn't recognize it. He was almost sure that the voice had purposely sounded scratchy and deep to make it hard for him to recognize.

As Bill thought about it, he wondered what possible reason the caller could have for telling him about the hay piles on Keaton's property. Was he calling to tell him where the explosives container was hidden? What reason would he have for doing that?

Maybe it was some kind of a trap to get Bill to go out in the backcountry where he could be killed and there would be no witnesses. But why would he suggest Keaton's place. Had something been hidden there in order to point a finger at Keaton as having something to do with the murder, or, at the very least, the theft of the container? After all, it was common knowledge that Bill was working on the murder case involving the man who had been murdered in the quarry.

There were a ton of questions running through Bill's mind, but there were no answers to any of them. One thought came to his mind. It would be almost impossible to get a search warrant of Keaton's property based on an anonymous phone call. Bill was sure of that.

Was the call a way to get Bill to break, or at least bend, the law enough to get him pulled off the case? Was that what the caller wanted? But why? The caller had to know that even if Bill was taken off the case, someone else would take over.

Bill thought about it. If he could see the tire tracks of the truck used to move the container from the quarry, and they led to one of the hay piles, he might be able to get a search warrant. It was a bit of a stretch for sure, but it might be enough.

Bill decided to call the sheriff and get his take on the phone call. He would also ask him about getting a search warrant if he could find tracks leading to the hay piles. He reached over and picked up the phone, then placed a call to the sheriff's office.

"Pennington County Sheriff's Office, how may I help you?"

"Hi, Mary."

"Hi, Bill. What can I help you with?"

"Is the sheriff in?"

"Sure. I'll put you through to him."

It only took a few moments before the sheriff came on the line.

"Morning, Bill. How are things going?"

"Well, sir," Bill said, then went on to tell him about the phone call he had received just a short time ago.

"I see. What do you think it means'?"

"I'm not sure, but the reason I called was to get your take on the call and to see if it would be possible to get a search warrant of the hay piles on Keaton's land based on the call?"

"I don't think so. Not with what you have so far," the sheriff said.

"If I could show where the truck used to remove the container from the quarry had driven onto Keaton's land, and the tracks went either to or toward a hay pile, do you think I could get a warrant to at least search the hay piles?"

"Do you think you can do that?"

"I think I might be able to, but at this point I'm not sure."

"It sounds pretty thin to me. How would you prove the tracks went to the piles without actually going on Keaton's property?"

"To be honest, I don't know. I don't know if the tracks would show up in a photograph of them, at least enough to make a case before a judge, but I might be able to get the photographs without going on Keaton's property."

"I'll go to bat for you if, and I say 'if', you can get me photographs of the tracks from a truck showing them leading to a hay pile. But if you go onto Keaton's property without his permission, you can bet the judge will throw out any application for a warrant, and will probably chastise you severely. And if he chastises you, he will make it a lot tougher for you to get a warrant in the future."

"I understand," Bill said thoughtfully.

"So, what do you plan to do?"

"I think I'll go up to the quarry and see how close to the hay piles I can get without going on

Keaton's property, and hopefully I will be able to see tracks. If I can, I'll try to get photos of them."

"Okay, but you be careful. They've tried to get rid of you once already. There's little doubt in my mind that they will try again."

"How well I know. If I find I can't show the truck went onto Keaton's property, I'll go to the local newspaper office and see what I can find out about the quarry and Keaton there."

"Okay. Keep me posted on your progress," the sheriff said.

"Yes, sir," Bill said then hung up.

Bill sat down and ate his breakfast. He had a lot of things running through his mind. Things like, would he be able to see the tracks, and if he could, would he be able to get pictures of them? Was the container really hidden in a pile of hay? Was the call meant to get him out in the backcountry so he could be ambushed? Once again, none of his questions were going to get answered without going to the quarry.

As soon as he finished his breakfast and put his dirty dishes in the sink, he grabbed his keys to the patrol car and headed for Jasper Quarry. It took him a little less than an hour to get to the quarry and turn in the gate. He stopped in front of the gate and got out of the patrol car. After looking around, he started looking for any new tracks in the dirt before he opened the gate. He didn't see any new tracks, so he drove on into the quarry. He parked the patrol car at about the same place he had parked it when he first came to the quarry to investigate the murder.

Bill took his time to look around the area of the quarry where most of the old buildings were located. He glanced at the old shed that had almost collapsed on him, then looked toward the rock crushing building where the victim had been tied to the large wheel. He carefully scanned the area looking for anyone who might be hanging around, or who might be a danger to him. He saw no one.

Bill reached into the patrol car, took out his binoculars and camera, and put the straps around his neck. He then locked up the patrol car and began walking around the outside edge of the quarry pit.

As he walked, he moved into the trees that were between the quarry pit and Keaton's property. It was close to a hundred yards between Keaton's fence and the quarry pit. Most of the area was covered with fairly dense tree cover which gave him some protection and made it difficult for anyone to see him or get a good shot at him.

He was only about fifty yards from where the fence turned and went along behind the quarry pit. Bill moved to the edge of the tree line and looked out into the pasture area of Keaton's land. He was a good hundred and fifty yards or so from the nearest hay pile. He took his binoculars and scanned the area very carefully. He could see three piles of hay stacked in the field.

As he looked out over the field, a sudden thought crossed his mind. He could not remember ever seeing, or hearing, anything about Keaton having any horses or cattle. Bill began to wonder why Keaton had so much hay piled up. He took a minute to look at the piles of hay and at the field through his binoculars. It quickly became obvious that the hay had not been cut this year. The piles of hay had the look of hay that had been harvested at least a year ago, probably two or three years ago, and none of them looked as if they had been disturbed as if something might have been buried under them.

Bill took a couple of pictures of the field and the hay piles. Since he didn't have a camera with a telephoto lens, he put the camera lens up against one side of his binoculars and snapped several more pictures using the binoculars as a telephoto lens. He hoped he would get one or two good pictures.

After taking the photographs, he began moving along the edge of the trees that were growing just a couple of feet from Keaton's fence. It wasn't long before he came to the corner of the fence marking the corner of Keaton's property.

Bill took a minute to look around. If he continued to move along Keaton's fence line, he would be moving out into an area with very little cover. The trees were not as thick, making it easier for someone to see him. It was time for him to make a decision. If he went out in the more open area, he might be seen. But if he didn't, he would not be able to get to where the tire tracks went onto Keaton's property.

He took his binoculars and put them up to his eyes. Bill carefully scanned the area in all directions. He could not see anyone or anything indicating there was anyone around.

Just as Bill was about to step out from the cover of dense trees and walk along the fence line, he heard a vehicle. He quickly stepped back into the cover of the trees and knelt down behind a large pine in the tall grass. He peered around the base of the tree as a one-ton stake truck came over a hill about two hundred yards away. It was headed right toward where Bill was hiding. Bill thought about retreating back deeper into the woods, but was afraid he might be seen if he moved.

The truck suddenly slowed down and turned toward the fence where it came to a stop facing the fence. The truck was sideways to Bill which allowed him to see that the bed of the truck was covered with a dark green canvas. He could not see if there was anything inside the bed of the truck.

Two men got out of the truck. Bill quickly recognized the driver. It was Mr. Frank Gordon, the man who owned a campground and several cabins just south of Hill City. Bill didn't know him very well, but he seemed like a nice guy. Bill had had very little contact with him as he never seemed to have any trouble at his campground.

Bill recognized the other man as well, but he didn't know his name. He was the same man he had seen talking to Keaton and two other local men in the café. If he recalled correctly, he had been told by Sandy in the café that he was an insurance salesman. He wondered what he was doing out there.

Bill pulled his camera up and took a couple of pictures of the two men and the truck. He was hoping someone in the sheriff's office might know who the 'insurance salesman' was, and why he might be out there.

While watching the two men, Bill noticed one of them kept looking around. It was almost as if they were expecting someone to come by, or looking for someone who might be watching them. It wasn't but a couple of minutes and a pickup truck came racing across the field toward where the stake truck was stopped. Bill recognized the pickup as belonging to Keaton. When it pulled to a stop, he saw Keaton get out of the pickup, hurry to the fence and begin talking to the two other men. Again, Bill took a couple of pictures of all three men and the trucks.

They hadn't talked for more than a couple of minutes when they all began to look around. Within a few seconds, the two men from the stake truck ran around and jumped into the truck, started it, then backed away from the fence. As it turned to go back the way it had come, the loose canvas flipped open for just a second, but it was long enough for Bill to see the olive green explosives container in the back as they sped off. Bill was able to get a couple of pictures of the back of the truck, but wasn't sure if he had gotten a picture of the explosives container as the truck sped away.

Keaton stood there until the stake truck went over the hill and out of sight before he returned to his pickup. He got in and turned around and headed back toward his house.

As soon as Keaton was gone, Bill stood up. It was time for him to get out of there and return to Hill City to call the sheriff. He needed the film from his camera developed as soon as possible. He wanted to know who the 'insurance salesman' was and what he was doing in the truck with an explosives container in the back. Bill was sure the container in the truck was the one he had been trying to find, but not one hundred percent sure.

He hoped the pictures would show some of the numbers on the container so it could be positively identified as the same explosives container he had seen in the quarry, and the same one that had been stolen from the Rapid City Air Force Base.

Bill pulled back away from the fence and began walking back to the patrol car. He hadn't gone far when he thought he heard something just ahead of him. He quickly drew his gun as he ducked down behind a tree with a bush growing beside it, and waited.

It wasn't long before he could see who it was that was making so much noise. It was Julie out walking in the quarry. He stepped out from behind the bush.

"What are you doing out here," Bill said rather sharply.

"Damn, Bill, you scared the hell out of me," she said as she stopped dead in her tracks.

"I'm sorry I scared you, but what are you doing here?"

"I was just out getting a little exercise. You know I like to walk around here."

"I thought you were going to be at work."

"I was, but it got changed. They want me to come in tonight and work the night shift for a couple of days. They are going to put me on a regular schedule next week," she explained.

"Oh."

"I called you this morning to tell you about it, but when I didn't get an answer I figured it didn't really matter because I would be seeing you later today anyway."

"I'm sorry I startled you, but I didn't expect to see you out here."

"I take it you were expecting to see someone," she said as she looked at the gun he still held in his hand.

"Sorry about that, but I was just being careful."

"It looks more like you were expecting trouble."

"Not really. I was just being ready if it came my way," he said as he put his gun back in his holster. "I'll walk you back. I don't think it's a good idea for you to be walking around here, at least until we find out what is going on out here."

"What is going on? What is it you're not telling me?"

"I can't tell you what is going on because I'm not sure myself, but I will tell you this much. It is not safe for you to be wandering around out here."

Julie looked at him as if she was thinking about what he was saying to her. She thought back for a moment and remembered him having trouble with his patrol car. She began to think the trouble with his patrol car may have something to do with why he didn't want her to hike around here.

"You're scaring me," she said as she looked up at him.

"I'm sorry about that, but at least until we have a handle on what's going on, I think it would be wise for you to stay out of here."

"Okay, if you say so. I'll walk back with you."

Bill took her hand and walked her back to the patrol car. She looked at the car, then looked at him.

"Where is your new patrol car?"

"It's in the garage getting fixed."

"Oh," she said, but decided not to ask him any more questions about what he was working on, and why he thought it was unsafe for her to be in the quarry. He had made it pretty clear he wasn't going to tell her anyway.

"I have to go into Rapid City as soon as I get you out of here. I should be home by five or five-thirty if you would like to come over tonight," he said hopefully.

"I'd like that," she said with a smile.

"Would you like a ride home?" Bill asked.

"Sure."

Bill held the door for her and then went around to the other side and got in. He started the patrol car then drove her back to her house. He got out and held the door for her. As he closed the door, she stepped up to him and put her arms around his neck. She tipped her head up and gently pulled his face to hers then kissed him.

"That's just to help you think about me until tonight," she said as she looked up at him.

"I don't think I'll forget you anytime soon," he said.

He leaned down and kissed her. He then straightened up and stepped back.

"I have to get going if you're coming over tonight," he said.

"Okay."

Reluctantly, she let go of him and followed him as he walked around to the other side of the patrol car. He got in and rolled down the window. She leaned in a little and kissed him again.

"See you about five," she said.

"If I'm not there, I will be shortly."

"I'll wait on your back porch."

Bill reached into his pocket and pulled out his key ring. He took a key off it and handed it to her.

"This is to the backdoor. You can let yourself in if I'm not back by the time you get there."

"Are you sure it's safe to let me have a key to your house. I might steal all that expensive furniture you have," she said with a grin.

"Very funny, but if it's missing I'll know who to come after," he said then reached down and started the patrol car.

Julie stepped back and waved at him as he drove away. As soon as he was out of sight, she turned and went into the house. Bill drove away, getting a quick glimpse of her in his rearview mirror just before he turned out onto the road.

CHAPTER FOURTEEN

It was getting close to lunchtime by the time Bill got back to Hill City. He stopped by his house and grabbed a bite to eat before he headed to Rapid City. He drove directly to the sheriff's office. Since the sheriff was out to lunch when he arrived, he went over to the lab where he found Ralph Wickum, the county coroner, and Chuck, a lab tech, sitting at a table in the coroner's office having their lunch.

"Hi, Bill. What brings you here? Have you got something for me?" Wickum asked.

"Yes, sir. I have a roll of film I would like you to develop as soon as possible."

"Okay. What's on it?"

"Pictures I took this morning of a truck with an explosives container in back and pictures of the men who may have stolen the container. I will need a blowup of the container. I hope it will show some of the numbers on the container so I can tell if it is the one I saw at the Jasper Quarry. I would also like a blowup of the license plate of the truck, if you can."

"Chuck will get right on it as soon as we finish eating. He should have it ready in about an hour, maybe a little longer," Wickum said as he looked at Chuck for agreement.

"No problem," Chuck said. "Are you planning on waiting for the pictures?"

"Yes. Can you make two sets of them for me?"

"Sure thing," Chuck said.

"I'll be over at the sheriff's office. I would appreciate it if you would give me a call when they're ready," Bill said.

"Sure thing."

Bill thanked Chuck, then turned and left the coroner's office. He returned to the sheriff's office to wait for the sheriff. It was almost one o'clock when the sheriff returned from lunch. The sheriff motioned for Bill to join him in his office.

"What brings you here? Are you here to pick up your car?" the sheriff asked as he sat down behind his desk.

"Not really. I didn't know my car was ready," Bill said as he sat down in front of the sheriff's desk.

"It is, so you can trade cars before you head back. I take it you want to discuss something with me?"

"Yes, sir. The reason I'm here is I brought in a roll of film for the lab to develop that might prove to be very interesting. I took several pictures of three men who met in a hay field belonging to Mr. Keaton. It looks like it was the same field with the hay piles I talked to you about earlier."

"The one that was supposed to have something hidden in the hay piles that would be of interest?" the sheriff asked.

"Yes, sir. While I was looking for a way to prove there might be something hidden in one of the hay piles, a one-ton stake truck drove up to the fence and stopped where there wasn't a gate. There were two men in the truck. They got out of the truck and just leaned against it. They seemed to be looking toward the hay piles and possibly waiting for someone. Within a few minutes, Keaton showed up, they talked for a moment or so, then the two men who had been in the truck quickly got back in it and drove away in a hurry. I got several pictures of the men, the stake truck and what little of a container I could see in the back of the truck as they drove away."

"Good work, Bill," the sheriff said. "Could you identify the two men in the truck?"

"Only one of them. It was Frank Gordon. He owns a campground south of Hill City where he has campsites and rents cabins as well. I don't know him very well, but he seems like a nice enough guy.

"The other man, I don't know. I've only seen him once before in Hill City. I was told by the waitress in the Hill City Café that he is an insurance salesman from Rapid City, but I have my doubts. I'm hoping he can be identified from the photos I took this morning."

"Are you any closer to figuring out what they are up to?"

"I'm afraid not," Bill said with a hint of disappointment in his voice.

"You're doing good work. What's your next move?"

"I'm going to spend a little time going over some old newspapers tomorrow to see if I can find out anything about the Jasper Quarry, and about Keaton. I hope to find out if he belongs to any questionable organization or group, or has shown any leanings toward the Nazi party. I'll also be looking into Gordon to see if there is anything in his background that might help.

"I plan to talk to the Forest Service to find out where some of those fire roads go, especially where they come out onto county roads or state highways. I know I said I was going to visit the library and the Forest Service Office before, but I keep coming up with things I think I should follow up on immediately."

"I understand," the sheriff said with a grin. "Keep plugging along and you will turn up something helpful. Let me know if I can help."

"I will, and thank you, sir."

"Are you going to wait for the lab staff to print the photos for you?"

"Yes, sir. They said they would call here when they are ready. I thought since my car is ready, I would go get it while I wait. I asked the lab staff to make two sets of photos. Maybe you can identify the man in the photos."

"I'll see what I can do. Stop in and see me before you go back," the sheriff said.

"Yes, sir," Bill said then stood up and left the sheriff's office.

Bill went to the parking lot, got in the patrol car he had been driving and drove over to the County Garage to pick up his patrol car. When he got to the garage, he took his personal belongings out of the patrol car he had been using and put them in the patrol car that was assigned to him.

After a brief talk with the mechanic, he drove his patrol car over to the parking area and returned to the sheriff's office. Mary called to him as he headed down the hall to the sheriff's office.

"Bill, I've got a message for you from the sheriff."

"What is it, Mary?"

"Sheriff Henderson had to leave, but he said to give you this," Mary said as she handed him a large yellow envelope. "He had to go out, but he said he has a copy of the pictures and will see what he can do to find out the name of the unidentified man. He also said he'll call you and let you know what he finds out."

"Thanks, Mary," Bill said as he took the envelope then turned to leave.

He went out and got into his patrol car. Instead of driving off immediately, he sat in his patrol car and opened the envelope. It contained a number of photographs. There wasn't any note along with the photographs, but since he had taken the pictures there was no need for a note.

He looked through the photos. The blowup of the back of the truck showed a large olive drab green explosives container in the back of the stake truck, and it was similar to the one he had seen in the quarry. He could make out a few of the identifying markings, but was not sure they were the same as those on the one he had found in the quarry. He would have to check his list of numbers when he got back home.

With nothing else to do in Rapid City, he headed for home. A quick look at his watch showed he should get home at least an hour before Julie was to arrive at his home. He smiled at the thought of her coming over for dinner tonight. He thought her grandfather might not be too thrilled with her having dinner with him two nights in a row. Wilbur just might have to fix his own dinner for a change.

The drive back to Hill City was uneventful. Bill had spent most of his time thinking about Julie. As far as he was concerned, their relationship was getting rather serious. He wondered if she felt the same way. The way things had gone last night was enough to make him think she was serious about their relationship, too.

As he turned into his driveway, he noticed Julie's grandfather's pickup was there. He also noticed someone was peeking out of the blinds over a window in the house next-door. There was little doubt his nosey neighbor lady was spying on him.

Bill got out of his patrol car, looked toward the house next-door and waved. The blinds immediately slammed shut. He smiled to himself as he stepped up on the back porch and opened the door.

As he walked into the kitchen, he saw Julie leaning down and reaching in the oven. From the smell in the kitchen, it was clear that Julie had been baking bread. He couldn't help but notice how nicely her tight jeans fit her.

"It's nice to come home to the smell of fresh baked bread," he said.

Julie turned and looked at him. She set the pan of bread on a hot pad on the counter, then turned to him.

"I didn't expect you so soon," she said as she walked up to him. "How did things go in Rapid City?"

Julie put her arms around his neck and pulled him toward her before he had a chance to answer her. Bill put his arms around her narrow waist and pulled her up against him. He leaned down and kissed her. The kiss was soft and gentle, yet it had a hint of passion in it. It lasted a minute or so before he let go of her.

"Things went pretty good. Things seem to be moving along on my investigation, but rather slowly."

"Can you tell me about it?"

"As much as I would like, I really can't at this point," he said.

"Will you tell me when you can?"

"I will. By the way, did you notice my neighbor was spying on my place? It would be my guess she saw you come in."

"She makes a pretty poor spy. I saw her the minute I drove in your driveway. She watched me bring in the groceries. I can only imagine what she was thinking," Julie said with a grin.

"Maybe I should call her and ask her if she would like to meet you since she seems so interested in you and what you're doing here."

"Do you think that's wise?" Julie asked, not sure if Bill was kidding her.

"Probably not. It would just get her more interested in what was going on here. I doubt that what we do would be nearly as interesting as what she will make up," Bill said with a grin.

"You're probably right. Dinner won't be ready for a little while," Julie said.

"In that case, I'll get out of this uniform and take a shower."

"I have a couple of things that need to go in the oven."

"I'll be out in a few minutes," Bill said.

Bill leaned down and kissed her, then turned and went into his bedroom. He got out of his uniform, then went into the bathroom. He took a shower and shaved, then returned to his bedroom to get dressed. He put on a clean pair of jeans and a shirt. As soon as he was ready, he walked out to the kitchen. The smell of fresh baked cookies was in the air.

"What are you cooking now?"

"I'm making some chocolate chip cookies. Your cookie jar was empty," she said with a grin.

"How did you know chocolate chip cookies are my favorite cookie?"

"Chocolate chip cookies are almost everybody's favorite cookie," she said.

Bill reached over and took a cookie off the cooling rack. It was still warm when he took a bite of it.

"These are really good," he said then took another bite.

"Don't spoil your dinner. It will be ready in about an hour."

"You sound like my mother when she would bake cookies for us kids. Is that something every girl learns from their mother?"

"I don't know about every girl, but that was what my mother always said," Julie said with a laugh.

"Have you been here all afternoon cooking?" Bill asked.

"No, not all afternoon, but most of it."

"Well, I guess the old saying is true."

"What old saying?" Julie asked.

"The way to a man's heart is through his stomach."

"Is it working?"

"Not really," Bill said.

"It's not?" Julie asked, looking a little concerned.

"You already have my heart," Bill said, then wondered if he might have spoken too soon.

A smile came over Julie's face. She put down the cookie sheet with fresh baked cookies on it and stepped over in front of Bill. She reached up and put her arms around his neck, drew him down to her and kissed him.

"That was nice," she said, kissing him again then smiled up at him. "But if I don't get the cookies out of the oven, you might not like them as well."

Bill let go of her, then sat down at the table and watched her work. A lot of thoughts of her ran through his mind. She was a very good cook, she was smart, she was beautiful and even sexy, to say nothing of the fact she loved him. He decided he would talk to her about her new job. It seemed to be the safest thing to do at the moment.

"How do you think your new job is going?"

"I think it is going okay, but I have to go in to work the night shift tonight."

"I remember you saying something about that. You have to work a couple of nights. Right?"

"Yes. Tonight and tomorrow night, then I will be put on a regular rotating schedule starting with two weeks of days, then two weeks of afternoons followed with two weeks of nights, then back to days again."

"What about weekends?"

"I will be on the rotating schedule that gives me Monday's off. I know it will be hard for us to see each other at times, but we can manage."

"I remember you saying you didn't get the job you wanted. What job were you trying to get?"

"I wanted to get the nursing job at the clinic here in Hill City so I could be closer to grandpa. He's doing okay, but his health is not good," she said with a hint of sadness in her voice.

"Are you going to still try to get on at the clinic?"

"Yes. I'm still hoping to," she said. "That's enough of talk about me. As soon as I get this last sheet of cookies out of the oven, I'll start dinner."

"I take it you are cooking tonight?" Bill asked.

"Yes. We are having meatloaf, mashed potatoes and corn."

"That sounds good. What's for dessert?"

"It just might be cookies, if there are any left," she said with a smile.

Bill and Julie talked about a lot of things while she made the meatloaf and put it in the oven. Bill got a lot of information from her about some of the people who lived in and around Hill City. It seemed to him it would be very difficult to keep any kind of secrets in this small town. Bill decided to find out if she could tell him anything about the Jasper Quarry.

"What can you tell me about the Jasper Quarry? I know a lot about it, but I would like to know why it closed."

"I'm not really sure why it closed; but from what I've heard there were a lot of accidents, and after awhile they couldn't get anyone to work there. I'm sure there's more to it than that."

"Did Wilbur work at the quarry?"

"Yes, but it was before I came to live with him. I didn't come to live with him until well after the quarry closed."

"Did he ever talk about it?"

"No. I've tried to talk to him about it, but all he said was they were killing the people who worked for them. I had heard about a few of the people who had been seriously injured at the quarry, but grandpa never talked about it. In fact, very few people around here talk about the quarry. I guess it has some sad memories for a lot of people."

"I take it your grandfather was not one of those injured at the quarry."

"No. He already had the farm and he didn't like working in the quarry. From what little he told me, he quit well before it closed."

"Do you happen to know what happened to Keaton? He walks with a limp."

"All I know is he was injured at the quarry. I did hear a rumor sometime ago that Rutledge had something to do with the accident causing Mr. Keaton's leg injury, but I've never heard anyone speak about how it happened, or about the cause of the accident," Julie explained. "I'm not even sure an accident at the quarry was the cause of his leg injury. I had also heard he served in World War One. He might have been injured during the war."

Bill sat there and thought about what she had said. He was sure he needed to take the time to look into the history of the Jasper Quarry. He had heard rumors it had closed due to a very poor safety record. He wondered what else had contributed to the closure of the quarry.

"Are you ready for dinner?"

"Yes," Bill said as he got up from the table.

Bill got plates and glasses out and set them on the table while Julie finished preparing the dinner. Once the table was set, they sat down to eat. Their conversation turned to more mundane things like the weather and other local news.

After dinner Bill and Julie cleaned up the kitchen then went into the living room to sit down. It wasn't long before Bill had his arm around Julie. He kissed her and held her close. She snuggled up to him and laid her head on his shoulder. It was a time for them to be close before she had to go to work.

When it was getting close to the time she should leave to get to work on time, they stood up. Bill drew her close and kissed her while she wrapped her arms around his neck. After a long kiss, he let go of her and walked her to her grandfather's pickup truck.

"I get off at six, but it would be about seven before I would get back to Hill City. Would you like me to stop by and have breakfast with you?"

"That would be nice, but right know you best get going. You don't want to be late for work at your new job."

He reached out and opened the pickup truck's door. Julie slipped in behind the steering wheel then looked up at him.

"See you in the morning," she said then reached down and started the pickup truck.

"Drive careful. Love you," he said as he closed the pickup truck's door.

Bill stepped back and watched her as she backed out of the drive, then turned and drove down the street. He watched until she was out of sight. He then turned and went back inside his house.

Since he had already taken a shower, he sat down and listened to the news on the radio then turned in for a good night's sleep. It didn't take him long to doze off to sleep with pleasant thoughts of Julie.

CHAPTER FIFTEEN

Bill was awake before his alarm went off. The only reason he could think of for being awake so early was that Julie was going to stop by for breakfast on her way home from work. A glance as his bedside clock told him it was six-thirty, and it was at that moment his clock went off. He reached over and shut it off. He got up and took a quick shower and shaved, then got dressed in jeans and a shirt. He decided he didn't need to put on his uniform just yet.

He went to the kitchen just as he heard a vehicle pull into his driveway. He looked out the window and saw Julie getting out of her grandfather's pickup. He looked at his watch as he walked to the backdoor.

"Right on time," Bill said as he held the door for her. "I was just about to start making breakfast."

"Good. I'm hungry," Julie said as she stepped up in front of him.

Julie put her arms around his neck and kissed him. After the warm, gentle kiss, they turned and went into the house.

"You look tired. Sit down and I'll fix you something to eat."

Julie sat down in a chair at the kitchen table, leaned back and stretched while she watched Bill break a couple of eggs into a pan on the stove. Her thoughts were not on the pan, but on the man at the stove. She couldn't help thinking about him and what it would be like if they were married. Would he fix her breakfast when she came home from working the night shift?

"What are you thinking about," he said as looked at her.

It was apparent he had caught her thinking about something. It was almost as if she had fallen asleep, but her eyes were still open.

"I was thinking about you," she said with a slight grin.

"Is that good or bad?" he asked.

"Oh, it was good."

"I'm glad to hear that. Breakfast is ready. I hope you like the eggs. I wasn't sure how you like them."

"They will be fine."

Bill set the plate in front of her and a plate where he was going to sit. He poured her a glass of orange juice and a cup of coffee, then sat down across the table from her.

"How did it go at the hospital?" Bill asked then took a bite of bacon.

"It was pretty quiet for most of the night. The ward I was assigned to was kind of quiet so they asked me to go down to the emergency ward and work there for a little while."

"I'll bet that was interesting."

"It was quiet most of the time I was there. About the only thing I saw was Mr. Gordon. He came into the emergency ward."

Her comment about Gordon caught Bill's attention. He stopped eating and looked at her. He remembered he had shot someone behind the quarry, but had no idea who it might have been, or how serious the injury had been. Bill knew Gordon had been back behind the quarry near the piles of hay at one time. He began to wonder if it might have been Gordon who had shot at him the other day, and whom he had hit when shooting back. It seemed a long time to wait to get a gunshot wound treated.

"What was Gordon in the emergency ward for?"

"I don't really know, but he was holding his arm when he left. I didn't treat him."

It was easy for Bill to think it might have been Gordon since the blood on the tree was about the right height if Gordon had been kneeling when the shot was fired.

"Did he see you?"

"No. I doubt he would have seen me. I was just coming into the emergency room from the lab and he was on his way out to the parking lot. We used different doors," she said wondering what interest Bill had in Gordon's injury.

"Is there a problem?" Julie asked.

"No. I don't think so."

"You seemed very interested in Gordon's injury."

"Not really. I was just interested from the standpoint that I know him."

"Oh," she said.

Bill and Julie finished their breakfast without any further conversation about Gordon. Bill didn't want Julie to get involved in what was going on in the backcountry.

After breakfast was over, Julie helped Bill clean up. When they were done Bill sat down at the table with Julie to have another cup of coffee.

"What are your plans for today?" Julie asked.

"Nothing very exciting. I'm going to spend some time at the library and at the newspaper office. I'm going to do a little research on the Jasper Quarry."

"Why so much interest in the quarry?"

"I'm trying to figure out why the murder took place there. I've heard a lot of negative things about the quarry. I would like to know if any of the things that happened in the past have anything to do with what is going on now."

"That seems like a lot of fun," she said with a hint of sarcasm. "I think I'll go home and get some rest."

"What? You don't want to spend hours going over everything I can find in the library and newspaper office on an old quarry that has been closed for twenty or more years?"

"No. Actually it sounds very boring. I think I'll go home."

"Okay. I'll walk you out," he said as he stood up.

Bill walked her out to her grandfather's pickup, kissed her then held the door for her. She got in and started the pickup.

"I'll stop by on my way to work tonight for a few minutes," Julie said looking up at him. "I should probably fix grandpa his dinner. I doubt he is eating like he should."

"I'd like for you to stop by. Drive careful," Bill said, then leaned in and gave her another kiss before he stepped back and watched her as she drove away.

As soon as she was gone, Bill started walking toward the local library. It was only a few blocks from his home. When he arrived, he went directly to the section of the library that had information on the history of the area. It didn't take him long to find a book with a lot of information on quarries and mines in Pennington County.

He took the book and sat down at a table and began going through the book looking for information on the Jasper Quarry. It took him awhile to find anything on the quarry. He discovered it had originally belonged to Harney Peak Tin Mining Company and was opened as a mine in about 1888, then sold sometime later. The article did not give the date it was sold, or to whom it had been sold. However, it did say it was renamed Jasper Quarry and that it became a quarry where the rock from the quarry was used for roads and other construction projects. The quarry was closed in 1929.

Whatever the reason for the closure of the quarry was, it was not given in the book. In fact, there was very little about the quarry at all.

Bill spent a couple of hours in the library, but was unable to find out anything more about the Jasper Quarry. The librarian was a fairly young woman, and was unable to give him any additional information about the quarry, or about anyone who had worked there who still might be living in the area. The one thing of importance was that Bill was able to find the approximate date the quarry closed. That bit of information gave him a starting point to look at newspapers that contained information about the quarry. The newspapers might supply him with information on why it closed down, and if what he had heard about accidents at the mine had been the reason for the closure.

Bill got up and left the library and walked down the street to the newspaper office. As he walked into the newspaper office, he was greeted by Ethel Wingate. Ethel had been working at the newspaper for almost thirty years, and was very knowledgeable about almost everything that happened in Hill City and the surrounding area. The only problem was she was also one of the town's biggest gossips. It wouldn't take her long to spread the word that Bill was looking into the Jasper Quarry.

"Hello, Deputy. What can I do for you today?"

"I would like to see some of the newspapers from about – oh – 1922 to say – oh – about 1930."

"That's a long time ago," Ethel said as she looked at him wondering what his interest was in that time period.

"Yes it is. I'm curious about what it was like around here during the late twenties."

"Is there something special you're looking for?" she asked, wondering what he was doing.

"No, not really. I've just heard a little about life in the area and wanted to see for myself what it was like, and there's no better place to find that out than in the newspapers of the time."

"That's true enough. Would this have anything to do with the Jasper Quarry?"

"No," Bill replied casually, and without commenting further.

"Oh," was all Ethel had to say.

It was disappointing to her that he would not share his reason for wanting to know about the area during the 1920's. From his answer, she was not sure what was on his mind, but it was clear he was not going to tell her, either.

"You do have newspapers going back that far, don't you?"

"Yes. Yes, of course."

"May I see them?"

"Certainly. Right this way."

Ethel led Bill to a fairly large room in the back of the building. He noticed there was a wall almost completely covered with shelves. When he got closer he could see dates written on the edge of each shelf.

"Here are the papers covering 1920 to 1924, and right below it are the papers for 1925 to 1929. The papers for 1930 will be on this shelf," Ethel explained as she pointed to a shelf. "You can use the table over there to lay them out. Please be careful with them, they are rather old."

"I will take good care of them," Bill assured her.

She looked at him for a moment before she left the room. Bill got the impression she didn't believe what he had told her, but he didn't care what she believed and he was not about to tell her.

Bill took the pile of newspapers from 1920 through 1924 and set them on the table. The newspapers had only four to six pages per newspaper, and the paper was only published once a week, which pleased him. It meant it would not take him long to find articles that would be of interest to him, and it would not take long for him to cover a long period of time.

The papers from 1920 through 1924 didn't contain anything very interesting to him. The Jasper Quarry was mentioned but only in a good light and only a few times. It seemed to be a good neighbor and employed a good number of people from the area.

When he finished, he put the newspapers back on the shelf where they belonged, then took the newspapers covering the period from 1925 through 1929 and set them on the table. He then sat down and began going through them one page at a time as he had the first stack of papers. He didn't want to miss anything that might have had something to do with the Jasper Quarry.

Bill was only into one of the 1925 newspapers when an article caught his eye. It was an article about a local quarry worker who was killed in an accident in the rock crushing building. It seemed the man killed had gotten his arm caught on one of the wheels of the crushing machine while trying to adjust a belt that ran around part of the wheel. His arm was completely severed, and he bled to death before anyone could get to him and stop the bleeding.

It was the name of the man who died that caught Bill's attention. His name was Mathew Gordon. In the list of surviving family members was a son named Frank Gordon. The only Frank Gordon that Bill knew was the man who had a campground just south of Hill City, the very same Frank Gordon who had been to the hospital in Rapid City last night. Frank Gordon was also the name of the man Bill had seen with the stake truck that had the explosives container in it just back of the Jasper Quarry.

That bit of information didn't have any real value in helping with Bill's case, at least that he could see at the moment. He made a quick note of the incident on his notepad, including name, date and cause of death.

Bill returned to the newspapers to continue his search for information. During the following weeks there were a couple of follow up reports on the incident, but they didn't provide any additional information to help Bill's case.

It wasn't until he got to a mid-July 1927 newspaper that he found anything else that caught his attention. There had been another accident in the quarry, but it didn't end in death of the person injured. The name of the person injured was not someone who currently lived in the area. However, Bill still made a note of the incident.

Bill continued to read on. Over the next six months there were five more accidents involving injures to workers to different degrees. Two had been able to return to work, and three were permanently disabled. One of the three was Keaton, John Keaton. It was interesting to Bill that he was the only one of the five who remained in the area. In fact, Keaton's property bordered on one side and part of the back of the Jasper Quarry property. The question that ran through Bill's mind was did Keaton own the property before or after he was disabled. If it was after, how was he able to pay for it?

Based on the information in the newspaper, the quarry settled out of court several claims of negligence against the quarry. That piece of information got Bill to thinking. Had the owners of the quarry bought off the injured workers to prevent a court settlement which would probably have been much costlier?

Bill returned to the newspapers only to discover there were several more accidents at the quarry over a fairly short period of time. Very few of the workers had stayed in the area after they settled. There were only a couple of names that came up in his search that he recognized as people who still lived in the area, or appeared to be relatives of the injured worker.

When he got to a mid-September 1929 newspaper, he found an article stating the Jasper Quarry would be closing the following week. It indicated the quarry was shutting down due to financial reasons, and that the quarry could no longer meet its payroll as requests for its product were down.

The interesting thing was, in the editorial section of the newspaper, the editor had written a scathing article claiming the quarry had closed because workers had complained so much about the unsafe working conditions and nothing had been done to correct them. It also indicated that the workers were going to walk off the job if the safety issues were not addressed. According to what the article said, rather than the company officials dealing with the safety issues, they were just going to close the quarry. There was also a repeat of the claim it would cost too much to keep it open.

Bill had found out as much as he could so it was time to leave. He couldn't see how anything he had discovered would be of any help in solving the murder case. The one thing he wanted to know was who owned the quarry when it closed, and who owns the property now. He was unable to find out from the newspapers who owned the quarry when it closed.

After putting the newspapers back where they belonged, he walked out to the front office. He found Ethel sitting at an old roll top desk. She looked up at him and smiled.

"Did you find what you were looking for?" she asked.

"Yes and no."

"Oh," she said, a look of disappointment on her face. "Is there something I could help you with?"

"I don't know. I was noticing in the newspapers that there was never any mention of who the owners of the Jasper Quarry were when it closed. Do you happen to know who they were?"

"No. All we know is it was owned by a big company in Chicago. Once it closed, the manager and assistant manager left. Actually, they left two weeks before the announcement was made that it was closing. They took all the papers on the property and left in the middle of the night. The announcement that it was closing was in the form of a letter attached to the front door of the office. Since the managers had left, no one seems to know who put the notice up."

"That's interesting. Has anyone tried to find out who owned it?"

"My husband tried to find out, but didn't have any success. The people at the company in Chicago said they never heard of the place."

"Do you know who owns it now?"

"As far as we know, it is still owned by the same people, but we don't know who they are."

"It's interesting that no one seems to know who owns the land."

"If you look it up in the records, you will find it is owned by Jasper Quarry Company. You will also find out that the taxes have been paid on the property every year," she said. "And before you ask, the checks are mailed from Chicago and signed by the quarry manager who was here when it was in operation."

"Interesting," Bill said as he thought about what he had been told. "Didn't the records show the names of those who owned the Jasper Quarry Company?

"No, and that is interesting, too," she said.

"Do you think the manager actually owns the property?"

"I don't know, but whenever he has been contacted about the property he says he was just the manager. He says his only contact with the actual owners had been by phone. He claims he does not know who they are, and that he has never seen them."

"That's the strangest thing I've ever heard," Bill said as he wondered what was going on.

"It sure is," Ethel said. "I think it's owned by someone who doesn't want anyone here to know who they are."

Bill smiled at her comment, since it was so obvious to him that stating it seemed unnecessary. Bill was sure he had found out all he was going to at the newspaper office. Maybe it was time to give the sheriff a call and let him know what was going on. The sheriff might be able to help him find out when Keaton had purchased or received title to the property he lives on. Bill had no idea what that piece of information would tell him, but he didn't think he should overlook it.

Bill left the newspaper office and returned to his home. As soon as he arrived, he made himself a cup of coffee then placed a call to the sheriff's office. The phone rang only three times before it was answered.

"Sheriff's office, how may I help you?"

"Hi, Mary. I would like to talk to the sheriff if he is in."

"The sheriff is out at the moment. He should be back in about thirty minutes. Would you like me to have him call you?"

"Would you please have him call me at my home?"

"Sure."

"Thanks," Bill said then hung up.

Bill took a quick look at the clock on the wall and found that it was almost noon. He was sure the sheriff had gone for lunch. He fixed his lunch and sat down to eat it. Bill had just sat down when his phone began to ring. He picked up the receiver.

"Hello"

"I hear that you have been looking into the Jasper Quarry and asking around in an effort to find out who owns it," the male voice on the other end of the line said. "There are some people in Chicago who don't want you to have that information."

"Now why would that be?" Bill said trying to remember if he had heard the voice before.

"Because it is none of your damn business, and it might be in your best interest to remember that. I recommend you stop your search for who owns the quarry and concentrate on writing speeding tickets," the voice said, then the phone went dead.

Bill stood there looking at the phone for a moment or two before he hung up. He sat back down and thought about the voice. It occurred to him that he had heard the voice before. It was at that moment he remembered where he had heard the voice. It was the same voice as the man who had called him to tell him about the piles of hay on Keaton's property. Bill was convinced the first call had apparently been used to set him up for an ambush, but it had failed, and the second one to get him to back off.

He was being warned to drop the investigation, but why? The only reason he could think of for someone wanting him to drop it was he was getting too close, but too close to who, or what? He would talk it over with the sheriff as soon as he called.

CHAPTER SIXTEEN

Bill sat down at the table to eat his lunch, but didn't pick up his sandwich. The call had directed his thoughts toward what he had found out so far, which seemed to be of little help in finding the murdered man's killer. He also thought about what was going on that would make someone threaten him. Was he getting close to someone, or to the answer of what was going on? Both were certainly possibilities.

His thoughts turned to those he still wanted to question. Keaton and Gordon were two of those he believed he needed to question in the hope he would get some kind of clue to what was going on and possibly who might be involved. It stuck in his mind that there had to be a connection between the missing explosives container, the shot at him, the phone calls threatening him and the dead man Rutledge had found in the quarry.

There was also the lapel pin, but what did the lapel pin have to do with it? Bill was sure that the 'insurance salesman' had something to do with it, too, but he had no idea how he was involved. He didn't even know his name, or if he was actually an insurance salesman. It was almost as if he had too much information, and it was scattered about like little pieces from a jigsaw puzzle waiting for someone to put it together. There had to be something out there that would connect it all together so it made sense, but what?

Bill picked up his sandwich and began to eat his lunch. It wasn't long and he had finished. He cleaned up the kitchen while he waited to hear from the sheriff, but his mind was not on what he was doing.

Suddenly the phone rang. He quickly tossed his dish towel on the counter then answered the phone.

"Hello," he said hoping it was the sheriff.

"I take it you want something."

Bill immediately recognized the voice. It was Sheriff Henderson.

"Yes, sir. I have found out some very interesting things about the Jasper Quarry, but what I really want to know is who owns it. I have not been able to find out who actually owns it. I'm hoping maybe you can find out for me."

"I've been looking into it. It apparently belongs to some big corporation out of Chicago."

"That's about all I can find on it, but I can't even find the names of any of the corporate officers. The only contact person is the guy who was the manager when it was operating," Bill said.

"That's all I can find," the sheriff admitted.

"I've got a feeling there is no corporation, at least not one with offices. I think it's a corporation on paper only, and the man who was the manager when it went out of business is the corporation."

"What gives you that idea?"

"It seems the manager is the one filing and paying taxes on the land. There doesn't seem to be any kind of contact with anyone else. The only person anyone had ever dealt with since it closed has been the manager," Bill said.

There was dead silence on the phone. For a moment Bill thought the sheriff had hung up, but knew he was probably thinking.

"I see what you mean," the sheriff finally said. "Do you have a name for the manager?"

"No, but everyone seems to think it is the same guy who was the manager during the time the quarry operated as Jasper Quarry."

"It sounds like you don't think it is the same guy."

Bill hadn't realized it, but that was just what had been floating around in his head. It wasn't until the sheriff mentioned it that it became clear.

"You might be right. I'm not sure, but I don't think it is the same guy."

"I'll take a look at the records in the courthouse and see who is paying the taxes on the place. If it's the same guy who managed the place, we'll have someone to contact."

"Sheriff, I have a feeling it isn't the same guy. The checks used may be old corporate checks, and they may have the same name on them, but it might not be the same person signing those checks," Bill said.

"You think someone is forging the manager's name to the checks?"

"I'm not sure of anything at this point, but think of this. Let's say the corporation was dissolved, but no one turned in any papers stating it was dissolved. Then let's say someone else got hold of the paperwork and a bunch of company checks. The one most likely to be able to get the paperwork is the manager, and he probably got them at the time it closed. The company checks would have Jasper Quarry on the heading. That person or persons kept the bank account open, or more likely opened a different account in Chicago using the same name and a post office box number," Bill explained.

"Why would someone keep paying the taxes on the quarry? Are there any signs that the place is being used for anything?"

"No, not that I have seen," Bill said then thought of something.

"Maybe," Bill said then paused.

"What does 'Maybe' mean?" the sheriff asked, almost afraid of what Bill might say.

"Maybe someone is doing something with the quarry. Think of this. We have a missing explosives container we now know was stolen from the Rapid City Air Force Base, and it was hidden and stored on quarry property for at least a month. That indicates that maybe someone was using the quarry as a place to store things until they could be moved to somewhere else.

"We also have the lapel pin for the Nazi Political Party I found in the quarry near where the container was hidden. The pin was clean and had not been on the ground for very long.

"When you add it all up, the quarry might be used as a depot for stolen items of military value until they could be transported safely to wherever they were needed," Bill explained.

"Okay. Like you said, when we add it all up, including the part about the lapel pin, you are saying the quarry is being used as a depot for stolen military items to be used by Nazis. Is that what you're getting at?" the sheriff asked.

"I guess that's what I'm saying."

"Where's the proof?" Sheriff Henderson asked bluntly in an effort to find out if Bill had any proof.

"Well, I'm hoping you can help me with that."

"How so?"

"What I would like is for all the military bases that have storage facilities where weapons, explosives and ammunition are kept, do a complete inventory of what they have in order to see if anything else is missing. It needs to be done so those running the storage facilities don't know they are going to be inspected until it's too late for them to cover it up," Bill explained.

"I might be able to get the commanding officers of the bases in our area to go along with it, especially since we already know of one storage facility with a missing explosives container. What else?"

"I need to know who is writing the checks to pay the taxes on the quarry. Any ideas on where I might find that information?"

"Not at the moment, but I'll work on it. The county treasurer should know who is signing the checks," the sheriff said. "Just a thought. Do you think someone is doing a little mining in the quarry and wants to make sure no one else is going to butt in on it?"

"I hadn't thought about that, but it is a possibility, I suppose. I haven't seen anything to indicate anyone is doing any mining in or around the quarry. I haven't seen any signs of fresh diggings."

"What about a tunnel mine somewhere in or on the quarry property?" the sheriff asked. "It wouldn't be very difficult to hide the entrance to a mine."

"I haven't seen anything indicating that, but then I haven't been looking for an underground mine. I'll have to check it out.

"I was also looking for information on Keaton. I would like to know when he bought his land next to the quarry. I found out he was disabled while working in the quarry. It would be interesting to know if he got the land as part of his settlement with the quarry for his injuries. He is one of the few who stayed around after he suffered an injury at the quarry and had settled out of court."

"I'll see what I can find out. Is that all?"

"Yes, sir."

"Good. Might I make a suggestion?"

"Of course, sir."

"Mary tells me you've been putting in a lot of overtime. I suggest you take the rest of the day off and hit it again in the morning. I want you to be at your best. By the way, that's an order."

"Yes, sir."

"I'll try to get the information you want today. I'll call you later to fill you in on what I'm able to find out."

"Thank you, sir."

"Good. Relax and get some rest. By the way, you're doing a good job. Keep it up."

"Thank you, sir, and I will," Bill said then hung up the phone.

Bill thought about what Sheriff Henderson had said. He knew he was putting in a lot of hours. He decided it would be a good idea if he stayed home.

It might not go over so well with the sheriff if he wasn't home when he called.

Bill looked around the kitchen and thought it looked clean. Since there was nothing else he could do and still be able to hear the phone ring, he laid down on the sofa and relaxed. It wasn't long before he had dozed off.

It was almost five when his phone began to ring. Bill quickly got up and answered the phone.

"Hello."

"Bill, I've got some information for you. First of all, the name on the checks is the same as the person who managed the quarry, Samuel A. Shepard. He is the one who seems to be the only contact we have with the corporation.

"Secondly, I contacted the commanders of the South Dakota National Guard here in Rapid City, the Rapid City Air Force Base, the Wyoming National Guard and the Supply Depot for the Army in Omaha. All the commanders agreed that it might be a good idea if they do a complete surprise inspection of the supply depots, and do a complete inventory at the same time, without alerting the staff of the depots first. The commanders of each base assured me they would let me know if anything was missing. I told them how the container at the air base had been hidden so they will look past the front row of stacked items.

"I also sent a request to the Chicago Police Department for information on the Jasper Quarry Corporation. It didn't take them long to get back to me. They told me the Jasper Quarry Corporation was dissolved about twenty years ago."

"It looks like Shepard is keeping the taxes paid on the quarry so no one will be able to buy the land for non-payment of taxes," Bill said.

"It kind of looks that way."

"Has the ME been able to identify the victim of the shooting?"

"Not so far. I'll call him again in the morning and see what he has found out. By the way, you may be onto something with your theory on the quarry," the sheriff said.

"I think we will have a better idea if my theory is valid when we hear from the commanders of the different bases. By the way, are you sure Shepard is really signing the checks?"

"No, I guess I'm not sure," the sheriff said after giving it some serious thought. "Do you still think it's someone else who is signing the checks?"

"I don't know why that thought keeps coming to mind, but, yes."

"Any idea who you think it might be?" the sheriff asked.

"Not that I can prove, but I've got a feeling it just might be the 'insurance salesman'. He never has a briefcase with him, he spends a lot of time talking to Keaton and Gordon, but I've never seen him talk to anyone else, except the waitress at the Hill City Café to order a meal. He was at the back of the quarry with Keaton and Gordon. He and Gordon were the ones I saw at the truck near the hay piles. Gordon was the one driving the truck with the explosives container in it."

"Is he in any of the pictures you sent to the lab for developing?"

"Yes. He's the one leaning on the hood in front of the stake truck. Gordon is the one leaning on the right front fender and Keaton is the one on the other side of the fence," Bill explained.

"I'll check the pictures you dropped off and see if we can find out who he is."

"Thanks. Do you think you can get a name for the 'insurance man'?"

"I'll see what I can find out and get back to you."

"Okay. I'll talk to you tomorrow."

"It might be late afternoon," the sheriff said.

"That will be fine. I'll be gone most of the morning, anyway. I have a couple of people I want to question. I'll make it a point of being around in the afternoon."

"Good. Talk to you later," the sheriff said, then he hung up.

Bill hung up the phone, then looked at the clock. It was a few minutes past five. Since Julie was planning to fix dinner for her grandfather, he didn't expect her to stop by for at least an hour or so. He decided to fix his dinner and clean up the kitchen as soon as he was done. It would give him something to do until Julie stopped by.

It wasn't very long and Bill had finished cleaning up the kitchen. He went into the living room and sat down with a pen and paper. He began to write down those things he wanted to do, things he wanted to find out, the names of those he wanted to question, and questions he wanted to ask those he was going to question.

As he wrote, he remembered seeing the curtains at Keaton's house move when he had been there. He added to his list a note to find out who was really living in Keaton's house. He had no idea if it meant anything, but just to know would go a long way in answering at least one of his questions.

As he leaned back and looked at the list of names and questions he wanted answers to, Bill heard a vehicle pull into his driveway. He got up and walked over to the window and pulled back the curtain and looked out. Julie had pulled into the driveway driving a Ford coupe. It wasn't a new car, but it was not more than a couple years old. Bill turned, went to the front door and stepped out on the porch.

"Nice car," he said as he stepped off the porch and walked toward the car.

"It's not new, but it's in good shape," she replied with a grin.

"It looks nice. Is it yours?"

"Yes. My grandfather helped me buy it. He said I needed a better vehicle than his old truck to drive back and forth to Rapid City every day. I don't think he liked me driving his pickup truck," she said with a grin.

"I have to agree with him. Have you got time for coffee before you have to head into Rapid City?"

"Yes," she said then took his arm and they walked into the house.

Julie followed him into the kitchen where he made a pot of coffee. They sat at the kitchen table while the coffee was brewing.

"Anything exciting happen today?"

"No, not really. Sheriff Henderson is looking into a few things for me. I hope to find out who the man was who was murdered at the quarry. I have a couple of rolls of film at the lab to be developed. I took the pictures at the quarry and would like to know what the sheriff thinks of them.

"We hope to find Shepard before long. We think he could shed some light on what is going on out there."

"Wasn't Shepard the manager of the quarry when it was open?" Julie asked.

"Yes. He is also the person who has been paying the taxes on the quarry all these years. But I would prefer to talk about us."

"Are you sure you want to talk?" she said with a grin.

"Now that you mention it, not really. I would like to move to the sofa to have our coffee," Bill said as he stood up.

Julie smiled at him then stood up. She watched him as he poured two cups of coffee and took them into the living room. She sat down on the sofa and waited for him to set the coffee down on the coffee table.

Bill sat down beside Julie, leaned over to her and drew her toward him. She reached out and put her arms around his neck. Their lips met in a soft and gentle kiss. They spent the next few minutes kissing and holding each other. She then curled up to him, leaning against him and feeling very much at ease as he wrapped his arms around her.

They spent their time together just enjoying each other's company. Not really talking, but being close. Time passed much too fast as it was soon time for her to go to work.

"I have to be going," Julie said, sounding a little disappointed.

"I'll walk you to your car," Bill said as he took his arms from around her.

He stood up then helped her to her feet. When she was standing in front of him, she put her arms around his neck and kissed him.

He held her for a moment or so, then leaned back away from her.

"I love you," Bill said.

"I love you, too, but I really need to get going."

Bill let go of her, then took her hand as they walked out to her car. He opened the door and held it while she got in the car. He leaned down and kissed her again.

"Will I see you in the morning? I'm off work tomorrow night." Julie asked.

"I have a lot to do tomorrow morning, and I need to get started early. If you get some rest in the morning, we could do something tomorrow evening if you like."

"I'd like that," she said with a smile.

"I'll come out to your grandfather's place and get you."

"Okay. I have to go."

Bill leaned down again, kissed her, then stood up and closed the car door. He stepped back and watched her as she started her car, then backed out of the driveway. He continued to watch her until she was out of sight.

As soon as she was gone, he went back into the house and got ready for bed. He wanted an early start tomorrow and he needed some rest.

CHAPTER SEVENTEEN

Bill's alarm clock went off at two minutes before six. The night didn't seem long enough to Bill, but he did get some much needed rest. He climbed out of bed, went into the bathroom, showered and shaved. He dressed in his uniform, then left his home and drove downtown to the Hill City Café. He sat down in a booth where he could see anyone coming in or going out, then ordered his breakfast.

While he ate, he thought about what he wanted to get done today. The first thing was to go out to the quarry and look for any activities that would show there was some kind of mining going on there. He would also be looking for proof that the quarry was being used as a depot to store stolen military items until they could be moved to where they were to be used or sold.

No one he wanted to question had shown up in the café before he was finished eating. He left the café and drove to the quarry. On the drive to the quarry, he didn't see anyone. There was no one on the road which was not unusual. There were very few people who lived in that area of the Black Hills. As he drove by Keaton's place, he didn't see anyone around, but then he couldn't see much of the house or the barn from the road.

When Bill pulled up to the entrance gate of the Jasper Quarry, he found the gate closed. He took a minute to get out of his patrol car and check the drive for any signs of anyone having gone in or out of the quarry. He found nothing indicating someone had gone in or out of the quarry, at least by the front gate.

He opened the gate, got back in his patrol car and drove onto the quarry property. Bill drove up close to the old office building, stopped and got out of the patrol car. He made a quick check to see if anything had changed since he had been there. He found nothing, so he returned to his patrol car and drove to the quarry pit. He drove into the quarry pit then turned the patrol car around and parked it facing toward the only way in or out of the pit. Bill left his patrol car and began a thorough search of the quarry pit, but found nothing to indicate there was any kind of mining going on, either above or below ground.

As he stood next to his patrol car looking around, he thought there might be a mine with an entrance located outside the pit, but still on the property of the Jasper Quarry. It seemed to make sense. With people using the quarry to sight in their hunting rifles or practice shooting, a mine entrance in the quarry might accidentally be discovered, and it could cause problems for whoever was mining on the property. It also might be a problem if someone discovered the hiding place.

Bill returned to his patrol car, drove out of the quarry pit and on around to where he had found the explosives container. He parked his patrol car off to the side of the road where it would be easy to turn around if he needed to in a hurry. He got out of the patrol car and started looking for anything that didn't seem to belong on the quarry property.

It didn't take him long before he found the shell of an old car. As he looked it over, it was obvious the car had been there for a long time. Looking inside the car, he discovered it had been pretty well gutted. He didn't find anything very interesting in the passenger's compartment. He walked to the rear of the car and tried to open the trunk, but it was locked. It struck him as odd that the trunk would be locked since the car had obviously been left there as junk, and it had the kind of latch that had to be turned to open the trunk. He got the tire iron from his patrol car and pried it open.

To his surprise he found several olive drab steel army ammo cans, the kind that small arms military ammunition came in. He was a little surprised to find them still at the quarry since the explosives container that had ammunition and explosives in it had already been removed from the quarry after the container was discovered.

Bill took his pad from his pocket and wrote down the stock number from each of the eight ammo cans. It gave him a better chance of tracking the ammo cans which would help determine where they had come from. It also convinced him that he had been right when he said the quarry was being used as a depot for stolen military weapons and ammunition. But the questions still running through his mind were who was stealing it, where was it going from there and what was its intended use. There was also the question of where had it come from.

Bill returned to his patrol car and placed a call to the sheriff's office. He needed to know what the sheriff wanted him to do with what he had found. If he left it there, there was a good chance it would be gone by the time he got back, especially if someone had seen him open the trunk. But if he took it, the lab might be able to get fingerprints off some of the ammo cans.

"Car eight to base."

"Go ahead, eight," Mary said.

"I've got something interesting the sheriff should know about. Can you get him on the radio?"

"Sure, stand by."

It didn't take but a couple of minutes for the sheriff to get on the radio. Bill explained what he had found and where he found it. The sheriff decided he didn't want the ammo to remain there. The sheriff told Bill to photograph the ammo cans where they were, then carefully remove them so any fingerprints would not be disturbed and bring them into the lab.

After Bill signed off, he photographed the ammo cans while they were still in the car. He then backed his patrol car up closer to the back of the old car. He carefully loaded the ammo cans into the back of his patrol car, being very careful not to handle them any more than he had to, and using his handkerchief to avoid leaving his fingerprints on the cans. He used the wire type handle on the end of the cans to remove them from the old car and place them in the trunk of his patrol car. It was the only place where he could get a good hold on the cans and not leave any fingerprints.

Once he had the ammo cans secured in the trunk of his patrol car, he did a quick check for anything else that might have been left in the car. When he removed the tire to see if anything had been hidden behind the tire, or in the tire well, he found the tire seems very low on air. It was not a surprise because a tire left in an old car would deflate over time. However, when he pulled the tire out of the wheel well, he saw the spare tire was loose on the wheel rim and there were tool marks indicating the tire seal on the backside had been broken, apparently on purpose. He pushed the tire away from the rim and found there was money inside the tire, apparently a good deal of money. He took several pictures of the spare tire before removing it from the trunk. Not wanting to disturb what he had discovered any more than was necessary, he took the tire, with the money in it, and put it on the floor in the backseat of the patrol car, being very careful not to have any of the money fall out.

Finding nothing else in or around the car, he closed the trunk. He got into his patrol car and immediately headed for Rapid City. It took him well over an hour to get to the lab.

When he got to the lab, he parked his patrol car just outside the backdoor. He rang the bell at the loading dock door then waited for someone to answer. One of the assistants answered the door.

"Hi. I need a cart to load some things on," Bill said.

"I'm sorry but we don't take deliveries here," the assistant said.

"Tell the lab supervisor that Officer Sparks has some evidence from the quarry," Bill said, but the assistant just stood there looking at Bill.

"Do it now," Bill insisted.

The assistant looked at Bill for a moment before he said, "Yes, sir."

It wasn't but a couple of minutes before the assistant returned with the lab supervisor.

"How can I help you, Deputy?"

"I have eight military ammo cans I found at the Jasper Quarry. I want them checked for fingerprints before they are opened. If you can get any fingerprints off them, I would like you to run them and see if they can be matched up with any known person."

"I'm sorry, but we can't just do things at the whim of a deputy. We have to have authorization," the supervisor said rather forcefully.

"Will authorization from the Pennington County Sheriff be enough?" Bill asked with a strong note of authority. "He told me to bring the ammo cans over here and have you check them for fingerprints, all of them. I'll give you his phone number if you want to call him to get your authorization."

Just then the ME, Doctor Harrison, stepped out of the door. He saw Bill and smiled.

"What brings you here, Deputy Sparks?"

"I have eight ammo cans I need checked for fingerprints, or anything else that might tell me who handled them, before we open them."

"We'll get right on it. Did you touch them with your bare hands?"

"I only touched the wire handle on the end of each box, and I used a handkerchief when I did that."

"Good. We'll get right on it. You want to wait to see if we get any prints? It won't take long to see if there are any fingerprints."

"Sure."

Doctor Harrison had the assistant remove the ammo cans from Bill's patrol car, watching him to make sure he didn't touch the cans anywhere but the wire handle on the front of them. Once all the cans were on the cart, Bill followed the ME into the lab.

"Have you been able to identify the murdered man?"

"Not yet, but we haven't given up."

"You might want to check his fingerprints against any you find on the ammo cans," Bill suggested.

"You think there's a connection?" Doctor Harrison asked.

"I don't know of any, but it wouldn't hurt to check."

"True enough," the doctor said with a grin. "We'll check it out."

Bill stood by the cart while the assistant began the task of looking for fingerprints on the ammo cans. Bill found it interesting that they only found one set of fingerprints on only one of the ammo cans. He remained next to the ammo cans while the assistant went to talk to the ME. It was only a moment or so before the ME came back to talk to Bill.

"They found only one set of usable prints. I'll have to check them and see if we can find out who they belong to. I'll have them compare the prints to the murder victim."

"Thanks."

"You can open the cans now."

"I'll take them to the Sheriff's Office to open them in his presence, but I have a good idea what is in them. I've handled a lot of ammo cans that were full, and these feel and sound like they are full of ammunition."

"Okay, but if you need anything let me know," the ME said.

Bill thanked him for his help then loaded the ammo cans back into his car. He had intentionally not said anything about the tire with the money in it. He wanted the sheriff to see it first and be a witness to the counting of the money.

Bill arrived at the sheriff's office with one of the ammo cans just shortly before noon. He found the sheriff in. He knocked on the door and was told to enter. When he stepped into the office, the sheriff was on the phone. The sheriff motioned for him to sit down. Bill sat down and waited for him to finish his conversation. It wasn't long before the sheriff hung up the phone.

"That was the ME on the phone," the sheriff said as he looked at Bill. "It looks like they have a match for the fingerprints off the ammo cans. They were a match to the dead man. How did you know they would match?"

"I didn't. It was just a guess on my part. We still don't know who the dead man is," Bill said.

"That's true. I see you have one of the ammo cans. Let's open it.

Bill opened the ammo can. It contained 30.06 small arms ammunition as Bill had suspected.

"The rest of the cans are just like this one and weigh about the same," Bill said.

"You can take them to the evidence room and log them in. Did you find anything else while you were at the quarry?"

"Yes. I also found a lot of money in the spare tire in the trunk of the old car that I found the ammo cans in. It looked like someone was trying to hide it, but they didn't do a very good job of it."

"Did you bring the money in?" the sheriff asked.

"I brought the whole thing in, tire and all. I wanted you to see how they tried to hide it," Bill said with a grin.

"Go get it. We'll take the money out of the tire and count it here."

"Yes, sir."

Bill went out to his patrol car and retrieved the tire. He carried it into the sheriff's office and set it down on the floor.

The sheriff knelt down on the floor and looked at the tire. He pushed the loose side of the tire in and began digging out the money. He handed it to Bill, and Bill stacked it on the sheriff's desk. When the sheriff got all the money out of the tire, they counted it. There was five thousand dollars, total.

"Well, that's a good sum of money. I wonder why it was kept in a tire?" the sheriff said thinking out loud.

Bill didn't say anything. The money was in several different denominations with none of them being larger than a twenty, indicating the money might have been gathered over a period of time, and possibly from several sources.

"I'll put this in a safe and hold it as evidence in the murder of the unknown man. It may have nothing to do with the murder, but then again there's a strong possibility that it does," the sheriff said.

"I was thinking it might have had something to do with the murder."

"How so?"

"There's the possibility the guy who was murdered got caught dipping into the till, so to speak," Bill said.

"I was thinking the same thing. What is your next move?"

"I still have a couple of people I want to question. I have no idea what questioning them will produce, but it might shake up someone who will make a mistake. Have you heard back from any of the military bases?" Bill asked.

"All of them agreed that an inventory of their supply depots is in order, and that a visual inspection of everything would be necessary. They are planning on hitting as many bases as possible at the same time in case there is a connection between any of the bases."

"Sounds like a good idea," Bill said. "I have a list of the numbers on all eight of the ammo cans. You might want to give it to them so they know what we have, and what they are looking for," Bill said as he reached in his pocket and took out his note pad.

"Good idea."

Bill gave the sheriff the page with the numbers on it. After the sheriff looked at it, Bill stood up.

"If that's all, I'll take the ammo cans to the evidence room, then be on my way."

"Okay, go ahead. Let me know how the questioning turns out."

"I will," Bill said.

"I'll get these numbers to the inspectors."

Bill nodded, turned and left the sheriff's office. He returned to his patrol car, then took the ammo cans out of it and took them to the evidence room for storage. As soon as he had a receipt for the ammo cans, he headed back to Hill City.

On his way back, he stopped off at a restaurant for lunch. He arrived back in Hill City about three-thirty in the afternoon. With the early start of his day, he had already put in a full day. He called in to check out.

Bill took a shower then sat down to make notes of some of the questions he wanted to ask those he intended to question. He decided the first person he would question was Gordon. He wanted to know how he injured his arm.

He also began to think of Julie, and remembered she didn't have to work tonight, and he had told her he would pick her up at her grandfather's place. A quick look at his watch showed him it would be about five o'clock by the time he got there if he left right now. Since he was ready, he decided to leave.

Bill arrived at Julie's grandfather's place just shortly before five. When he pulled to a stop he saw Julie was sitting on a porch chair. She stood up and smiled as she walked to the steps. Bill parked his car, got out and walked up to the porch.

"Hi," Julie said as Bill stepped up onto the porch.

"Hi."

Bill stepped up to her, reached out and put his hands on her narrow waist, then pulled her close. She reached up and put her hands on his shoulders. He leaned down as she tipped her head to one side. Their lips met in a soft, loving kiss that lasted only a moment. Julie leaned back and looked up at him and smiled.

"You said last night you would pick me up. Where are you planning to take me?"

"There's a movie in Rapid City I thought you might like to see. I thought I would take you to dinner and to a movie."

"I'd like that. It's been a long time since I've been to a movie. What movie did you have in mind?"

"I thought we could see *Key Largo* with Humphrey Bogart and Lauren Bacall, or we could see *Easter Parade* with Fred Astaire and Judy Garland. You pick," Bill said with a grin.

"I would like to see *Key Largo*. I've always liked Humphrey Bogart films."

"Okay. Are you ready to go?"

"Yes, but I better tell grandpa what I'm doing. I would guess we will be back late?"

"Probably," Bill said.

Julie went inside the house and told her grandfather she was going into Rapid City for dinner and a movie with Bill, and they would be back late. Bill and Julie left and went into Rapid City where they had a nice dinner and took in the movie.

It was fairly late when they headed back home. The ride home was a quiet ride. Julie rested her head on Bill's shoulder almost all the way back.

When they arrived at Julie's grandfather's farm, they sat in the car and did a little necking before they decided it was time for her to go in. Bill walked her to the door, and kissed her again before saying goodnight. He waited until she was in the house before he returned to his car and left for home.

Bill returned to his home in Hill City and went directly to bed. He slept well with pleasant thoughts of Julie.

CHAPTER EIGHTEEN

Morning came early for Bill. He was up, dressed in his uniform and on his way to the Hill City Café by six. As he walked into the café, he noticed Mr. Frank Gordon was sitting in a booth by himself.

Gordon was sitting sort of slumped over with his elbows on the table and his hands holding a cup of coffee as if he were trying to keep his hands warm. He was looking into the cup as if he was trying to find the answer to something very important and that the answer was in the cup. He seemed to be deep in thought, and the expression on his face gave the impression he was worried about something. Bill walked up to Gordon's table.

"Good morning, Mr. Gordon," Bill said politely as he stopped at the end of the table.

Bill had obviously startled him. Gordon looked very surprised to see Bill standing there. In fact, so surprised he spilled a little coffee, but he didn't say anything about it or even seemed to notice it.

"Do you mind if I join you?" Bill asked.

"Ah - - No. I guess not. Please have a seat," Gordon said as he set his coffee cup down on the table and leaned back in the booth.

"How have things been going at the campground?"

"Ah – Okay. I think we will have a good year if the weather stays nice for the next month or so."

"That's great. I heard you injured your arm. How are you doing?"

Bill noticed Gordon started to reach for his arm, but quickly withdrew his hand. His reaction was involuntary, and it showed on his face that he was a little upset with himself for reaching for his arm.

"It's getting better. It was just a scrape."

"I heard it was bad enough that you went into Rapid City to have it cared for. Why didn't you have it looked at right here, at the clinic?"

"Well, - ah – you see, I guess I didn't get the scrape cleaned up as well as I should have, and it was getting a little red around the edges. You know, showing signs of an infection. It started bothering me while I was in Rapid City on business, so I went to the hospital to get it looked at and get a shot, just in case."

"That was probably a good idea. How did it happen?"

Gordon seemed to be getting a little nervous. Bill wondered why? Had he actually been the person Bill shot after he was shot at?

Gordon was beginning to wonder just how much Deputy Sparks really knew about his visit to the hospital. Did Bill know that he was the one who had taken a shot at him?

"You know the hospital is required to report all gunshot wounds to the police."

"I didn't know that," Gordon said, looking a bit scared.

"It was a gunshot wound, wasn't it?" Bill said, not one hundred percent sure he was right, but willing to take the chance that he might be.

Gordon just looked at Bill for a minute, then looked around the room as if he was trying to make sure no one was close enough to hear them or was watching them.

"What do you say we go back to your place and have a little talk?" Bill asked quietly while looking into Gordon's eyes.

"I don't really want to arrest you in front of everybody."

Gordon looked at Bill for a minute, then tipped his head down and took a deep breath while looking at his coffee cup. Slowly, he looked up at Bill.

"I think you know it won't do you any good to try and run," Bill said softly. "It wouldn't take me two minutes to have an all-points bulletin out for you. If I do that, everyone will know it by the end of the day."

Gordon sat looking into Bill's eyes. All he could think about was that it was over. There was no need to play games with Deputy Sparks. Gordon was sure he knew most, if not all, of what was going on.

"Where do you want to meet?" Gordon finally asked quietly, looking as if his world had come to an end.

"Let's meet in your office at the campground. We can talk there."

"I'd rather meet somewhere more private," he said, the tone of his voice almost pleading for Deputy Sparks to concede to his request. "We might get interrupted in my office."

"All right. We'll meet just off the highway on the Forest Service road that runs west from your campground. You can leave now. I'll be right behind you to make sure we are not followed."

Gordon didn't reply; he nodded that he understood, then got up, put money on the table to cover his coffee and walked out of the café. Bill waited a minute or so, then got up and followed him out of the café. Gordon turned right and walked toward his car, while Bill turned left to go to his patrol car.

Bill got in his patrol car just as Gordon pulled away from the curb. Bill waited until Gordon was down the road a little ways, just to make sure no one was going to follow him. He then pulled away from the curb and headed south out of town. He kept a close eye in his rearview mirror to make sure he was not being followed.

With all the curves in the road, Gordon had not been in Bill's sight all the time. In fact, Bill could not see him for at least a minute or so when Gordon turned onto the Forest Service road well ahead of him. When Bill got to the Forest Service road, he turned onto it. He could make out Gordon's car through the trees around the next curve.

As Bill pulled up behind Gordon's car, he could see the backdoor on the driver's side was open, but he couldn't see Gordon. He got the feeling there was something wrong, very wrong. Bill got out of his car, drew his gun then started walking toward Gordon's car. As he moved closer to the car, he kept a careful watch for any surprises Gordon might have in mind.

As soon as he was close enough to look in the car, he looked in the backseat of the car. It was empty. After a quick look around to make sure there was no one who might cause him harm, he moved up to the driver's side door and looked inside. He found Gordon lying down across the front seat of the car.

The first thing he noticed was the blood running down the side of Gordon's head, and there was blood all over the passenger's side of the car. On closer look, he noticed Gordon's left hand was hanging lifeless down toward the floor. There was a gun lying on the floor near the end of his hand.

It looked as if he had taken his own life, but yet it didn't. There was something about what Bill was seeing that didn't add up. It just didn't look right.

Bill took a minute to look around, not only at the inside of the car, but at the ground around the outside. He found a couple of footprints near the backdoor of the car and at the front door. It didn't look like Gordon had gotten out of his car, and he certainly wouldn't have gotten out from the backseat. A quick look at Gordon's shoes made it clear he had not stepped out of the car. It had rained a little the night before and the road was a little muddy near the car where Gordon had stopped. There was no sign of mud on his shoes from the wet ground next to the car.

Also the footprints were pointed toward the car, not away from the car, the way the footprints should have been pointing if Gordon had gotten out from either the front or back of the car. Bill doubted Gordon would have had time to get out of the car, then get back in and shoot himself, plus, it made no sense. There was also a question of why would he get out, then get back in to kill himself. The position of his body indicated he was shot while sitting in the driver's position in the car, and probably not by his own hand.

As Bill looked over the scene, he began to wonder how anyone would have known they were going to meet there. He quickly concluded, they wouldn't. Someone had to have gotten into Gordon's car while it was parked on the street in Hill City. Someone must have seen Gordon and Bill talking in the café. The only questions were, who saw them, who killed Gordon and why was he killed? That last question was the one Bill really wanted answered. Bill returned to his patrol car and placed a call on his car radio to dispatch.

"Car eight to base."

"Go ahead, eight," Mary said.

"I need to talk to the sheriff."

"I'll get him," she said.

It didn't take very long before the sheriff was on the radio.

"Got a problem?"

"Yes, sir. I was following Mr. Frank Gordon to a place where we could talk privately. I lost sight of him a couple of times, but none of them for more than a minute, maybe a few seconds more. When I pulled up behind him, I found him dead. He had been shot in the head," Bill explained.

"Dead? What happened?"

"I'm not sure, but I think there must have been someone hiding in the backseat of his car. When he pulled to a stop on the Forest Service road where we had agreed to meet, he was shot in the head by the person in the backseat. That person disappeared into the thick forest before I came around the corner. I found footprints in the wet ground indicating someone got out of the backseat of the car."

"Do you think you can follow the tracks?" the sheriff asked.

"No, sir. They quickly went off the road. The ground just off the road is pretty rocky."

"What was your interest in Mr. Gordon?"

"I think he was the one who shot at me. The same one I'm sure I hit when I shot back. I started to talk to him in the Hill City Café this morning. He agreed to talk to me, but wanted to talk away from the café."

"Who else was in the café?"

"No one, except the waitress and she hadn't come out from behind the counter. It had to be someone who saw us talking and got in the backseat of Gordon's car while it was parked on the street and we were talking in the cafe."

"I'll get a coroner out there as soon as possible. I'll send someone to get any fingerprints from the car. Wait there and don't touch anything."

"Yes, sir. I'll make casts of the footprints while I'm waiting," Bill said.

"Good idea."

Bill gave the sheriff directions to where he was located before he hung up. While he waited for the coroner, Bill made plaster casts of the footprints. While he was making the plaster casts, he noticed that the footprints were of dress shoes, not the kind of shoes that Gordon was wearing. Gordon was wearing work boots. Bill also noticed the shoe's right heel had left an impression showing there was a metal lift plate on it.

He looked around for any evidence that might help him find Gordon's killer. He found nothing but a few footprints leading away from Gordon's car, but quickly lost the trail on the rocky ground.

Bill spent some time thinking about what had happened. All he could think of was someone had to have been in the backseat of Gordon's car when he left Hill City. It was the only way anyone could have found out where they were going to meet. Gordon had not talked to anyone after they had decided on a meeting place. For the question of who had killed Gordon, Bill had a couple of suspects in mind.

It took about an hour before the coroner arrived. There was a fingerprint specialist from the lab with him. They pulled up behind Bill's patrol car and got out.

"What have you got this time?" Ralph Wickum asked.

"I've got a dead body. He's in the car."

"I'll take a look," Wickum said, then walked to the car.

Bill stood back and watched as the coroner looked over the body. He wore rubber gloves so he wouldn't leave any fingerprints. After a few minutes of looking at the body and the inside of the car, he stood up and looked at Bill.

"Bill, I don't think he committed suicide. It looks to me like he tried to turn his head as he was shot. The angle of the shot and the placement in his head would make it very difficult for him to hold a gun in that position."

"I didn't think he had committed suicide. I'm sure he was shot by someone who had been hiding in the backseat. I'm hoping he might have left some fingerprints on the car's door handles or something. I made casts of the footprints close to the car."

"Have you taken pictures?"

"No, not yet," Bill said.

"I'll take them."

Bill stood back and watched while Wickum took pictures of the area around the car, of the car itself, the interior of the car, both front and backseat areas, the body and the footprints left in the mud beside the car. When he was finished, he removed the body and placed it in the coroner's truck. The fingerprint specialist went over the car in the hope of finding fingerprints they could use.

"Did you get a good look at the gun on the floor?" Wickum asked.

"Not really. Why?"

"I don't think it's the gun that killed him. There's no blowback of blood on it; and if I had to guess, and it would be a guess, the gun that killed him was a different caliber. Were you very close to this location when he was shot?"

"I had slowed down to turn in so I wasn't more than twenty-five to thirty yards behind him. He was around the corner from me where I couldn't see his car for maybe a minute, possibly a minute and a half at the most."

"Did you hear a shot?"

"Not a sound. As you can see, the side window of my car was rolled down. I was never so far away from him that I wouldn't have heard a gunshot." Bill explained.

"He was probably shot almost as soon as he stopped. And he was probably shot with a gun with a silencer on it."

Bill had to agree with the coroner's assessment. He stood back and watched the fingerprint specialist do his work. It wasn't long and he was finished. He walked over to Bill.

"Deputy, did you touch the car at all? Be sure of your answer."

"No. I did not touch the car at all. I looked in. It was obvious Mr. Gordon was dead. I then placed a call to the sheriff."

"You didn't touch the car when you leaned in?"

"No. I didn't touch the car at any time. I made it a point not to touch the car."

"Good. I think I have a couple of good prints from the backdoor handle, both inside and out. I have fingerprints from the steering wheel and front door handles, which are probably the victim's."

"Good, because I think the shooter was lying in wait in the backseat of the car."

"We'll be hauling the car in for a complete going over. Will you be able to stay with it until the wrecker can get here?"

"Sure."

"Good. The wrecker should be here shortly," he said then returned to the coroner's truck.

Ralph said goodbye to Bill then backed down the road. Bill watched as the coroner's truck disappeared from sight.

While he waited for the wrecker, Bill walked the area around the car, moving further and further away from it, but never letting the car out of his sight. He found a few places on the edge of the road where someone had been. From the looks of the footprints, the person had been running away from the scene. There was no need to take casts of the footprints that were not close to the car as they were not good enough to get anything useable in court. The tracks quickly disappeared in the rocks where the person turned off the road and went into the woods.

Bill didn't move his car until the wrecker got there. He didn't want Gordon's car out of his sight until it was hauled off. Once it was gone, Bill drove to the campground Gordon and his wife owned. He was not looking forward to telling her that Frank was dead.

Bill pulled up in front of the office to the campground and got out of his car. He had just gotten out when Mrs. Gordon stepped out of the office onto the porch.

"Good morning, Deputy Sparks," she said with a smile.

"Good morning, Mrs. Gordon."

"What brings you out here on such a beautiful day?"

"I'm afraid I have some bad news for you."

Bill noticed the smile quickly disappeared from her face and was replaced by a concerned look.

"Could we go inside," Bill suggested.

"Yes," she replied softly, then turned and went back in the office.

Bill followed her into the office and pointed to a chair.

"I think you should sit down," he said then waited for her to sit down.

"Something has happened to Frank, hasn't it?"

"Yes. I'm sorry to have to tell you this, but Frank was shot about two hours ago."

"Oh God," she cried as she put her hands over her mouth.

Bill stood by and watched her. Telling someone of the death of a loved one always made him feel uncomfortable. It was several minutes before she seemed to get her emotions under control and looked up at him. Her eyes were filled with tears, but she didn't say anything to him for several more minutes. She wiped her eyes and took a deep breath.

"You said he was shot?"

"Yes."

"Is he - - dead?" she asked, but the expression on her face showed Bill she seemed to know.

"Yes."

"How did it happen? He said he was going into town for for a cup of coffee and would pick up the mail."

"We are not sure, but - - - ."

Bill went on to explain how her husband happened to be parked on the Forest Service road. He told her someone must have been in the back of his car when he left Hill City.

"Can you think of anyone who might have had a reason to kill your husband?"

"No. He seemed to get along with almost everyone."

"Can you tell me what organizations he might have belonged to?"

"The only one he belonged to was the one most of the campground owners in this area belong to, but that is an organization to promote and advertise campgrounds."

"Does he belong to any political organizations?"

"No. Why would you ask that?" she asked with a concerned look on her face.

"It was just a routine question. We are just trying to find a reason for someone wanting to kill him. Who are some of his close friends?"

"Ah, there's Keaton, that's John Keaton. They have been friends for years. Ray Rutledge was also one of his friends."

"I'm a little surprised that Frank would have much to do with both Keaton and Rutledge because they don't get along."

"Oh, they patched up that disagreement sometime ago. It was after they resolved their differences that Frank became friends with Rutledge."

"Do you know what the disagreement was about?"

"No, I just know it lasted far too long," she said.

"Do you have any idea what it might have been about?"

"I heard at one time that John blamed Ray for the death of his son at the quarry, but Ray couldn't save John's son even though he tried. But I think it had something to do with the war, but I'm not sure what. It might have been their differences in their beliefs. I don't think Ray thought we should be involved in the war in Europe, but I'm not sure about that. I had never even met Ray until the war was over for more than a year."

Bill found that interesting. He wondered if Rutledge, or possibly Keaton, might have been members of the Nazi Political Party and had eventually convinced Gordon to join in. That thought confirmed Bill's suspicion that someone had seen Gordon talking to him in the Hill City Café. That someone probably didn't trust Gordon to keep his mouth shut about what was going on, and thought it was better to kill him than have him spill the beans by naming names.

"Did your husband buy any insurance lately?" Bill asked.

"No. Why do you ask?"

"I saw your husband along with Keaton talking to a man who was reported to be an insurance salesman. I thought you might know something about the man, maybe his name."

"Do you think he had something to do with Frank's death?"

"No. He was a man I'd seen with your husband and I'd never seen around here before."

"Frank never mentioned talking with an insurance salesman. I would know if he bought an insurance policy. I handle all the bills."

"Well, I guess that's about all I have to ask you at this time. Is there someone you would like me to call to come and stay with you?" Bill asked.

"No. I would like to be alone for a little while."

"Do you have someone who could deal with your campers until you feel a little better?"

"I'll get our groundskeeper to watch the office," she said.

Bill turned and left the office. After talking to the groundskeeper, he walked out to his patrol car, got in and headed home. He had reports to fill out which would take him awhile to get done.

When Bill got home, he sat down at the kitchen table and began writing out his reports. He described in detail everything that had happened from the time he first talked to Gordon up to, and including, his questioning of Mrs. Gordon.

It was well after lunch before he was finished with the reports. He took time to have his lunch. He decided to take a few minutes to think about this morning. He had three people who might have a reason to kill Gordon. Those three were John Keaton, Ray Rutledge, and the "insurance salesman". The three all had a connection to each other. Bill knew it was possible there was a fourth, or even a fifth, person involved, but he had no idea who they might be.

The more he thought about it, the more he wondered if what he had stumbled on in the quarry had anything to do with the body that was found in the quarry. All he knew for sure was there was a good possibility there was a connection. The fact that Gordon had been murdered, with the apparent reason to keep him from talking to authorities, led Bill to think the murder of the man in the quarry might have been for the same reason. If that was the case, what were they planning to do with the weapons and explosives in the stolen Army explosives container?

After spending sometime thinking about what was going on, Bill placed a call to the sheriff's office. He was immediately put through to the sheriff.

"I was about to have dispatch give you a call and have you come into the office," Sheriff Henderson said.

"Oh. What's going on?"

"Let's just say, it's better if you come in to not only hear what information we have, but that you see some of it."

"Okay. I'll be there in about an hour."

"Good. Bring your reports, along with any evidence you have with you."

"Yes, sir," Bill said then hung up.

Bill gathered up his reports then went to his patrol car. He got in and headed for the sheriff's office in Rapid City.

CHAPTER NINETEEN

Bill arrived at the Pennington County Sheriff's Office at two-thirty in the afternoon with his reports in hand. He had just walked in the door when Mary pointed toward the sheriff's office.

"He's waiting for you. Just go on in," she said.

"Thanks," Bill said as he walked down the hall and into the sheriff's office without knocking.

As he stepped into the office, he saw Sheriff Henderson looking at photographs laid out on a long table against one of the walls. Sergeant David Johnson from the U.S. Army Ordnance Depot was also looking at the photographs. The sheriff turned to see who had come into his office.

"Bill, I want you to see this. Most of the photographs on the table you took," he said as Bill walked over to the table. "What I have done is to take all the photos, the ones you took, the ones the coroner took, and any others relevant to your investigation and put them in chronological order.

"Hi, Dave," Bill said as he stepped up close to the table.

Bill took a few minutes to look at all the photographs. He immediately recognized the ones he had taken. Most of the others were new to him. It seemed the other photos filled in a few of the gaps.

"As you can see, there are a lot of photographs from the coroner in the field, some taken by the ME during the autopsy, some of them were taken by you in the field. The man you found murdered in the quarry was Airman First Class Jason Olson of the U.S. Air Force. He worked in the supply depot at the Rapid City Air Force Base," the sheriff explained.

"If he worked there, why didn't Captain Walker say anything about him? He had to have been missing for some time."

"He was on leave for two weeks, and was supposed to be in New York while he was on leave. At the time you first talked to Captain Walker, Olson had only been on leave for six days. He wasn't expected back for another eight days."

"It looks like we found our inside man," Dave said with a grin.

"Did the eight ammo cans come from the air force base?" Bill asked.

"No. We are still trying to track them down. We still have two bases that have not sent us their reports on their inspections," the sheriff said.

"What about the markings on the ammo cans? Didn't they tell you where the ammo cans came from?"

"No. None of the bases we have talked to have a listing for those ammo cans," the sheriff said. "All we can conclude from that is they were stolen from a base somewhere else. We have a request in to the Army Master Supply Office requesting information on where those ammo cans had been sent. We have not heard back from them, yet."

"It would appear we have only one of the inside men, if those ammo cans came from some base out of our area," Bill suggested.

"I would think so," the sheriff said. "I'm hoping our request to the Army Master Supply Office comes up with a possibility."

"It's possible the ammo cans were from sometime ago. Maybe they were stolen from a supply depot out of country. It wouldn't be the first time things came up missing in, say Europe, then showed up here in the states," Dave said.

"Did you find anything more about Gordon?" the sheriff asked.

"I visited with his wife, but nothing much came of it. I have my reports for you. The only thing I found interesting was that Gordon was fairly close friends with Keaton and Rutledge."

"Any idea why Gordan was murdered?"

"I think he was murdered because someone saw me talking to him and was afraid he would talk too much, but that's speculation on my part. I have no proof."

Bill spent the next fifteen to twenty minutes giving the sheriff a complete rundown on what had happened and what evidence he had found at the scene of Mr. Gordon's murder. He also told him about his talk with Mrs. Gordon.

The sheriff sat and listened very carefully to Bill. He began to understand why Bill thought Gordon was killed to keep him from talking.

"What's your next move?" the sheriff asked.

"Do you think I could get a search warrant for Gordon's office and home?"

"Under the circumstances, I think we can. I'll call the judge and see if he will let us have one," the sheriff said.

"I would like to search his home, his office, his tool shed, his shop and any place else on the property where he might have hidden things. I want to see if I can find anything that might help us find a reason for someone to kill him. I also plan to have a talk with Keaton and Rutledge. I think they are involved, but I don't know how."

Just then the phone on the sheriff's desk began to ring. The sheriff reached over and answered it.

Bill could only hear the sheriff's side of the conversation. By the look on the sheriff's face, it appeared to interest him a great deal. It was a fairly long conversation with the sheriff not saying very much, mostly just listening.

"Thanks for the information," the sheriff said then hung up and turned toward Bill.

"The ammo cans were missing from a supply depot at an air base in England. The best guess of the supply officer was that they were put on an airplane returning to the states after the war by whoever stole them."

"That would have been almost three years ago," Bill said.

"Right. This is the most likely scenario. When the plane landed, it was parked off the runway while other planes landed. Sometime, maybe when it was dark, the ammo cans were removed from the plane and taken off base."

"Do they know which plane the ammo cans were on?"

"No. They don't even know which squadron of planes the ammo cans came in on. With all the troops coming home, it seems no one paid a whole lot of attention to what was brought in on the planes. There is no way of knowing who brought them in, when they were brought in, or where they went," the sheriff said.

"So we're right back where we started," Bill said.

"It would appear so," the sheriff said with a look of disappointment on his face. "There's nothing we can do about it. Let me see if I can get a warrant before you head back to Hill City. Maybe a search of Gordon's place will shine some light on it."

The sheriff picked up the phone and called the judge. He was still in his chamber. After a brief talk with the judge, he hung up.

"Go over to the judge's chamber. He will have a search warrant waiting for you. Once you get it, you can head on home and serve it. If you need any help, give me a call."

"Yes, sir."

Bill put his reports on the sheriff's desk, then left his office. When he got to the judge's chamber, he had to wait for a few minutes for the judge to finish the warrant and sign it. Once he had it, he headed back to Hill City.

When Bill arrived in Hill City, he drove through town and out to Gordon's campground. When he drove in, he saw a man in a suit coming out of the office. The man stopped suddenly, then turned as if he didn't want to be seen or talked to by, Deputy Sparks, but Bill had seen him.

"Hold it right there," Bill said as he slipped his hand over his gun.

The man stopped and looked at Bill. He was clean shaven and looked every bit the epitome of a businessman, right down to the expensive suit and tie, and the briefcase he was carrying.

"What is it officer?" he asked.

"May I ask what you are doing here?"

"I came to see Mr. Gordon, but he isn't here."

"What did you want with him?"

"I don't think that is any of your business, officer."

"Let's go back in the office and talk. By the way, that was not a request," Bill said forcefully.

The man looked at him for a moment before he slowly turned around and returned to the office.

Once inside the office, Bill pointed to a chair for him to sit on. Bill walked up to the counter and rang the bell, then waited. There was no answer. He rang it again. Within a moment or so, Mrs. Gordon came in from outside.

"Hello, Deputy Sparks."

"Mrs. Gordon," Bill said with a slight tip of his head, but not taking his eyes off the man. "Do you know this man?"

"Why, no," she said looking a little confused.

"He was coming out of your office."

"I didn't know he was in my office. I was out of the office showing a camper where his campsite was located."

"First of all, what is your name?" Bill asked the man.

"I don't think that is any of your business."

"Well, it's a long ride into Rapid City. You can either answer my questions here, or I can take you into the sheriff's office and you can answer them there. What's it going to be?"

The man looked at Deputy Sparks for a moment before he began to think he really didn't have a choice.

"I'm Richard Stassen," he said reluctantly.

"What was your business here?" Bill asked.

"Now that IS none of your business," he said sharply.

"Stand up," Bill ordered.

Stassen just looked at Bill for a moment. He didn't move until Bill looked at him with a stern look and motioned for him to stand up. As soon as he stood up, Bill frisked him for weapons. When he was done, Bill told him to open his briefcase.

"I don't have to do that. You have no right to search my briefcase."

"You were in this office without the owner's knowledge. I want to know what you took from here. You acted like you had something to hide when you saw me. Now open the briefcase," Bill demanded.

Reluctantly, Mr. Stassen opened the briefcase and set it on the coffee table. He then sat down on the sofa.

Bill looked in the briefcase. All he saw were a number of papers and a couple of file folders. He looked at the names on the file folders, but didn't recognize any of the names. There was nothing in the papers that would indicate he had taken any of them from the Mrs. Gordon's office.

It wasn't until Mr. Stassen went to close the briefcase that Bill got a glimpse of one of the file folders that fell open and he could see just the edge of a paper. He couldn't see all it said, but he could make out only part of a name. It was the end of a name and looked like the name was the end of the word, Keaton. All he could see was the "a-t-o-n". Bill didn't say anything. He would contact the sheriff and ask him to find out all he could about Stassen.

Once Stassen had closed the briefcase, he looked at Bill.

"You may go," Bill said, having no reason to detain him any longer.

Bill watched Stassen as he left the office and walked out to his car. As he was getting in the car, Bill wrote down the license plate number. He continued to watch Stassen until he was out on the highway and out of sight. He then turned and looked at Mrs. Gordon.

"Mrs. Gordon, are you sure you don't know who that man is?"

"I've never seen him before," she replied.

"Have you ever heard his name?"

"No, I don't believe so."

"Okay. The reason I'm here is I have a warrant to search your home, Frank's office, his shop and his tool shed."

"My goodness. What do you want to do that for?"

"I will be looking for anything that might give us a reason for someone to have killed Frank."

"Oh. I don't know what you will find to that end, but I guess I don't have a choice."

"I'm sorry, but you are right. You do not have a choice. I would like the keys to his desk, file cabinets, any buildings such as a shop or a shed, or anywhere Frank might have stored things."

Mrs. Gordon just looked at Bill for a moment before she walked around behind the counter in the office. She picked up a set of keys from under the counter and handed them to Bill.

"These are Frank's keys. The two larger keys are to his tool shed and his workshop. The smaller keys are to the file cabinets and his desk."

"Did Frank spend a lot of time in his workshop?"

"Yes. I guess you would consider it a lot of time. He was always making something or repairing something."

"I'm going to start in his office. I do not want you to go into his workshop or his tool shed. In fact, I don't want you to leave the front office until I'm finished here and in his office. Do you understand?" Bill said.

"Yes. I guess this is official business."

"Yes. It is official business. I will try not to make a mess of things."

"Thank you."

Bill turned and began looking into drawers and cabinets in the front office. When he was done, he left Mrs. Gordon in the front office while he went into Frank's office. Bill started with Frank's desk. He searched every drawer, looked for hiding places in the desk and even turned over desk drawers and checked behind them, but found nothing. He moved on to check out the two file cabinets, but found nothing of interest. After going over every inch of Frank's office, he found nothing that would shine any light on what Frank had been doing that might be related to his death.

Bill returned to the front office and saw Mrs. Gordon still sitting on a chair. She looked like she was afraid of what Bill might find.

"I've finished with his office. Was there any place else in the house where he might have kept private papers or boxes of things?"

Bill wasn't sure she would tell him the truth, but it seemed right to ask her. He might be able to tell by the look on her face and the way she answered his question if she was telling him the truth.

"No, I don't think so," she said. "But you can certainly look around our living quarters if you wish."

"Let me ask you a question. Do you know of any organizations Frank might have belonged to or showed an interest in?"

"No. He didn't belong to any organizations except for the Campground Owners Association. He never showed any interest in any other organizations that I know of."

"Did he go out regularly, like once a week or once a month?"

"He went out to play a little poker every other Tuesday night, but he was home by midnight or one in the morning at the latest."

"Do you know who he played poker with?" Bill asked.

"The only one he ever mentioned by name was John Keaton. He did say there were different men at different times."

"So it was Keaton, Frank and different men?"

"Yes," she said.

"He never mentioned those other men by name?"

"No. He said I wouldn't know them anyway."

"I see. Do you know where they met?"

"I know they met at John Keaton's house a few times."

"Did they ever meet here?"

"No. Well yes. They met here twice, maybe three times, during the winter, but they didn't play here in the house. They used one of the cabins. They're empty most of the winter."

"But you didn't see any of them?"

"No. They went right to the cabin to play. I can't see all the cabins from here."

"Did Rutledge ever play cards with them?"

"No, I don't think so. Frank would have mentioned it, if Mr. Rutledge played with them."

"Thank you," Bill said then went out to the workshop.

Bill let himself into the workshop. There was a table and a workbench with shelves. The shop seemed to be very well organized. Everything seemed to have a place, and everything seemed to be in its place. After a brief look around, he decided the best place to start was the workbench and the shelves on the wall behind it.

Since Bill had no idea what he was looking for, he would have to check out everything. There were several old boxes under the workbench, he decided to start there. The first couple of wooden boxes had nothing of interest to him, except that they were old boxes from the Jasper Quarry, the same kind that Mr. Turnquest had found on his property.

It was the fourth box that got him interested in his search. Inside the box were several small black notebooks, the kind that could be carried in one's jacket pocket. He opened the first one and found it had a few letters and some numbers. The numbers didn't seem to make any sense. He studied them for several minutes, but still could not make heads or tails of what they might mean. After looking at the rest of the notebooks, he decided to take one of them with him to study at home. Since they had dates on them, he put the latest one in his pocket.

He continued his search of the workshop. It wasn't until he looked in a small tin hidden behind some other tins full of nuts and bolts that he found something of interest. It was a small lapel pin. It was the second pin like it he had found. The other one he had found near the Army explosives and weapons container in the quarry. Finding the pin tended to connect Gordon with whoever lost the first pin he found. Bill continued his search of the workshop with little success.

When he finished in the workshop, he moved on to the tool shed. He did a complete search of the shed without finding anything. As he stood looking around the tool shed one last time before he was going to leave, he noticed a mark on the floor that resembled part of a circle or part of an arch. It looked as if a panel from the wall had been dragged across the floor, scratching the floor from the wall outward into the room. It wasn't very big which led him to believe the eight-inch-wide board that was part of the wall would move out if it was hinged on one side.

Bill got a pry bar from the corner, then pried the board loose. Behind the board, between the two-by-fours that were part of the wall, was a cylindrical tube. Bill wondered why anyone would keep such a thing hidden in the wall. He opened it up at one end and looked inside. It looked like a flag was inside the tube. He carefully began to pull it out of the tube, but stopped when he had only about one-forth of it out of the tube. He immediately recognized it as a Nazi flag, a dress flag, complete with gold braid around the edge. He had seen a flag like it when he and his platoon broke into a German officer's office in Paris, France, when they retook the city.

Bill quickly pushed the flag back into the tube. The evidence he had reinforced his belief there was a Nazi Political Party operating in the area, and there was a very good chance Gordon was part of it, possibly a major part of it. The only question he had at this point was who else in the area belonged to it. He could think of several possibilities.

There was time to think about it later. It was time to get the evidence out of there and in the hands of the sheriff. The sooner they found out who was involved, the better the chances of ending any destructive activities they might have in mind. Bill took the tin containing the lapel pin, and the tube with the flag inside and put them into his car.

After he was done with his search of the workshop and tool shed, he returned to the office. Mrs. Gordon was sitting in the office when he walked in.

"Are you done," she asked. "I saw you take something from the shed."

"That depends. Is there any place else where he might have hidden things he didn't want you to see?"

"Not that I can think of," she said. "What did you take from the shed?"

"I would rather not say,"

"Was my husband into something I should know about?"

"Do you know what political party Frank was affiliated with?"

"Frank? Why, he wasn't the least bit interested in any political party. Why do you ask?"

"No reason."

"I know you well enough to know that you don't ask questions without a reason. Frank was into something he shouldn't have been, wasn't he?"

"I don't know for sure," Bill said.

"You may not know for sure, but you suspect he was involved in something illegal."

"Yes, but I would like to wait until I'm sure before I say anything. And it might be a good idea if you say nothing to anyone else. It would also be a good idea if someone gets to asking you a lot of questions about Frank's activities that you give me a call."

"Oh, I will."

"I will be back to talk to you again."

"Anytime, Deputy Sparks. I've had a feeling Frank was doing something behind my back," she said with a hint of anger in her voice.

"What gave you that idea?" Bill asked.

"He seemed a bit nervous lately, and he was sort of jumpy. That wasn't like him."

"Did he offer any reason for his nervousness?"

"No. He wouldn't talk to me about it.

"Thank you. I'll see you again soon," Bill said then walked out of the office.

Bill got in his patrol car and sat looking at the office. He wasn't sure how much she knew, but he got the feeling she knew more than she was letting on. He leaned forward, turned the key and started his patrol car. He then drove back to his home in Hill City. A look at his watch showed him it was too late to get the sheriff in his office.

Bill fixed himself some dinner, then called Julie. They talked for a few minutes and made plans to have breakfast in the morning after she got off work. He took a shower and turned in for the night.

CHAPTER TWENTY

Bill was up a few minutes before six. He got dressed and started preparing breakfast for Julie and himself. He had a pretty good idea about the time she would arrive. He made baked eggs in a muffin tin with strips of cheese on top. He also had slices of hickory smoked ham in the frying pan ready to turn on the heat as soon as he heard her drive in the driveway, and bread was in the toaster ready for toasting, too, and the coffee was ready. Everything was ready for her to sit down and eat as soon as she arrived.

The baked eggs were just about done baking when he heard Julie drive in the driveway. He was taking the eggs out of the oven when she walked in the backdoor.

"Oh, it smells good in here. I'm hungry."

"Good, because it is almost ready. Sit down and relax."

"If I relax too much, I'll fall asleep."

Bill put a couple of the eggs on a plate with a good sized piece of ham and two slices of buttered toast then set it on the table in front of her. He leaned over and kissed her lightly on the cheek, then set a plate in front of his chair and sat down.

"This looks good," Julie said with a smile as she stuck a fork in the ham and began slicing off a piece.

From the look on Julie's face as she began eating, the meal was just what she needed. When they were about halfway through the meal, Julie looked up at Bill and smiled.

"I'm going to have to hire you to do the cooking."

"It's just something my mother used to make on Sunday mornings. It's easy and fairly quick."

"And it's good," she said then took another bite of ham.

They didn't talk much until breakfast was finished. When they were done, Bill stood up and cleared the dishes from the table and set them in the sink. He glanced over at Julie in time to see her yawn.

"You look tired. Why don't you stay here? I have a lot to do this morning. You can sleep in my bed, and you will have the house to yourself," Bill suggested.

"I think I'll take you up on that, but I need to call grandpa first so he doesn't worry about me."

"Go ahead and call him while I clean up the kitchen," Bill suggested.

Taking Bill's suggestion, Julie nodded in agreement and went to the phone. Bill could hear her side of the conversation as he washed the dishes from breakfast. Bill glanced over at her when she hung up the phone and smiled.

"What did he say about you staying here?"

"He said he wasn't worried about me. He figured I would stop here for breakfast. He did thank me for calling him and letting him know where I was and that I wasn't coming home. He worries about me."

"What do you have to do this morning?" Julie asked.

"I have a couple of people to question. By the way, have you heard that Mr. Gordon was killed yesterday?"

"No. What happened?"

"I can't get into details, but he was shot in his car on a Forest Service road near his campground."

"Was it suicide?"

"No. He was murdered. How well did you know Mr. Gordon?" Bill asked as he washed up the last of the dishes.

"Not very well, really. I think grandpa knew him fairly well. At least, they talked to one another from time to time, mostly when they ran into each other here in town. I don't think they socialized at all. I've never seen Mr. Gordon out at the farm."

"Well, I'm done here. I'll get out of here so you can get some rest."

"Aren't you going to tuck me in?" she asked playfully.

"Only if you will go to sleep and get some rest."

"I don't have a nightgown to wear. Could I use one of your shirts?"

"Sure."

Julie gave him a kiss then went into his bedroom. She undressed, put on one of Bill's shirts, crawled into his bed and covered herself with just a sheet as it was warm. When she was ready, she called him into the bedroom.

Bill went into the bedroom and saw her lying in his bed. He couldn't help but think that she looked like she belonged there. He walked over to her, leaned down and kissed her.

"I had better get going, or you just might find me in bed with you," he said as he looked down at her.

"I might not mind if you come to bed with me," she said softly, then yawned. "Then again, it might not be such a good idea."

"You get some rest. I'll be back later," he said with a smile.

"Will you be back for lunch?"

"No. I'll get something to eat downtown. You need to rest. I'll fix dinner for us tonight."

"Okay," she said then yawned again.

"I love you," Bill said as he leaned down and kissed her again.

"I love you, too."

Bill smiled at her then turned and left his bedroom. He went out to his patrol car and headed out to Keaton's place.

It took him almost an hour to get there. He drove up the driveway to the house and stopped out in front. As he got out of his patrol car, he looked at the upstairs window where he had seen the curtain move the last time he was there. He noticed the curtains on one of the upstairs windows move slightly as if it had been held open and then released. Since the other window curtain didn't move, it was obvious someone had been looking out.

He had just gotten to the front of his patrol car when Mr. Keaton stepped out on the porch. The look on Keaton's face gave Bill the impression he was not happy to see him.

"What do you want now?" Keaton asked rather sharply.

"I would like to know how well you knew Frank Gordon."

"What's that to you?"

"Just answer my question."

"I knew him, so what?" Keaton said, but offered no further information.

"Did you socialize with him?"

"Yeah, a little. Why all the questions about Frank?"

"He's dead," Bill said bluntly while watching closely for a reaction from Keaton.

The look on Keaton's face was that of someone who was surprised to hear the news.

"When did that happen?" Keaton asked, but the expression on his face changed suddenly as if to hide the fact he really might have cared about Frank.

"Yesterday morning."

"I didn't hear anything about it. Did he have a heart attack or something like that?"

"No. He was shot to death, shot in the head. In other words, he was assassinated," Bill said clearly without any indication of feeling.

The look on Keaton's face confused Bill a little. It was almost as if he expected it. Yet, it was more like he was afraid, but afraid of what? Keaton seemed to be a little short of breath.

"Are you all right?" Bill asked, a little concerned for Keaton.

"Yeah," he said softly.

"You and a couple of others used to get together from time to time. What did you do when you got together?"

"Ah – ah, we played cards occasionally. Nothing much, a little penny ante poker. We actually spent more time just talking than playing, it seemed."

"What did you talk about?"

"Oh, about people, things going on in the world, nothing much, really," he said, but without the anger he had first shown Bill for being there.

Bill got the impression Keaton was worried about something. He wondered if Keaton might be worried that Bill had found something that would point to what they had been doing at the meetings, and in the quarry. Maybe Keaton knew he had seen the "insurance salesman" and Gordon back of the quarry at the hay fields, and might have seen him as well.

"Do you know how Gordon got the injury to his arm?" Bill asked.

"What?"

His question startled Keaton. It had interrupted his thoughts.

"Do you know how Gordon got the injury to his arm?"

"Ah – no. I didn't know he had injured his arm."

Bill wondered what was going on in Keaton's mind. Keaton seemed confused and unsure of himself. It was clear that Bill's question had shaken Keaton.

"Who is staying with you?" Bill asked, hoping that he had caught Keaton off guard.

"What?" Keaton asked with surprise.

"I asked you 'who is staying with you'. I saw someone in the upstairs window."

"No one," he said, but with little conviction in his voice.

"I saw someone. I want to know who is in your house." Bill demanded.

"There's no one in my house," Keaton insisted.

Bill stepped closer to the door of the house.

"You can't go in my house," Keaton said as he moved toward the door to block him from reaching for the door to open it.

Bill moved up close to the door and looked inside. He couldn't see very far into the house, but was a little surprised by what he could see as it looked like it had been well taken care of. The part of the living room he could see appeared to be neat and clean. That didn't seem right to him, especially since the rest of Keaton's property was far from neat and organized. The thought running through Bill's mind made him think there might be a woman living there.

"I don't know who's in the house, but you best come out with your hands where I can see them." Bill called out as he reached down and put his hand on his gun.

"You've got no right," Keaton said as he stepped in front of the door.

"Step aside," Bill ordered sharply.

Keaton looked at Bill, then at his hand resting on his gun. He looked up at Bill again then reluctantly moved away from the door. The look on Keaton's face gave Bill the impression he had given up. It was at that moment a rather nice looking woman who looked to be in her early thirties appeared in the doorway.

"Step outside," Bill said softly.

The young woman stepped out on the porch and stood next to Keaton. The woman was wearing a simple cotton dress and no shoes. She had long dark brown hair and deep brown eyes. Even in the simple cotton dress, he could see that she had a very nice figure. She also looked like she was rather nervous. Bill wondered why.

"What is your name?" Bill asked as he looked into her brown eyes.

The young woman looked at Keaton. From the look on her face, she wasn't sure she should answer him. Keaton nodded that it was okay for her to speak.

"I'm Anna Keaton," she said her voice clear and firm. "I'm staying here with my uncle."

"You're John's niece?"

"Yes."

"Where are you from?"

"I'm from New York City, New York."

"How long have you been here?"

"Two months. I'll be leaving in a few days. I'm going on to the west coast to visit another of my uncles," she said.

Bill wasn't sure she was telling the truth. There was something about her that just didn't set well with him. It was almost as if she was trying to hide something, but he had no idea what it might be. His thoughts may have been because she had made it a point to remain unseen by anyone. What was she hiding from, or more to the point, who was she hiding from? If she was there to visit her uncle, why the secrecy?

Bill would have to do what he could to find out if she really was Keaton's niece. From what he had been able to find out about Keaton, which he had to admit to himself was very little, he was pretty sure Keaton didn't have any brothers. With no brothers, it would be hard to have a niece with the same last name.

"I'm sorry to have bothered you," Bill said as he looked her over closely.

She didn't say anything as she looked at him. She simply turned on her heels and went back inside the house.

"Are we done?" Keaton asked sharply. "Because if we are, you can get off my property."

"We're done, for now," Bill said, then turned and walked back to his patrol car.

Bill got in and sat behind the steering wheel while looking at Keaton. He slowly reached forward and turned the key to start his car, but didn't take his eyes off Keaton. As soon as the car started, he shifted it into first gear and drove toward the road. He watched Keaton in his rearview mirror. He remained on the porch until Bill reached the end of the driveway and turned out onto the road.

When Bill reached the end of Keaton's drive, he turned and went down the road toward the quarry. Turning into the quarry, he stopped and opened the gate. He drove in, then closed the gate. He drove the patrol car behind one of the old buildings and parked it where it would be hard to see.

He grabbed his binoculars, locked up the car, then began walking toward the trees that separated the quarry from Keaton's property. He carefully worked his way along the tree line until he was at a place where he was sure he would not be seen by anyone in or around the house, but he could see the house and barn. He settled in to watch Keaton's house. He had no idea what he was looking for, but something was not right there. There was something about the young woman that caused him to think she was not who or what she was trying to get him to believe.

CHAPTER TWENTY-ONE

Time passed slowly with nothing happening. No one came to the house and no one left the house. As he waited, he took a few minutes to scan the grounds, especially the house and the barn, using his binoculars.

As he looked over the barn using his binoculars, there was something that caught his attention. At first he wasn't sure what it was. There were some wires hanging on the back of the barn very close to the roof. Bill could not think of one reason the wires needed to be there. But after he thought about it for a few minutes, he remembered seeing wires strung on buildings like that on the German countryside during the war. The wires were for two-way radios the Nazis used to report the location of U.S. troops moving in the area.

Bill began to add up in his head all the information he had been able to gather so far. Stolen ammunition and weapons, the Nazi lapel pins, and the Nazi flag in Gordon's shed, and now the wires for a two-way radio all seemed to add up to a group of people who had not surrendered their beliefs, nor their desire to continue to fight to overthrow the U.S., or at least, to cause trouble and instill fear among the people.

Bill wasn't sure what to do at this point, but he remembered one thing that was said by the woman staying with Keaton. She had said she was planning to leave in a few days. He couldn't help thinking she had something to do with what was going on. Why would she stay out of sight if she was just visiting "her uncle", John Keaton?

Bill continued to watch the house and barn while he thought about what he should do. He was pretty sure he didn't have enough evidence to get a search warrant for Keaton's house and barn. He needed to get more, but how was he going to do it. It was at that moment he came up with an idea.

Bill quickly returned to his patrol car and got his camera, then quickly returned to the place where he had been while watching Keaton's house. He could hold the camera's lens up to one side of his binoculars and snap a picture using the binoculars as a telephoto lens. He knew it could be done because he had done it before, but it was not easy to get a good picture. It was still worth a try.

After making sure the binoculars were adjusted for what he wanted to take pictures of, he carefully lined up the camera with one side of the binoculars then snapped a picture. He repeated the same thing as he took several pictures of the house and the barn in the hope of getting at least a couple of pictures that would show the kind of detail he needed.

Suddenly, he saw Keaton and the young woman come out of the house. Bill took several pictures of the two of them as they walked toward the barn. He only hoped he had gotten a couple of good pictures of the woman. He noticed the woman was no longer wearing a simple cotton dress. She had changed into well-tailored slacks, a fitted blouse and riding boots.

As they walked toward the barn, Bill got the impression the woman was unhappy with Keaton. In fact, it looked like they were arguing. He couldn't hear what they were saying.

Once they disappeared into the barn, Bill sat back and waited. He thought about the woman and Keaton as they walked across the yard. The more he thought about what he saw, the more he was convinced the woman had been chewing Keaton out. He wondered if she might be in charge, and Keaton was a subordinate. It appeared that the woman was the leader, and she had a lot of authority over some men.

Bill continued to wait and watch. If the woman had been hiding out at Keaton's, and she had been discovered, there was a good chance she would disappear as soon as possible. Maybe before the couple of days she had said. It was time to find out what was going on.

Bill looked over the place to see if there might be someone else around, and to see if there was a way for him to get closer to the barn without being seen. He carefully laid out a path in his head that would take him closer to the barn without being seen. It meant working his way between old farm equipment and old vehicles strewn around the yard. There were other things like bales of hay, trees, high weeds, and just plan junk that would provide him with some cover, too.

Bill started working his way toward the barn. It was slow going, moving from one bit of cover to the next. He only hoped they didn't leave the barn before he got close enough to hear what was going on.

When Bill finally got to the back of the barn, he saw a small place in the siding where a knot in the wood had fallen out. Bill moved over to it and carefully leaned down to look through the hole. He found that he could see inside the barn, but he couldn't see anyone. However, he could hear the woman talking, but could not understand what was being said. He did not hear any response to what she was saying from the only other person Bill knew to be in the barn, Keaton.

Bill moved along the outside of the barn to the corner. He peeked around the corner to make sure there was no one there. He didn't see anyone. He moved around the corner and saw a small window. Two of the four panes of glass were missing from the window. Standing next to the window, but staying out of sight, he could hear the voices of two people clearly. One was Keaton's and the other was the woman who called herself, Anna Keaton. They were apparently arguing.

"What did you do to get that damn deputy nosing around?" Anna asked, the tone of her voice showing she was angry.

"I didn't do anything. He never would have been nosing around if you and Ralph hadn't killed Olson and left his body in the quarry. I told you Rutledge was a scavenger and was always rummaging around in the quarry. He's the one who reported the body to the sheriff," Keaton said angrily.

"What were we supposed to do when those kids showed up?" she retorted sharply.

"You should have waited for the kids to leave, then gone back immediately and got the body out of there. I don't know why you killed him there in the first place."

"He knew too much. What's done is done, besides, he was expendable," Anna said.

"I suppose that goes for Gordon, too."

"Yes. It was necessary. He was going to talk to that deputy."

"What you have done is to put all of us at risk," Keaton said angrily.

"Ralph thought Gordon had shot the deputy, but found out Gordon missed him. Instead, the deputy shot Gordon," the woman said.

"Yeah, and then Gordon was murdered. Whose idea was that?" Keaton asked.

"Ralph's. He saw Gordon talking to the deputy in the Hill City Café. He was afraid Gordon was going to spill everything. Ralph took care of Gordon, too," Anna said.

"Yeah, he sure did," Keaton said sarcastically. "He took care of it, all right. Now the deputy is looking at us."

"You've got nothing to worry about. He can't prove anything."

"Oh, really? He has seen you. Your picture is in every Post Office in the country, and probably in every law enforcement office as well. Do you think he will not recognize you sooner or later? He'll go back to the sheriff's office and see your picture. When he figures out who you really are, he'll be back, and the next time he comes back here, he will have help, and lots of it."

"By the time he figures it out, I will be long gone," she said with a grin. I'm going to leave as soon as it gets dark."

"And I'll be left behind to face charges of harboring a wanted criminal. No thanks," Keaton said sharply.

"What do you plan to do? Are you going to run?"

"I'm not going to stay around here and end up in jail."

"Ralph won't like that kind of thinking."

"What's he going to do, shoot me like he did Gordon?"

Bill didn't hear an answer to Keaton's question, but he had heard enough. It was time to take action before either of them escaped to somewhere where they could hide, and he could not find them. Bill drew his gun and moved quickly, but quietly, to the front of the barn. He looked around the door and could see them clearly. They had their backs to him. He ducked into a stall near the door and waited for them to turn around to leave. As they turned around and started for the barn door, Bill stepped out in front of them.

"Put your hands in the air and don't take another step," Bill ordered holding his gun on them.

For a couple of seconds, they just stood there surprised to see him.

"Put your hands in the air," he demanded.

Slowly the two of them put their hands in the air. Bill noticed that Anna took a step back which put her just back and to one side of Keaton.

"Turn around and put your hands on your head," Bill said as he moved closer to them.

Bill watched the two of them very carefully. He was sure that one of them would try something. He would be very careful, because he had no plans to let either of them get away.

As Keaton started to turn around, the woman shoved Keaton toward Bill, but Bill didn't grab Keaton as he fell forward. Instead, he stepped aside and hit Keaton on the back of his head with his pistol as Keaton stumbled by, knocking him out. He immediately raised his gun and aimed it at the woman as she turned and began to run toward a door at the back of the barn.

"Halt, or I'll shoot," Bill yelled, but she didn't stop.

If she got outside the barn, there were a number of places she could hide where he might not be able to see her. He couldn't let her escape. Bill leveled his pistol and fired one shoot. The bullet hit the edge of a large wooden post in the barn just as she was starting to pass it. The slug from his gun scattered small pieces of wood from the post, several of them hitting the woman. She quickly stopped, turned around and looked at Bill as if he was some sort of strange creature.

"You shot at me," she said with a surprised look on her face.

"You're right. If you hadn't stopped, the next shot would be to stop you."

"You would shoot a woman?"

"One like you, in a heartbeat. Now, put your hands on your head and walk over here," Bill ordered.

Looking defeated, she put her hands on her head and walked toward him. When she was close enough, Bill turned her around and put a handcuff on one of her wrists, then pulled her over to a heavy post in the barn. He wrapped her arms around the post and handcuffed her other wrist.

"That should keep you for a while," Bill said.

"You can't leave me here like this," she said sharply.

"I can and I will."

Bill turned and reached for a rope hanging on the wall next to a stall. He knelt down and hogtied Keaton, then drug him into one of the stalls where he took another rope and swung the end of it over a rafter. He tied one end of the rope to the rope that he used to hogtie Keaton. He hoisted Keaton up and suspended him almost ten feet off the ground from the rafter and secured the other end of the rope to a post next to the stall.

"I'll be back in a little while. Don't go away," Bill said with a grin.

Bill left the barn and returned to where he had left his patrol car. He drove back to the barn and parked his car inside toward the back of the barn where it would be hard to see. He then sat down in his patrol car and placed a call to the sheriff's office on his radio.

"Car eight to Dispatch."

"Go ahead, eight."

"Mary, is the sheriff in?"

"Yes. I'll put you through to him."

It only took a minute or so before the sheriff was on the radio.

"What's on your mind, Bill?"

"I have two people under arrest. One is wanted by the FBI."

"Who is the one the FBI wants?"

"So far she hasn't been willing to tell me her real name, but she passed herself off as Anna Keaton, John Keaton's niece. Keaton doesn't have a niece. I think she's probably wanted on several charges, but I'm arresting her for accessory to murder, the murder of Gordon, and possibly the murder of Jason Olson."

"Really? You said two people. Who's the other one?"

"John Keaton. I'm arresting him for harboring a criminal and accessory to murder. He had been hiding her here at his place for the past two months.

"Okay," the sheriff said.

"I would like to have you come out to Keaton's place as soon as you can. There is one other who could cause me problems if he should get here before you do. All I know about him is he goes by Ralph, no last name. I think he's the guy I've been told is the 'insurance salesman' that I've seen around town, but I don't know him. From what I've heard, he is the one who killed Gordon."

"I'm on my way. I'll have anyone who might be closer get over there as quickly as possible. Out."

Bill turned and looked at Anna. She was just standing there looking at Bill. He thought he could see the fear in her eyes.

"You feel like talking?" Bill asked.

"Why would I talk to you?"

"You never know. It might help you if you would tell me who Ralph is."

"That's a death sentence for me, and for you, if I give you his name."

"He's that important to your organization?"

"Yes."

"If he's that important, you realize once he finds out we caught you, your life is over. If he thinks for a minute you talked, he'll have you killed whether you talked or not."

The look on her face showed Bill that she already knew it. Bill got up and walked over to her. She just looked at him, but didn't say anything. He watched for any sign she might change her mind and talk to him.

Suddenly, Bill noticed a change in her expression when she looked past him. It was as if she saw something behind him. Bill quickly dove to the right, grabbing his gun as he fell on the barn floor. He heard a shot behind him as he rolled over and quickly fired two shots at a man standing in the doorway of the barn with a gun in his hand. Both of Bill's shots hit the man, one to the chest and one to his right shoulder, spinning him around and knocking him to the ground face down.

Bill got up and slowly walked over to the man, keeping his gun on him. As he approached the man, he noticed the heel of his right shoe had a metal lift plate on it. The man was lying face down in the doorway of the barn. Bill knelt down and turned him over. He recognized him immediately. It was the "insurance salesman", and he was dead.

Bill turned and looked at Anna. She was looking at him. The expression on her face was one of surprise. It was at that moment he noticed blood on her blouse. He stood and ran to her. It was obvious that the shot the "insurance salesman" fired to kill him had struck Anna.

Bill uncuffed her and laid her down on the floor of the barn and held her in his arms. She was still alive, but she was going fast.

"Anna, can you hear me?" Bill asked.

Anna opened her eyes and looked up at him. She was breathing in short shallow breaths and looked like she was in pain.

"Anna, can you hear me?"

"Yes," she whispered softly.

"What is your name?"

"It's - - Anna - - - Hoff – mann."

"What's his name?" he asked, but she didn't answer.

"Anna, what is his name?"

"Ralph - - - Gutt - - Guttmann," she said softly, then closed her eyes and fell limp in his arms.

Bill looked at her for a moment, then laid her down. He knew it was not over, at least for him. He may have gotten who was responsible for the murder of Olson in the Jasper Quarry, and the man who killed Gordon, but he hadn't found out what was going on, and who had stolen the weapons and ammo from the supply depot. Bill's only hope was to get Keaton to talk. Maybe he could tell them what they needed to know.

It was a little less than an hour before another deputy showed up, and a little over an hour before the sheriff was on the scene.

"You want to tell me what happened here," Sheriff Henderson said as he looked at the two bodies lying in the barn.

Bill started explaining what had happened from the time he arrived at Keaton's up until the time

Anna died. He explained who everyone was, and what he knew about each of them. The sheriff listened very intently.

"There is a two-way radio in this barn somewhere. I have no idea who is on the other end, but it would be my guess they are not very far away."

"We'll find whoever it is," the sheriff said.

"I think Keaton might be able to tell you the rest of what has been going on, but it looks like a faction of the Nazi Political Party has been operating in the Black Hills with the purpose of getting weapons to cause chaos and instill fear in people. I think Keaton will talk if he thinks by talking he will not end up in the gas chamber," Bill said.

"A search of the barn and house might provide you with more information. It seems to me that almost everything centers around this place," Bill added.

"By the way, do you know where Keaton is?" the sheriff asked.

"Yes, sir. He's hanging in the rafters above that stall," Bill said.

Bill pointed to the rafters above the stall, then looked at the sheriff. At first the sheriff looked a little surprised to see a man hogtied and suspended by a rope in the rafters. His surprised look soon turned to a grin, then he looked at Bill.

"I didn't want him running off while I went to get my patrol car so I could call you," Bill said with a grin.

Bill and the other deputy began to laugh, but the laughter quickly ended when they looked at the two dead bodies lying on the floor of the barn. They cut Keaton down, untied him then handcuffed him. They put him in a patrol car and had him taken to jail in Rapid City.

After the coroner had taken the two bodies to the morgue in Rapid City, the sheriff and his two deputies gathered and logged all the evidence they could find in the barn and in the house.

A search of the property produced code books, papers on the goal of the small group and names of members of the group, including the name Richard Stassen. Richard Stassen was the leader of the group, and he lived in Rapid City. They even found the explosives container. It was hidden back in the corner of the barn under a pile of hay. There was also a two-way radio in the tack room of the barn.

The sheriff called the sheriff's office and had a couple of deputies go to the address of Richard Stassen and place him under arrest. Before they were finished gathering all the evidence, Sheriff Henderson received a call that Mr. Stassen was in custody and being taken to jail, and the officers were getting a warrant to search Stassen's home.

Once all the evidence at Keaton's farm was gathered together, listed and piled in one place, the sheriff called for a truck to take it to Rapid City to the Pennington County Building where it could be gone over before it was put in storage. As soon as everything was cleared out, Bill drove his patrol car out of the barn then locked the barn doors. Bill saw the sheriff had just come out of Keaton's house and was locking the door. Sheriff Henderson walked up to Bill.

"Well, I guess that's about it," the sheriff said. "I'll call in a couple of deputies when I get back to Rapid City to round up those who are involved. Most of them live in Rapid City. If I get right on it, we should get all of them before they find out what happened here."

"I hope so," Bill said.

"By the way, we found a bunch of checks for the Jasper Quarry Company in Keaton's desk. It seems Keaton was forging Shepard's name to checks from the Jasper Quarry Company for the payment of property taxes. He would send the checks to someone in Chicago. The person in Chicago would put the checks in a Jasper Quarry Company envelope and send them back to the County Treasurer to pay the property taxes, so the envelope would have a Chicago postmark on it," the sheriff explained. "So you were right."

"So Shepard never signed the checks used to keep the taxes paid. Any idea what happened to Shepard?" Bill asked.

"No. No idea what happened to him."

"Did you ever find out how Keaton got all the land around the quarry?"

"He got it as part of a settlement for injuries he received while working at the quarry," the sheriff said.

"Is there anything else?"

"No. We've got all the evidence and will get it back to Rapid City. It's now up to the district attorney to figure it all out, and prosecute those we arrested," the sheriff said.

"I guess I'm done here," Bill said with a sigh."

"You are done here," the sheriff said with a grin. "You did a good job. Why don't you take a couple of days off and spend some time with that young lady you've been seeing?"

"I think I will," Bill said with a grin. "I'll bring in my report tomorrow, if that's all right with you."

"That will be fine. See you sometime tomorrow afternoon," the sheriff said, emphasizing "afternoon", then turned and walked to his car.

Bill went to his patrol car, got in and drove home.

CHARTER TWENTY-TWO

It was well after dinnertime when Bill arrived at his home. He was sure Julie was probably worried about him. He knew he should have taken a minute to call her, but things happened pretty fast.

As he drove into his driveway, he saw Julie come running out of the door. He hardly had time to shut off the engine and get out of his car before she was in front of him. She threw her arms around his neck and kissed him hard. He wrapped her in his arms and held her close to him. The tearful kiss lasted for at least a minute before he was able to say anything to her.

"I'm sorry," were the first words he said. "I didn't mean to make you worry so."

"I'm just glad you're safe," she said as tears rolled down her cheeks.

"Things got a little out of hand, but it all turned out okay."

"Are you done with your investigation," she asked looking hopefully into his eyes.

"This one. I just have some paperwork to do and turn in. I have a couple days off except for turning in my report tomorrow afternoon."

"Good. I have a couple of days off, too. I will be starting to work here in the clinic in two days," she said with a grin.

"Great, but would you mind if we go in. I'm starving."

She smiled at him and took her arms from around his neck, then grabbed him by the arm. They walked into the house together.

Julie fixed dinner for the two of them while Bill sat down at the table and watched her. After dinner, they sat on the sofa and just held each other.

"I'm really tired," Bill said, then yawned.

"Why don't you get ready for bed while I clean up the kitchen?"

"The kitchen can wait. I'll walk you out to your car."

"Oh, I'm not letting you out of my sight. Go get ready for bed. I'll join you as soon as I get done in the kitchen."

"Do you think that's a good idea?" Bill asked.

"I think it is a very good idea. Now, go get ready for bed so I can get done in the kitchen."

Bill looked at her for a moment, then turned and went into the bedroom. He took off his uniform and took a quick shower. After his shower, he went directly to bed.

While Bill was getting ready for bed, Julie cleaned up the kitchen. When she was done, she went to the bedroom and looked in. Bill was lying in bed sound asleep. Julie smiled to herself, then got ready for bed wearing one of Bill's shirts.

As soon as she was ready, she climbed into bed and laid down beside Bill. She didn't want to wake him, but she needed to be near him.

"I love you," she whispered softly.

"I love you, too," Bill said.

Julie snuggled up against him as he wrapped her in his arms. It wasn't long before they were both asleep.

www.ingramcontent.com/pod-product-compliance
Lightning Source LLC
Chambersburg PA
CBHW061320170626
46817CB00001B/247